THE AMERICAN GHOST

by

SOMSY CAMVAN

Published worldwide by BabalonBOOKS
Front Cover Design by BabalonBOOKS
www.BabalonBOOKS.com

Set in Garamond, Matchbox and Caslon.

ISBN 978-1-926716-36-7
The American Ghost by Somsy Camvan

BabalonBOOKS is a division of 8th House Publishing, Montreal, Canada.
www.8thHousePublishing.com

8th House Publishing
Montreal, Canada

THE AMERICAN GHOST

By Somsy Camvan

1

A LONG TABLE was set on the flattened, trodden ground of the village center. Five chairs were arranged behind it in a row. The chief had told the men to set them up the night before in preparation for the witness interview and testimony.

Later that morning in May 1997, the chairs would be occupied by government officers from the Ministry of Defense, police officers and a translator. They would observe and record the testimony of the sole witness to a jet crash that had occurred twenty years earlier. They say this man had been living with "The Ghost" ever since, this *peetyhoung*—the spirit of the pilot killed in that crash that had come to him in a manner that possibly no one would ever understand.

‡ ‡ ‡

Wagner, the American MIA team leader, occupied the middle seat. He looked severe with thick eyeglasses in black frames, a short-sleeved shirt the color of eggshells and long khaki pants. Sitting still, impatiently, he wasn't smiling. To his right, was the swarthy translator, looking like a military student. His sharp brown eyes, wide and alert, surveyed the gathering. Two officers in green uniforms, their kind faces surrounded by soft grey hair sat to Wagner's left. As the children passed near, they would smile, waving in greeting or gesturing to them to stay still.

Everyone quieted down when Thamu was brought into the circle before the committee. They watched as he was led in his khmu fisherman pants, three inches short of his bare feet and a homemade black cotton shirt of the same material, to the empty chair opposite Wagner. Everyone took a deep breath when Thamu just stood there motionless. Then as if to allow the crowd to exhale and breathe again, Thamu sat down. He responded to the committee's greeting with a simple bow of the head. His hands were trembling when he raised his head again. He appeared hesitant and it seemed that in the silence of the expectant crowd, everyone could hear the thunderous bellows of him swallowing nervously.

Thamu waited. Everyone waited. Wagner then leaned over, handing two pages of handwritten notes to the translator as he conversed briefly with him. The translator read the pages aloud before addressing anyone particularly. Then he told Thamu to take a deep breath and instructed him to tell the committee everything he could remember, and that he should be quiet if someone raised their hand to him. The translator advised Thamu that he was not a suspect, that he was not accused of any wrongdoing. The translator assured him that the committee simply needed information from him in order to do their job, that it would be much more difficult without his cooperation for them to locate the remains of the pilot.

While all this was being said, Thamu's eyes were darting about as he twisted in his seat in search of his family, his mother, an aunt, somewhere in the crowd.

Not sure of his attention, the translator asked Thamu to confirm whether he understood.

Thamu nodded.

The translator reminded him again of the importance of determining the exact location of the site of the crash.

Thamu stood up. "In the name of my deceased uncle and that of our deities," Thamu began, "I will tell you everything I saw, everything I know and my uncle's wish for the *peetyhoung*."

The translator urged Thamu to take his seat explaining that it was not necessary for him to stand.

Thamu sat down again. A small chuckle rose up from the crowd.

The translator continued. "So... You witnessed the crash of the American plane?"

"Yes, sir," Thamu continued unperturbed. "I saw the crash and found the body of the pilot twenty and more years ago. I was sixteen then."

"Please tell us how it happened."

The crowd though accustomed to hearing the tale, all leaned in as though hearing it for the first time. "It was a February morning," Thamu began. "I was on my way to the bamboo grove to hunt wild chicken as I usually did then. I was walking the trail, listening, hunting... I saw the plane crash to the ground below the mountain top from the trail."

Thamu remembered it as though it were yesterday. The mountain was bare, with only exposed rocks here and there at the top. Below were groves, mostly bamboo mixed with some bananas, ferns and tall grass. They were green and the ground was wet. Not from rain—there had been no rain that February, but from the fog and mists fell continually during the night. In the early morning it was slippery all along the trail. If something unexpected were to happen, it would be very difficult to run to safety until high noon, and Thamu was forced to keep to a slowly steady pace.

"Sir, the jet no longer made any of the sounds of a machine," Thamu was now saying. Thamu said 'jet' because that's what they told him it was. Thamu had never seen one before. "I saw it from a distance. It came toward me from the east trailing black smoke. It went down very fast! With the speed of an arrow. As it passed over me it made the sound of a strong wind blowing through a hollow of rotten wood. *Woo! Woo!* And then the booms. The last sound I heard was that of the horns of two bulls fighting. *Klak, klak, klak, klak!* It went silent a few minutes later and there was only the sound of a forest fire. A hundred things went through my mind. But I was sure I had seen something fall from the sky."

Thamu was shaking again. His thoughts returned to that day that had taken him beyond what he knew of his everyday world. He had wondered if the sky had fallen, or part of it. And then he'd get control of his thoughts again and assure himself it couldn't be. But how could he know for sure that the sky wouldn't fall? There must be a world above this one or else, where could it be falling from? He felt like the fish in the lake that he'd spear, living all that time, ignorant of the world above the water, unable to reach it. He was bewildered, his mouth agape, trying to look in all directions, but everywhere he turned there was only the bush around him. He could no longer see the object, but could still see the fire, the sound of the raw bamboo cracking and exploding, sounding like gunshots.

Thamu recalled how all alone, he felt no shame, but

only fear. Every thought you could imagine ran through his head, but he couldn't bring himself to act on a single one.

"I could not see for sure where the jet had crashed," he told the committee, "so I climbed a tree to have a better look. The smoke was not exactly black. It was thick, inky grey, but I couldn't smell anything. It curled into the air. I wasn't far away, but the smoke seemed to touch the sky parting the white clouds above. It was more than half an hour before I decided to move. I slid down from the tree, and crept down the hill."

Thamu remembered how slippery the rocky trail was. The stones still wet from the morning fog, it was a treacherous descent on foot. Instead, he sat down and pushed himself along the ground with his arm until his body began to slide on its own. Reaching the bottom, he realized he was bleeding, his thighs, buttocks and back scratched from the stone edges. He hadn't noticed in his panic, not until he was home did he feel the pain.

"The whole thing was burned," Thamu told the translator. "A piece of metal hung from the rock, but the fire was too hot. I couldn't get closer. There was a smell that made my stomach turn. I didn't know what else I could do, so I turned back to the trail and returned to the village to tell the others."

Wagner leaned over to the translator after Thamu had finished. Then the translator was asking Thamu if he remembered the precise site where the plane came down. Thamu had taken the moment to scan the crowd again for some comforting faces. Everyone looked back eagerly at him. He felt bolstered.

"Yes, Sir, I can take you to the site, but I must warn you," Thamu began. He looked to the crowd again for support.

"There is a poison snake there, guarding the place. We kill all snakes that come near the village, but before the Chief died, he told us not to kill the snake   by the site."

The translator broke in before Wagner had a chance. "And why would your Chief say that?"

"Because it is the guardian of the American *peetyhoung* – the American ghost spirit. Why it is so poisonous I don't know."

"The snake is the guardian of this… ghost?" the translator said uncertainly.

"Yes, Sir. When someone dies they go and live in the air. They are no longer attached to the body; they are not prisoners of the senses. Sometimes they become animals and smell things differently."

"This is the myth of your tribe," the translator broke-in, half-chuckling as though discounting Thamu's testimony.

"All of life is connected," Thamu asserted. "Not just for our tribe. The stars are millions of sleeping suns which keeping rising each day to show us."

But neither the translator nor Wagner were satisfied and there soon followed the usual barrage of questions, insinuations and thinly-veiled insults that Thamu bore with patience.

"No, I wasn't dreaming, Sir." "No, Sir, I do not know how to read and write." "No sir, I never went to school; school did not exist in our village."

When it seemed that the translator had given up, Wagner leaned in again to whisper something into the translator's ear. The translator nodded and then stood up again to address Thamu.

"Well, perhaps your Chief was lying, to keep a secret," he said. "Do you think that might be possible?"

And now Thamu was incensed. The memory of Thabo

their village chief was still fresh and sacred to Thamu and all the villagers. Thamu almost stood up again, but caught himself with a deep breath. "Thabo was a great man, a good man and he cared about his people. He does not lie."

"Okay. Well, let's see if we understand this then. The American pilot—I mean his ghost—came into your Chief's dreams and told him that he had died on the other side of the mountain overlooking the village. So that this sacred responsibility belonged to your Chief."

Thamu nodded. "Not just Chief," he corrected. "But entire village."

"Then he provided your Chief with instructions on how to handle the remains?"

"When the night is lit by a full moon, ghosts come out looking for a new place or a permanent tomb where they are able to rest. Sometimes they need the help of the living and speak to them through dreams."

"And so the Chief dreamt that the pilot came to him to ask him for help. Is that accurate?"

"The *peetyhoung* entered the chief's home and introduced himself. He said he was the pilot of the plane that had crashed in the jungle near the village. He said his name was Tom Moorlock. 'I am come from America,' the ghost said, 'and I wish to remain in this place.'"

Everyone on the committee looked up in surprise. "The ghost told you its name?"

"Not me sir, the Chief."

"Yes, of course, the Chief... Tell us how it happened."

Thamu remembered the day well. When Thabo woke the next morning, it was with sympathy in his soul. He kept silent about the dream at first, but Thabo new his duty to the spirit world.

"The next morning, Thabo came to my home and

asked me to take him to the site of the crash. Before we set off, Thabo called two of my neighbors, Long Num and Matuke. The four of us then set off for the site. We arrived at noon. The dampness of the foggy night had been burnt up by the hot sun. I took them to the valley near the path where I had first seen the column of smoke. We climbed. I led the way, followed by the chief and my neighbors.

"Over the ridge was the wreckage just as I knew it would be. Thabo stopped us the moment he noticed it, and we said a prayer before the remains. Then we approached the wreckage. At first we saw only dust, but then later we found a tooth. Most everything was burned beyond recognition. Thabo told us to push everything together in one place and pile rocks over the pyre. We worked until sundown and then left for home. That night, the adult villagers gathered to pray, drink and eat. Many cried for the ghosts to follow. Crying is a way for the lost souls to find the place they wish to go," Thamu explained. "Then Thabo announced that from then on, the crash site would be a sacred place for the villagers and every month we had to bring animals for sacrifice and remind the *peetyhoung* to remain in place in its new home. Now it has been twenty years and I can tell you only that it was Thabo's wish that we not let the ghost leave us."

No one on the committee had expected this.

"That's very well," the translator commented. "But we are not concerned with ghosts. We want only the remains of the pilot to return to his home."

"But the pilot wished to remain here. He told Thabo. He does not wish to return to America."

"The ghost can stay here with you. We will take the remains."

"But the *peetyhoung* must follow where the remains

go," Thamu insisted.

"You must tell us where the remains are."

Thamu had been at this juncture before. He feigned fatigue. "I don't know where the Chief hid the remains," Thamu claimed and stood up. "With your permission, I am tired now and must return to my home." He walked away through the crowd, the villagers each nodding their support to him.

And that was that. The group of Americans from the MIA team, with their translators, guards and other officers, made no qualms about showing their dissatisfaction. They entered the Russian-made helicopter, with Wagner trailing behind. He took one last look at the village around them and then climbed aboard. He would have to return without the remains and with no official confirmation from Thamu or the villagers that they would be relinquishing the remains anytime soon.

11

IT WAS A SHORT FLIGHT for Frank Wagner. He still had no clear understanding of Thamu's motives for keeping the dead pilot's remains. Deep in thought, searching for reasons, it seemed the plane had barely taken off before it was pitching for a landing. The more thought he gave it only served to increase his confusion and he was soon feeling distanced from his team members.

He risked looking weak before his team. He felt they had already begun suspecting he was adrift without a plan, that he was buckling under doubt and confusion. Wagner felt that perhaps they were right. He didn't know how he would approach the Laotian authorities, nor explain to them the difficulties he was having with the jet crash witness and this backwards tribe. He was unaware that the authorities in Laos, even some of his team members, had prior knowledge of the tribe and their stubborn, closed ways.

Returned from that impromptu meeting in the village, Wagner chose to lock himself in his room going over his translator's notes and compiling his own from his research papers: Thai magazines printed in English, a National Geographic feature, the terse Ministry briefing and some vague anthropological studies by the National

University. He pored over them again, hoping to glimpse some insight into the tribe's deep set culture, their mores and practices. Clues—he needed clues to overcome the tribe's and Thamu's resistance. He was scheduled to give a statement tomorrow at the Ministry of Defense, before the minister himself, and he hadn't the first clue of how he'd make this mess actionable, resolvable… palatable to the ministry.

Too stressed to concentrate, Wagner returned his notes along with his research papers into the folder file inside his travel bag. Thinking about tomorrow's meetings had made him uneasy. A walk might clear his head, he thought.

Outside, he wandered through the hotel lawn, smoking a cigarette and assuming his best official air. The evening breeze wafted over him as he watched the sun set over the Mekong river. But even there, among the coconut trees and the fragrant perfume of *Dokjampa*, Laos's national flower, sprouting along the six foot stone walls surrounding the hotel estate, he was unable to forget. The situation had utterly surprised him; he never imagined anyone would want to keep the remains of the dead pilot.

He needed to learn more about the tribe's beliefs to understand their motives. Perhaps then, he might be able to solve the dispute. But there was no written history about them, no books written, no studies made—just unreliable information from local oral storytellers. No one knew precisely the origins of the tribe, how long they had been there, where they had come from. Since the crash, they had learned that the tribe actually spanned several villages and that the dialect spoken was diversified in each village as well. This only added to the difficulty.

Obviously no one in the team suspected Wagner's deepening interest in the tribe and its culture. Returning to the hotel he was accosted by his staff. They had been waiting for him and wanted to see the statement he had prepared for the meeting tomorrow. Wagner had always consulted with his staff on their opinion and second ideas before submitting final copy on official papers.

"Just go to the meeting and see how it goes," he told them now.

They looked at each other in surprise. "But sir," Liam, his most senior aide, spoke up. "We need to have the statement."

"It's done," Wagner said bluntly. "We have communicated our intentions and they have assured us that they are willing to co-operate. Tomorrow's meeting is to discuss how to deal with the witness. I have already requested, in letter, not to bring in the military. I want to avoid violence."

Wagner knew that Thamu was not using the dead to gain political power or leverage of any sort. He had understood it almost immediately during the committee interview. Thamu had been emotional during the interview and seemed actually frightened at the prospect of being separated from the pilots' remains. What's more, he was forthright and honest in his testimony—unreasonable as it might seem to anyone from 'civilized' society, to his team and later to the defense minister.

"We must understand the culture of his tribe," Wagner resumed. "I think once we understand them and the psychology of the witness, we will also see how the Lao tian police can work with us and the villagers in securing the remains while preserving the harmony of the tribe and its ideology of life and spirituality."

↟ ↟ ↟

It was late before Wagner got to bed. Then well into the middle of the night, stretched out in bed, he was still tossing and turning. He worried if what he had said to his staff had made any sense to them. Hopefully, they'd be able to understand and see the bigger picture with all its implications. "If they do, it will make things easier," he thought. It was almost a prayer, or a plea to the darkness above his bed. "But if they don't, it might end with bloodshed." These tribal villagers had no experience of the state and its brutal arm of law. Wagner knew the government would sweep aside any concern for the villagers for the cause of foreigners. It always did this in protection of its political relations. In this case, Thamu and his tribe had little value comparative to the economic support and state pressures the US might apply to secure their military wreckage.

III

WAGNER AND HIS TEAM were ushered into a conference room when they arrived at the ministry. It seemed that all had already been prepared in anticipation of their arrival. Wagner and his team took their seats at the end of the table. A water bottle and a glass had been laid out for each of them on a silver tray. Wagner thought back to the modest garments Thamu wore and the conditions the village had subsisted in for centuries. All was quiet in the room and then there was a rushing din of papers that reminded him of his student days at the University—all of them seated at their desks for the examination, waiting for the clock to strike before taking up the papers.

The deputy minister introduced the case. He gave a brief history of the jet, its crash, the requisition from the US State department, the location of the crash site. Wagner remained still, without looking up when he heard his name mentioned and his team's role in the assignment. Then the deputy minister announced Wagner would be briefing the assembly on his progress and turned the meeting over to Wagner.

Wagner began by describing Thamu and the village. He told the assembly how Thamu and the villagers had reacted to their presence. Thamu appeared frightened, desperate. These were simple, honest folk Wagner was attempting to make clear to them. But it was made obvious by the grumbling and shifting at the head of the table that there was little interest for Wagner's assessment of the villagers and the area.

"Please go on with your interview of the witness," the deputy now broke in.

"Yes, of course." Wagner cleared his throat. "The witness confirms witnessing the crash and disposing himself of the remains. However, he claims to have forgotten where he did so."

The minister nodded at his deputy.

"Please explain," the deputy urged.

"The witness's testimony, collaborated by others in the village, is that the American pilot appeared to the village chief, the witness's uncle, and instructed them on how to dispose of the remains. The site of the crash is hallowed ground to them now. It is protected by a guardian spirit they claim."

"He would not tell you where they disposed of the remains?"

"When he speaks of the dead pilot, it is like he is speaking of a relative." Wagner explained. "And to ask after the remains is to inquire about a holy idol or relic. The witness is clearly emotionally attached. I believe they know where the ashes are stored. I believe they know very well, that they even keep it safe or guarded. Feeling as they do, they would not abandon nor forget the remains."

"You believe then, that the witness is withholding this information?"

Wagner hesitated, but he knew his first duty was to the truth. "Whenever I asked him where they might be, he refused to tell me. When I insisted, he complained of fatigue and excused himself."

Sera Vong Savang, the minister had been seated quietly at the head of table. He had listened to Wagner's address at first without reaction—his eyes behind thick lenses purposefully avoided eye contact. He sported the traditional ministry black suit, white shirt and tie and now appeared impatient of the proceedings and of Wagner's hesitation. Still glancing at the files in front of him, he now spoke up:

"This should be a simple matter," he said somewhat annoyed. "What we can do to help our friends find their pilot's remains is to dispatch a police squad in full armament just in case, to accompany you and your team on your next visit," he said and now looked up at Wagner for the first time. "Anytime you want as of today. That should impress your villagers or at least secure their cooperation. These peasants understand only one thing: Force. They will know we mean business. Now," the minister began somewhat mollified. "If you can find the remains and return them to his family with the cooperation of the tribe, I personally will be more than happy to help assist you. This Thamu, you mention—this witness—if he refuses to help or to comply with our requests, then we shall have no choice but to use force. I will order the police to restrain him until he complies. Our only job here gentlemen," the minister made it a point to remind them, "is to find and collect the remains of that American pilot."

"We must also do all we can to avoid violence or loss of life," Wagner interjected. "My bosses at the Deparment of—"

"Of course," answered the minister. "If Thamu cooperates, there will be no need for force. If he refuses to cooperate, then he is defying Laotian law, and it becomes a matter for the police."

But Wagner wasn't convinced. "Forgive me minister, though I agree that this show of government support and police presence may help in... in…" Wagner had to be careful with his choice of words here. "…persuading the tribe to cooperate, I'm not sure that restraining Thamu will help our cause. I've been researching this tribe and its culture a great deal. They believe the dead return and live with them, that is, co-habit their bodies and minds."

But the minister was growing impatient again. "I don't mean to harm anyone," he says. "Certainly that is not the intention of the ministry. If what you say is true, that he believes the ghost of the American pilot has possessed him, then perhaps we should have him treated and evaluated by a mental health specialist. In that case, the best course of action would again be to restrain him for his own well-being and move him to an institution where he can be properly treated."

Now Wagner was backtracking. "I understand, minister. All the same, it is a little early sir, to take that route. Based on my interview, he appears healthy, and I would prefer to leave the mental health issue out of it for now if you permit me, sir."

The minister raised his bottle of water and took a sip. There was a pregnant pause that he appeared to enjoy while everyone waited for what he would say next.

"I'm a fair man." he began. "I think we both agree, we want what's best for the tribe. We will send a mental health expert along with the police squad. This way we all have all the tools to help these people," the minister concluded. He began collecting the file reports before him onto a pile on his right before looking around the table and then at directly at Wagner. "Anything else?"

"No, sir. Thank you. I appreciate your support," Wagner said. We would like to return to the village in three days if possible."

"We will make the arrangements and have your medical expert and police squad ready for you in the next three days."

Wagner stood up and made motions to leave. He turned around at the door however, and stopped. "In Vietnam," he said, before leaving the room, "an American delegation once contacted the local authorities for assistance in retrieving the remains of the missing soldiers, with the same end of returning them home for burial. This here, is a new experience," Wagner warns them. "We Americans have no experience of small tribal communities like these located in the higher ground in the country. The Hmong and Khmu of the Lao ethnic group are a mystery to us. My superiors have assumed that we can secure the tribe's cooperation through the use of communication. They believe that sending officials with an official request would have been enough to have them victory. We see that this has not worked. The witness refuses to cooperate--but not out of malice, self-interest or for gain. The tribe subscribes to what they perceive to be higher, spiritual authority and duty. Now, you propose to use force. I'm not sure that force will win the day."

"I understand," the Minister said, eschewing Wagner's concerns away with a wave of his hand. "I know that in Vietnam you were dealing with peasants, not tribes. It is somewhat different here, though on the surface there are many similarities. The peasant communities in Vietnam are literate; here in Laos the tribes are very backward and still mostly illiterate. We will have to deal with them differently."

Wagner nodded, as though to say, "I see," and left the conference with the same concerns he had walking into it, now amplified.

There's always a hidden agenda when dealing with the authorities here in Laos, Wagner had been warned. Leaving the Ministry, he knew they were signing the approval documents that he himself had helped to draft. Soon, the Ministry would receive a cool half million in US funds wired directly from the US State Department. This money would act as a deposit to assist in the deployment of operations to recover human remains from American soldiers in Laos territories after the Vynay site was discovered. This money was meant to defray expenses and if human remains couldn't be found, Wagner knew the the Laotian authorites would have the Laoloums—as the tribes people were called—manufacture them out of the trees if need be. The grant agreement would cover three years. The half million alone was enough to paint dreams of opulence at the Ministry, and three years of it would turn it upside down.

IV.

BACK AT THE HOTEL, Wagner was again turning over Thamu's testimony in his mind. Thamu's behavior, his suspicion was what bothered Wagner the most. The words Thamu had told him kept echoing in his memory. *"Yes, I can bring you to the site, but you cannot remove the remains…"* even though it had been clearly understood and again reiterated at the committee meeting that recovering the remains was the only objective. This wasn't a misunderstanding. Thamu was clearly refusing. It was the detail Wagner's subconscious had been nagging him about—the one detail he had been hoping to avoid.

Alone in his room, Wagner was restless again, pacing back and forth, smoking at the balcony. He was worried that Thamu was going to be the kind of problem that wasn't about to go away. In fact, he *knew* it. He picked up the phone and dialed Liam's room.

"Liam, join me on my balcony."

A couple of minutes later, they were both staring out at the horizon beyond the hotel.

Wagner lit another cigarette and then turned to Liam. "I found the little guy wasn't tell us everything, don't you think?"

"Possibly. Did you see something? What makes you say that?" Liam asked.

"All the while he was telling us of how and where he

saw the crash, his eyes kept searching the crowd."

"Searching the crowd?" Liam echoed, not understanding.

"For someone that might have known he was not telling the truth."

"I noticed he was fidgety. But you can't prove that, can you?"

"No, of course not. But I want all of us to be aware when we return to dig for the remains. He might be leading us down the proverbial garden path."

"Yes sir."

"He'll likely not reveal the site or mislead us if he believes we will try to remove the remains by force."

"Possibly. It is too early to determine whether or not he would do that."

"Maybe," Wagner said and added, "Sera said he would restrain Thamu, if need be."

"That will not get him to talk, if he doesn't want to."

"No, I don't think so," Wagner agreed.

"We can offer him money, sir."

"I'm not sure that would work, either. Anyway, Thamu is the key witness, but he is not acting alone. The entire village acts as one. If we pay him, we'll have to pay everyone."

↟ ↟ ↟

THE room was quiet. The only sound Wagner noticed was coming from the air conditioner. He woke again from his fitful sleep. He could see the day dawn through the window. He had been dreaming of the time back home, before he had made the trip to Southeast Asia. At his desk, reading the profile of the deceased pilot he was assigned to find the remains of; one of them was Tom Moorlock.

Wagner had promised Henry Moorlock that he would find the remains of his son and bring them home. Wagner had visited the Moorlock home prior to departing. He wanted to personally assure their families that he would do all he could to find their sons and bring them home.

The Moorlocks were from an agricultural town near Des Moines, Iowa. After Tom returned home from College, his father told him how they were watching a news report on television about the war in Vietnam one day. It was the summer of '63. Soldiers on both sides were being slaughtered. Henry told Wagner that he remembers his son was very much struck by the news reports. Later when they assassinated Kennedy, Tom was angry, said that he wanted to participate and perform his duty. "There was no dissuading him," Henry recalled. "I didn't want him to go. He was too young. What did he know about war? He thought the airstrikes would greatly support the ground troops and that the Americans were going to win the war. I tried to tell him the few pilots and soldiers that survived were scarred for life. Physically and mentally. The war I told him, was not about freedom. It was and always is just about money. But he wouldn't listen to me."

That same month, Henry's wife, Tom's mother passed away. The loss devastated them. Tom would enlist a month later.

TOM Moorlock's remains had now become Wagner's focus and his sole purpose. Wagner wouldn't bother commencing the other retrievals until he had Tom's remains found, collected and sealed to be shipped home. He planned to return to the site the following day, ahead of the team the minister would send over.

V.

THAT NIGHT, in the village Thamu was dreaming of his *peetyhoung*. He could see Tom and Ann again back in the land he only heard of as America. But when he dreamed of Tom, of his *peetyhoung*, he seemed to know everything his *peetyhoung* knew.

Tom and Ann were sitting together on her parent's back porch.

"We should delay the wedding," Ann was telling him.

"I guess you're right," Tom agreed.

"I don't want to wait, of course, but—"

"I know, it's too soon."

Thamu knew they were talking of Tom's mother's funeral.

Ann and Tom were both in their mid-twenties. Marriage was not the priority except their desire to be together. They were in love and wanted to be together as much as they could—that's all that mattered.

Toward the final year of her university, Ann moved out of her parent's home and into a one bedroom apartment downtown. Tom moved in the following year. It was a heady time in America and everything seemed to be changing. They often talked of the political and social issues ravaging their country. Ann was adamant that no

American, man or woman, should lose their life on foreign soil. But when it happened, it was the government's responsibility to conduct a mission that would bring the body back to heal the loss of families and properly honor the dead. No one should be left like that anonymously.

"If you live and I die, I want you to visit my grave every Friday night", he told Ann, kidding. "But if you die and I live, I will keep your remains in a fancy jar in my bedroom."

It was just a joke; but somehow it stuck.

"AMERICA is boiling," Tom was now telling Ann in Thamu's dream. The scene had shifted from the porch to their downtown apartment. "It's in the newspapers," he says. "The civil rights movement, the Martin Luther King assassination, the John F. Kennedy assassination, the Vietnam conflict..."

"What can *we* do about it?" she said.

"We can fight," he told her.

NOW Tom was in his parent's kitchen again. "You didn't bring Ann with you," his sister remarks.

"She went to her parents," he told her. "Marie, I want to talk to you. I have something to tell you."

"Oh?" she said sitting down. "What is it?"

"You know how I've been training to be a pilot?"

"Of course...."

"Well, I've finished my technical training.... Field training is next. I..."

"Field training?" she asked, looking him in the eyes.

"I won't be training for commercial flights. The air force needs men. I am signing up for fighter jet training," he told her.

"What is that supposed to mean?"

"We're postponing the wedding. Chances are I will be sent to Nam at the end of my training."

"What?"

"I'm not getting married this summer", he said. "I already spoke to Ann about it. She understands."

"You're going to Vietnam?"

"Most likely."

"For how long?"

"Tours are usually a year… Dad's gonna be here any minute. I want you to be there when I tell him."

"He's not going to be happy…" Marie said. "Are you sure? What about Ann? What did she say?"

"She knows. We decided together. She understands this is something I have to do."

IN his dream, Ann was now bringing Tom an envelope posted from a US Airforce Florida Airbase to him: "Confirmation of your departure to Saigon, Vietnam #317-AT-2. Report to base and C.O. two weeks prior to date of departure."

He hands the letter back to Ann after reading. Ann turns into Marie, Tom's sister in the dream, and she is hugging him tight, trying not to cry and Thamu knows Tom is leaving for the war. And now Tom's father is parking the tractor by the barn. The next moment, he is already in the kitchen.

"Hi Dad…."

"See your sister around?"

"Yes, but she left a while ago. She brought the groceries."

"I told her many times, she doesn't need to do groceries

for me. I need to get out of the farm myself sometimes."

"She or I can take you, dad."

TOM is now at the dinner table with his father. "Dad", Tom begins. "I was planning to come see you with Ann on Saturday."

"Oh?"

"I've received my commission papers. I am going to Vietnam."

Tom's father took a pause. "When?"

"They won't say exactly…. in the next six weeks."

"Are you ready?" he asked Tom, looking him in the eye.

"Of course, it will be a great experience. And after a year, when I come back, I will get married."

Tom's father sat back in his chair. He had long given up trying to argue his son out of it. "Well, you know how I feel. All the same, I'm proud of you, son," he said, but Tom felt his father was worried and that he didn't approve. Thamu felt it too in the dream.

NOW he and his father were arguing in the living room.

"What did they tell you were going to do in Vietnam? Save the world?"

"I'll be flying fighter jet as I have been training to do. I'll be protecting the ground troops below."

"By dropping bombs? How do you protect people by dropping bombs. If they need protection, why don't they just go home."

"Dad, the communists are enslaving those people. We need to stop it before it spreads. We can't wait until it hits our shores."

"OK! I don't want to hear the rest," his father said, in exasperation.

"I know... But we'll have to stop them eventually. And the sooner we stop it the better—there will be less suffering... And I have to do what my country asks me to do, dad!"

"What your *country* asks...! Son, it's not your country doing the asking, but politicians and business interests."

THAMU feels that Tom himself is no longer too sure. Doubts have crept in and his resolve was faltering. Leaving Ann, his friends and family for a war far away seemed foolish suddenly. But he couldn't back out now. And he knew he'd feel better once he had done his 'bit'. A year would be over shortly, he told himself.

"No son, you will not doing this for your country, you're doing it for some politician's love of money and power," he heard again as if in echo; and then his father's voice telling him, "I don't want to hear the rest."

IT'S late afternoon and the sky is a pale blue that Thamu had never seen before, even in the deepest of winter in his village. Ann is helping Marie clean up the party left-overs. Tom and Glen, his brother-in-law, are carrying the picnic tables to the shed for storage.

"I will build my own house when I return." Tom tells him.

"Let me know... I'm pretty sure, I can help. I'm not bad with a saw either. I restored my dad's barn last spring." They laid down the table and were returning for the next load. "So... you're leaving next week?"

"Yes, to Florida, and three weeks after that we'll head to Saigon."

"We will miss you buddy."

"I'll be back in a year," Tom promised.

"Watch out for those Vietnamese woman. I hear they can wrap their legs around you and you're stuck a vice," he said laughing.

"No, I don't think so," Tom smiling for his brother-in-law's sake. "I'll miss Ann too much. I'll be thinking of her all the time."

ANN was dropping Tom off at the terminal. She didn't have the strength to go in. Tom also thought it might be better, "easier" this way. They barely spoke in the car. They were hardly speaking at all these days. Last night, their last night together, they laid in bed, awake all night, lying back to back. Tom kissed her and stepped out of the car. He turned back to wave and smile at her, but Thamu knew Tom felt worried. Thamu felt it like Tom did that day he left Ann—an uneasy feeling turning in the pit of his stomach.

VI

THE TRAIL had grown larger with the years and as the villages grew in size. The path was now about four feet wider since Thabo's time. The path was everyone's responsibility and the villagers maintained it as they went along it, clearing it of weeds, branches and small stumps. Snaking up and down between the hills and through valleys, the path allowed the villagers to avoid the steep trek across the range. The trails ran from village to village as always, connecting them, but many smaller trails had sprung up giving access to every mountain that the villagers used for hunting and gathering wild plants for food and medicine. The main trail had become a sort of highway; traversable by horse or ox cart now, and even used by travellers and adventurers hiking. Along the trail, one could smell the wild flowers and ripe fruit's perfume in the air. Wagner wondered if this panoply of perfume and color would still be here in the years to come. The place had never before seen foreign hikers to say nothing of falling jets and American officials trampling through the ground.

There was no open space large enough in the village for the helicopter to land. Instead, they had to set down in a rice field near Barn Vinay village and hike the rest of the way. Wagner knew that if the helicopter had to come back a second time, a landing area for it would be cleared in or next to the village. They would set fire to the brush and then get the villagers to turn the soil.

Thamu was there to greet them at the village. As agreed, they set out for the crash site where Thamu said he had buried the remains. He told them he no longer remembers where it was precisely, that the underbrush had grown over and the jungle had swallowed the site up again. Based on what Wagner had gathered from this tribe and their customs, Wagner knew Thamu was misleading them. Wagner was fairly sure that Thamu knew precisely where the remains were. The place would be like a shrine to them. He had only to point to the spot and sure enough they would find the remains ceremoniously arranged and laid out in its burial ground. Wagner had a secret hope that they would find the remains themselves after some investigation, despite Thamu's reticence. This would absolve Thamu of any guilt, or the need for them to force his cooperation. If she showed him the wreckage and the site of the crash, then surely the remains would be found somewhere close by. They would have no reason to take him very far, Wagner surmised. Not back them anyway.

Thamu for his part, was silent and pensive the entire way. He went before the team leading them to where the wreckage was to be found all the while telling himself, that this would be the first and last time, he would bring them there. If they were allowed to return whenever they chose, they would eventually find the jar where the remains were kept. Thamu was certain he would never bring them back to the site, and he was equally stubborn about avoiding the other villagers and any authorities. He didn't want any conflict. He himself, would never impose his will on anyone, not the Government officers nor any villagers who might desire to allow these men to take the *peetyhoung*'s remains away—so why should *they* impose upon *him*? The agreement the government had made with the Americans included war reparation funds to rebuild the country's infrastructure that had been destroyed during the ten year conflict. Thamu understood that this meant new roads and bridges and prosperity for the village. It also meant the removal of the land mines in Siengkhaug in the Eastern province and Samnuer in the North East. But this too, was not his business, Thamu thought. If they want to build bridges and roads, and clear the jungle of mines then certainly Thamu was not stopping them, nor was his *peetyhoung*. What business was all this war and reparation and road building of theirs? The *peetyhoung* followed the laws of the spirit world and Thamu must follow the laws of his heart. Thamu knew, not only through dream, but through the dying words of his chief Thabo, that this is where the *peetyhoung* wished to be—it was their duty to protect the site and not disturb the spirit world or disaster would befall them all.

THE team arrived at the site at noon and decided to break for lunch before starting out on the digging expedition. All of them sat down, weary from the long trek up the trail. All but Wagner that is, who chose to remain standing. They laid their packed lunches on the ground before them, on dry fallen leaves, sitting or squatting around in a circle, eating in attentive silence—they looked very much like a commando unit to him. Perspiring and weary they sat about dazed, the sweat like a sheen on their faces in the jungle light transformed them all to shellshock victims in Wagner's mind.

They began the search after lunch and the necessary toilet visits in the bush were done. The field expert took his metals spectrometer and sonar equipment out and began making a spiral sweep of the grounds. Everyone watched as he went about in ever-widening circles, hoping for the same thing. He went on for two steady hours, trampling through the fallen bush and cut branches, checking his monitoring equipment and its steady, unflinching beeping, while the bush cutters went clearing the way ahead for him. Thamu insisted this was ground zero and that he buried the remains nearby. So after those two hours, the field expert began doubling back before he said the batteries on his equipment were dying. Two hours and no human remains found. Parts of the fuselage and cockpit debris were found. Too many other smaller parts to identify, but no human remains.

Time was running out for today and Wagner knew it. The sun was starting to set and the sky was turning darker. He tried to hide his disappointment and frustration from the team. It wasn't a total failure after all.

"Well, we've found the site!" he said with a bright voice, eager to sound cheerful. "Thanks to Thamu. And we've recovered much of the jet... Let's get these all packed and labeled. I want some soil samples, too. I will have them all analyzed and examined by laboratory experts at the University. I think we will soon find the pilot's remains," Wagner concluded, though not really believing it. He paused and stepped to the side, looking in Thamu's direction only, but not directly at him. "Unless you remember something else, Thamu?"

Thamu looked Wagner in the eyes. Wagner stared back.

⚑ ⚑ ⚑

THEY were all packed and gone before sundown. They returned the way they came, along the trail back to Thamu's village. The sun was already setting behind the mountains to the West. Shadows came out over the trail and it became harder to see. Each man had to be careful where he stepped. Thamu who knew the trail well, led them slowly and patiently. They seemed to him like blind hatchlings crawling along. Even the children of the village seemed more surefooted than these world-travelled men, Thamu thought.

Wagner climbed into the helicopter with his team. He closed the hatch and the helicopter began to rise. Wagner watched as the waving villagers grew smaller beneath him. The windblast of the propellers or maybe the smell of the burning fuel had the villagers cover their faces, but Wagner had noticed what he thought was relief on Thamu's face before he disappeared out of sight.

Thamu was feeling joyful about the remains he had hidden deep inside the stones. He felt nature had conspired to secure his and the *peetyhoung*'s interests. He had noticed that the roots had grown over the stones in an obstinate mesh over the spring. The zigzagging roots and vines resisted the bush clearer's machetes and protected the remains from the field experts probing. Thamu told himself that perhaps the *peetyhoung* had something to do with it, that it had acted in its defense and so communicated its desire to remain where it was. This idea gave Thamu particular pleasure, as though the Ghost had won, and he was smiling behind the hand that he had brought to his mouth to cover the poison air the flying machine the Americans brought was bellowing out.

But most of all, Thamu was relieved. He knew however, it was a risk he could not take again. He had made the preparations. That night he would return to site and himself take the remains to a sacred place he knew of in the jungle. Thamu knew the jungle, and some of the village men knew the jungle; but no American, foreigner or even women from their tribe knew the jungle. And among all the men in the village, no one knew the jungle better than Thamu.

VII

THAMU GREW UP believing in his tribal convictions. Everything else he needed to learn of the world, the jungle taught him. He had already understood, and his uncle Thabo, the tribal chief hadn't needed to say anything. Thamu knew that when a natural spirit or *peetyhoung* selected his or her home, then it was the duty of the living to respect it. No living souls should ever remove the *peetyhoung* from its place even if they had the power to do so. It would be a thing too dangerous to even contemplate. The *peetyhoung*'s capabilities varied depending on the situation. Sometimes the ghost would remain in place for generations. They might later spread their spirits out to another place or to the sky after their work was done. The *peetyhoung* could help or harm the village depending on how it was treated and if it was assisted in its work. Thamu knew of *peetyhoungs* sending swarms of insects to destroy crops. Sometimes they sent floods and spread disease through the villages. They could strike men with madness and death. They could make lightning strike and set the whole forest jungle to fire.

So Thamu already knew from an early age that the *peetyhoung* of any man must be respected and honored by the living. To not do so would be to invite calamity. Thabo had already explained that the ghosts, though they don't eat, must have nourishment and so take food from the living. Food, stocks, even people would start disappearing if the *peetyhoung* wasn't attended to. Thabo had instructed Thamu in the precise particulars. Sacrifices in the form of fruits, nuts and meat from the hunt would be laid out before the *peetyhoung*'s resting place. Most importantly, prayer and solemn words were recited aloud to honor the ghost while laying the sacrifice before him. Thabo explained that without these words, the *peetyhoung* lacked the power to take the food laid before him; and both Thabo and Thamu knew that a starving *peetyhoung* would wreak havoc on their tribal villages. And this was no regular *peetyhoung*. Never before in the history of their tribe did a *peetyhoung* from so far away come to their village. The responsibility was doubly great. Furthermore, it was *his* responsibility. Thamu couldn't help but reflect upon his life, his past, his uncle and those critical moments that had led him here.

Long after the jet crash, but still many years ago when Thamu was sixteen, his uncle had sent him to the Northern village to search for a wife. Young women in those days were reserved. They waited for their young men to come to the house to court them. Of course, if the young man was wealthy, he wouldn't need to court her. As was tradition, he might go to this young woman's village with his fastest horse at night and kidnap her. But of course that meant not only having a horse, but also the strength to carry her off and knowledge of her village, her home and her bedroom which meant bribing someone close to them. Then the kidnapping suitor would have to pay a fortune in dowry and slowly build the intimacy with his wife that he would have already had if they had courted. No, this type of nasty affair was not what Thamu had envisioned. He preferred a drunken breakthrough. The spirit of the alcohol would give him the courage he needed. Many of the tribesmen used the firewater to summon strength and courage in battle and during the hunt. Thamu hoped in this way to be emboldened to his purpose.

He set off to his future wife's home in the distant Northern village. His mother and uncle had already made arrangements for his arrival, but he didn't know it at the time. Even so, Thamu was already well known throughout the villages. His fame began when he shot his first deer at the age of eleven. It was a feat unheard of before and the news spread quickly. His mother of course contributed. She wasted no time. She promptly set to hacking the deer meat and sending pieces of the carved animal to every family in the villages—courtesy of Thamu, of course. When the meat ran out, she sent a cotton string as an apology. The villagers tied the string to their wrists and wore it like ornaments—it was said to bring good fortune.

The families that received the gifts of meat were happy and spread word of them: Thamu is a handsome boy; his father would be proud of him; his mother is a generous soul. But those that did not; those that received only the wrist band slowly grew jealous and resentful. They began to say that Thamu and his mother would sooner or later be punished for their presumption. Thamu knew the story of how the Braches deities punished those that offended the village law. They watched over all aspects of village life and were even said to have favorites. The deities would send grasshoppers, sparrows, rats and even wild boors to destroy crops, create miscarriages and bring disease.

But Thamu didn't feel he had done wrong. Before he was old enough to hunt, Thamu was already dreaming of being the best hunter, of having the lightest step, silent even on the dried leaves of the forest. He dreamt he could run, invisibly, silently, his step deftly avoiding twigs, leaning in and out of the brush. His father had died when he was three years old; Thamu's mother was a bamboo harvester—a good bamboo harvester. But she couldn't help him and Thamu taught himself all he knew about hunting and the forest. By the time he was a young man, his prowess with the bow was already well-known and when Thamu was making his way through the villages to see about taking a wife, people were coming out to greet him and word of his arrival had already begun to spread at the northernmost village. His future father-in-law was already at his door when Thamu arrived.

"Come," said the father warmly. "Come inside."

Thamu entered and was surprised to find a throng of villagers already gathered. The matriarch of the house led him to a seat near the fire place. The drummers stopped their beating the moment his rear touched the chair, all their eyes turned on him. He was surrounded. It seemed the entire family was there. Nang-Dee, the daughter however was nowhere to be seen. Thamu would later learn that she had fled to her bedroom and hid herself there.

Thamu understood what she must have felt that day. Everyone in the village was out in a circle about him and he too, had just wanted to hide.

VIII

TOM WASN'T EXPECTING a warm welcome from
the senior pilots and officers at the Vietnam air base. But
as soon as he descended the transport plane, he was met
with champagne and an impromptu party in the mess hall
with more than a hundred other service men and women.
This is crazy, he thought; and the doubts began to settle in
again. After the party, awake on his bunk, he couldn't help
but think of Ann. He played the scene in his head again.
A week before his deployment to Vietnam was confirmed,
Ann was reluctant to return home after work. Tom had
gone to meet her at the bank. She needed to be by herself
she told him. Later, that night, sex had been awkward;
she was distant. The following morning, saying their
good-byes—she was in such a hurry after dropping him
off. There was no parking she insisted and she couldn't
leave the car idling on the curb. Before he knew it, she was
speeding off down the embankment.

Now he realized Ann wasn't going to wait for him
as she had promised. But then no—he couldn't be sure.
He didn't know *what* she was feeling. Perhaps she felt
betrayed. Had he in fact, abandoned her by running off
to Vietnam?

It was already late and Tom realized thinking about

Ann and the past wasn't going to change anything. The best thing to do right now was switch his civilian mind 'off' and concentrate on his new mission—piloting the lightning-speed machines designed to rain death on targets below. Perhaps what didn't occur to him, even then, was that the enemies below would be targeting him also. Young and inexperienced at war, he naively felt conflicted about his supposed immunity flying high above clouds where no human eye could possibly see him, too fast and hot for any bullet to touch him. He knew the Vietnamese from the north were armed with lower tech weaponry that was still a risk to his more 'sophisticated' aircraft. He was told so at the briefing and he had heard stories of planes going down in the jungle on dangerous reconnaissance missions. But Tom was feeling confident. Perhaps he needed to be to get his mind off Ann—but he hadn't got that far yet in his thinking, when he was interrupted by a knock on the door..

"Come in," he said. "It's open."

"Sorry," said the man at the door in an officer's uniform with his hat under his arm. "I'm Jack. Thought you might need company. It being your first tour and all…Newbie, right?"

"Yeah. Tom's the name," he said taking his hand. "And it's fine, I was about to send my mind off."

"Oh? Why is that?"

"Nothing, just don't want to think too much about anything."

"Well, I don't think we can control our thoughts."

"Maybe you're right," Tom answered, but he knew he wasn't. "So how long have you been here?"

"A month."

"Just a month, eh? You see any Viet-Cong yet?"

"No...God no, and I'm not expecting to see them," he answered taking a seat on the bunk across from Tom's. "To tell you the truth, I don't think we ever get a chance to see them, or any of our targets. It's a good thing that we don't, I think."

That feeling of uneasiness was again sweeping over Tom and his confidence was waning. Even during his pilot training he felt conflicted. He couldn't understand it. He had always felt it was the right thing, the heroic thing, to do. But he was already feeling conflicted back then. Trouble sleeping, drop in appetite, anxiety... He had been told that he had been *given* the opportunity to take part in fighting for his country, and when he was accepted into the Air Force Academy he believed it. He felt privileged as if he had won by dint of devotion and skill some place in the hallowed halls. But it wasn't long at the Academy that he was questioning what or who he was really fighting for. Certainly, not his country. Standing before all that gargantuan weaponry with their death-bestowing payload, learning of its firepower and scale of devastation, the cost of its development and all the enterprise that went into it and being touted under pressure by fear of an unknown enemy, as ideological generals and politicians on both sides of the spectrum plotted the destruction of nations in their imperialistic take-overs, commanding a great war-machine with men like him at the helm told to destroy a target five thousand miles away—it was all beginning to get surreal to him. The dream of heroics had been overwritten by the script of cold duty and Tom was feeling less and less like a hero. Looking at the officer across the bunk, he was reminded of the global Air Force objectives in Vietnam: to destroy enemy buildings, cut-off access to food, communications and transportation; destroy key infrastructure points: bridges, power plants, army bases, ammunition depots, etc; undermine stability in the region by tasking the population: destroying villages, roads, farms stocks; generally use every bomb and weapon one had to the optimized maximal effect. This meant 'winning the war' for the ground troops.

But Tom began to see another side of the conflict. He already knew of the strength of the human spirit and of a nation when facing adversity. Sure, the Viet-Cong had their vulnerabilities. Their lack of sophisticated weaponry, for one. No air superiority for the other. This should be enough according to the politicians. But Tom was seeing it from the enemy's perspective. They had long term goals, generational duties. They were fighting for their homes, their families and for future generations. Many of the Viet Cong were already committed to dying for his or her country. All this made Tom's vague, suburban longings for heroics seem ridiculous. Their stakes here, beached on this foreign shore weren't on the same level. They were or thought they were fighting for patriotism, advancement and money.

Tom remembered Ann again.

"You got a girl back home?" he asked Jack.

"Married," Jack answered. "And to the most beautiful woman in all of Nebraska, too."

Tom couldn't resist a smile. "How long?"

"Two years." he says.

"Did she mind you leaving? I mean for Vietnam? Did you know that you'd be sent here?"

"Hey, I'm fighter pilot. It's what I do. I didn't know I'd be sent to Nam, but sure I figured I'd end up here sooner or later," he confessed. "After all, it's where the action's at. Who else are we bombing these days?"

"I suppose," Tom said absentmindedly.

Jack took a stretch and then stood up. "Anyway… it's been pleasant chatting with you. Morning jog starts at 6 AM sharp. Be there for the Captain roll call. You'll be assigned a squadron. Report to the base commander after your morning training. I'll see you on the tarmac."

Tom was thankful to be left alone again. At least he had walls, unlike the camps he had seen on the way over where the G-men slept on bunks in open areas. They had plumbing, sanitation, showers, a mess-hall… Hell, they had champagne! But all that didn't matter. It was farcical, like a vaudeville piece and all part of the new surreal taint the world had taken for him. He was thinking of Ann again. Maybe Jack had been right—there's no controlling one's thoughts.

"I'm not sure, Tom…" she said, twirling the golden crucifix hanging from her neck, "that God wants us to be life partners." Tom heard her voice telling him again.

That was a fu…nny thing to say.

IX

TOM WAS UP by 5:30. When the blare horns rang out the wake-up call ten minutes later, he was already dressed and ready to go. By 5:50, he was already standing to attention to the Captain's roll call. On the mark, at 6 AM sharp, they began their morning run. The muggy air of the jungle had them all sweating profusely in a matter of minutes. The jog took them through the banana fields where buffalo was being herded and used simultaneously to fertilize the land. Panting heavily, they were met with an air wall of buffalo urine and feces and whatever other animal remains and human waste the villagers were using to fertilize the fields, festering in that open heat. Deep in the field the Captain ordered them to stop. "Attention!" he called. "Drop and give me thirty." They all dropped at once, noses to ground for thirty push-ups. "That's it boys, breathe her in!" the Captain said, pacing up and down their rank. "Take a deep breath! We're gonna come here every morning until you learn to love the smell of the buffalo shit were in."

Some vomited and were told to start over and do forty. Tom passed undaunted and was soon on his feet again. He had been raised on a cattle farm and wasn't about to be overtaken by an odor. They continued on through the field on a narrow red dirt road when the final push-up had been completed and the last man was on his feet. Another steep mile through the hill and back down again, and they were back at the base.

⇡ ⇡ ⇡

TOM went straight to HQ after his shower.

"Tom Moorlock reporting for orders, ma'am," he said saluting the petite woman behind the desk.

"Oh, you don't have to salute me," she said. "Save that for your C.O. and Base Commander, who by the way would like to welcome you personally, but is too busy at the moment." She took out a large manila envelope and put it on the counter before him." "He asked me to give you this," she said. "Make sure you read it and understand it. The Colonel will be briefing you further on your flight mission."

"Yes, ma'am."

He took the envelope and opened it on his way out. He glanced briefly at its contents, scanning for his mission details. He was relieved for one thing to not be assigned to a carrier. He dreaded landing on a ship. His assignment was clear; he would be flying to the northern border, to Dong Temp near Laos. Tom stuffed the papers back into their envelope.

Alone again in his quarters, Tom took out his order papers and mission briefings. He read the briefings over and then re-read them. The actual targets of each mission would only be given once the Saigon Air Campaign department received location coordinates from intelligence on land. Tom began feeling that sense of purpose and even of heroism return to him. He was a critical link in a chain. Men on the ground were risking their lives and depending on him. President Johnson's speech on the need to send Americans to Vietnam to end the rise of communism and defend liberty returned to him—the memory of his family's living room back home as they all watched the presidential address attentively on the television. And Tom felt again the need to prove his manhood, to win honors and that these things could be given to him.

That Thursday standing to attention while the Colonel gave his speech, Tom felt filled with that same great motivation and earnestness that he had first felt when he dreamed of being a fighter pilot.

"Destroy all you see of an enemy," were the concluding words of the Colonel. "Before they destroy you."

Tom made up his mind that to worry about his role and his future was a form of cowardice, a surrendering to fear and the sort of trick he was warned his mind might play on him. He would leave it to God, he resigned. He would play the hand he was dealt. The outcome was already decided.

✈ ✈ ✈

THE heat of the Vietnamese summer reaches its peak in the early afternoon. The sky begins to darken as the pear white clouds of morning grow heavier and more threatening with every passing hour. The air grows increasingly humid and oppressive. Even a shower does little to relieve the heat. Vietnamese don't take baths in midday; they wait for the sun to go down. Of course, on a day like this, no one can see the sun through the cloud cover anyway. And though there is nowhere on earth that one can control the weather, Tom feels annoyed by the climate of South Vietnam, so different to that of Iowa. He couldn't seem to cool off, nor find relief from the perspiration running down the length of him, clinging to him. His hands were sticky—something distressing to a pilot—and he kept opening his fingers to cool and dry them in a breeze that never came. He longed to be up in the cold, cool air of the sky again in his cockpit cabin far above the sweltering heat. He remembered the first time he heard of Vietnam back in Iowa—all he knew of it then was that a free, capitalist south was trying to resist the communists from the north. It sounded distressingly familiar perhaps.

But Tom Moorlock had made up his mind. His concern was not for political rivalries nor the grander scheme of things on which he could have no impact. He was a man, and a pilot in the United States Air Force. He would do what he was trained to do, and to comply with orders and fulfill his missions would suffice to content him. He would work hard, dutifully discharge his missions and proudly serve. He would gain experience, eventually maybe even formal recognition of his service. These small vanities still persisted within him. Perhaps he was thinking then, that after the war was over, he might even get to meet the president and be hailed as a hero. He felt American again, that is to say, patriotic. He belonged to the best nation on earth, founded on independence and ready to bring independence to other countries in need.

His first flight mission was scheduled to depart tomorrow morning. Tom lay in bed, anticipating the morning run, going over all the details, the spot checks, safety checks, control measures…. He could still taste the buffalo-meat stew that was served as supper that night. It had tasted stronger than beef, sweeter and metallic as though he could taste the iron in its meat. There would be a lot of buffalo meat, he was warned—and that was if he was lucky. Otherwise, it would be army rations. Buffalos and rusting metal drifted in and out of his mind as he fell asleep. Then Ann came to him in a dream right there in Vietnam. She had traversed the ocean to visit him and was standing before him in a thin night gown almost transparent in the lamplight.

"Before you leave," she says and the night gown drops to her ankles. "Will you make love to me?"

↑ ↑ ↑

IT took only a couple of minutes to walk from his sleeping quarters to his jet. The light of the new dawn was on the hills and the camp. Everywhere the morning was filled with life; not just human life, but plants, fowls and beasts living by instinct unfettered by human fears. It wouldn't be long before the humidity brought the clouds inland, but for a moment the skies are open and clear and the sun emerges brilliant and dazzling. Tom read nature's blessing into this sky, granting him such clear conditions for his first take-off. It never occured to him that this might not only be his first mission, but also his last.

Tom's first mission was to destroy the Red River Bridge some kilometers north of Hanoi Square near Dong Temp. He had been flying now for over 10 minutes when he turned and broke left to avoid the enemy's gun-trucks that intelligence reported were stationed up the river. A minute later after a bend in the river, he saw the bridge cutting across the snaking river. He leveled out, cruised, counted, waited and dropped the payload. He continued north and then banked hard right to double back and check on mission success or drop a second round. It was while turning that he noticed erratic jet trails coming off his starboard wing. Taking a further look, he spotted anti-air blast holes in his wing. His other wing looked undamaged. Behind him however was a serious problem. He could see flames billowing out the tail of his plane. He instinctually veered north again thinking new gunships might have been stationed or that the intelligence was wrong. A moment later, a flash lit up the tail and exploded it off. The plane careened to left and began spiralling. The explosion hit the fuel line and spread to the cabin. A fire so intense it would melt the cabin blew through the cockpit. Tom didn't have time to register the pain. He saw his uniform disintegrate into ash. His right arm sizzled and split open. The next thing he saw were thick canopies of green from the jungle beneath.

Tom's burning body seemed to him to be floating silently in the air while the jungle below burned and sizzled about the plane wreckage. He descended slowly and set upon on a bamboo branch. He was looking for the body of the pilot though he knew somehow that the pilot was himself. He couldn't seem to make anything out of that molten disaster, when some feet away he noticed a village boy climbing up to a body that had fallen out some yards away. Charred, black to a crisp, it was still smoldering. He saw the boy circle the corpse with a hand up to his face for the smell it gave off, and then leave.

"Hey!" Tom called out, forgetting or not fully-accepting yet what he was. "Over here! I'm talking to you!"

The villager apparently ignoring him continued

walking. Tom decided to follow the boy and the moment he did so, he was carried afloat in the air behind him all the way to the village. For all of Tom's shouting and insistence, the villager never once stopped ignoring him. The boy passed on through the center of the village and entered a hut. Tom followed and took a spot in in the corner next to the door and watched. Tom soon realized the boy was speaking to the village chief, that they seemed related and that the plane crash and some great fire up beyond the hills in the jungle was the subject of their conversation. The older man stares at the village boy in amazement and then concern. He looks around the room, and then seems to stop where Tom had been hiding.

But Tom finally realizing what has happened, slinks further into the shadow, suddenly frightened of the living and that they should discover his place among them. The chief's eyes pass over. He looks again to his nephew and they both walk out the door, with Tom following after a moment's hesitation.

TOM'S FATHER, HENRY MOORLOCK, was sitting on his back porch looking over his sprawling corn field. He realized suddenly that it had been weeks now since he received news that his only son, Tom had gone missing. The passage of time had been one big blur since then. Weeks later now, and still no one had any more news of him to tell. He'd begun thinking of his late wife. He recalled how devastated Tom was when she died. He wiped the tears off his eyes. He wanted to get up as if leaving the room would be leaving these thoughts, but he hadn't the strength and he sat there tormenting himself with doubts. He was glad at least that his wife didn't have to suffer through this.

Immobile, he heard someone entering in the house from his chair. The front door opened and shut. He held his breath.

"Dad? Dad are you home?"

All at once, the hope that had welled inside him unexpectedly dissipated just as quickly as it had appeared.

"In the back," he told his daughter. "Over here."

He heard her footsteps getting closer, and finally, for his daughter's sake, he mustered the strength to rise.

She came in full of concern. Tom mustered a half-cocked smile.

"How are you Dad?"

"It's been weeks," he felt like telling her. "Weeks! If they haven't news now, it won't be good news, later." But he didn't. "Fine, fine…" he said instead.

Marie moved in closer and held his eyes. "Dad. I want you to prepare. Get cleaned up. I've invited some people up to the house," she tells him. "Some of Tom's friends, our friends… Glen and Adam are at the grocery store with Joy and her family and will be here soon. I want you to tell them Tom's missing Dad. You need to tell them. You can tell them anyway you like."

"There's nothing to tell yet," he insisted.

"Dad," she said again stepping to catch his face as he turned away. "Tom's missing, Dad. He's been missing for almost three weeks now. They deserve to know. We all miss Tom."

Henry nods, but returns to his chair again after Marie leaves him to prepare for the gathering in the yard.

☝ ☝ ☝

HENRY'S front lawn was soon filled with all those people he least wanted to see. Each one of them reminded him of Tom in their own painful way. Almost everyone was there though Henry failed to notice Ann's conspicuous absence. Marie had called to invite her to the house, but before even knowing why, Ann had declined. She had an errand to run, and was busy, though she was sorry. Then Marie told her it was regarding Tom. That they had important news. Ann was silent for a moment. "If he's back," she began to say angrily, "then…" But Marie cut her off. "No.

His plane went down and he's missing." "Oh," she said almost as an afterthought. "Well, I'll see if I can make it." And Marie knew somehow that she wouldn't. She had heard in fact, that Ann had taken up with someone else.

Henry descended the porch steps slowly. He dreaded what followed. It was as though by announcing it, he was making it real. Marie wanted him to come to terms with it, but what he really felt was that they all wanted him to give up hope. Henry cast a wistful glance at the barn and corn silos that he and Tom had worked on for so many years, that he would have inherited—*will* inherit one day, Henry corrected himself. He picked up a glass and fork. Raising the glass, he struck it repeatedly with the fork, until he got everyone's attention.

"I have sad news," he began, once everyone was turned his way. "My son, your friend Tom is missing. The news reached us two weeks ago, but it had been already twenty-nine days already since Tom hadn't reported back from his mission and was declared Missing in Action. His plane went down on his first mission, somewhere between the Saigon base he was stationed at and Hanoi on February 17th, 1969. We have yet no confirmation if he is alive, captured or killed in the line of duty. And my daughter and I thank all of you who came today for caring and supporting us. Whatever's happened to Tom, we wish him well and a speedy return. Please remember him in your prayers and join me in a toast," he said, raising his glass. "To Tom, my son, we love you and miss you. Come home soon!"

All raised their glass in a sort of dumbfounded way, looking at each other in surprise and talking to each other in whispers after the toast was made. Henry made his way back up the porch for his chair at the other end of the house.

Ever since his son's disappearance, Henry had taken to listening and watching for any news of development in the war. Marie feared that it was growing into an obsession. Henry remembered vividly a news report from Vietnam, where the reporter interviewed an American pilot, an escaped POW. Henry played the scene over and over in his mind. He had the dialogue down pat and kept replaying it as though it might tell him something about Tom's whereabouts. The pilot looked happy, healthy, even talkative. You might even say that he was in a good mood. He was a hero now, and maybe Tom would be one, too.

Reporter: Your plane went down in enemy territory and you were taken prisoner.

Pilot: (Smiling at the camera.) That's right. My fuel tank got shot. I was losing fuel. I tried to make it back, but crash landed in the jungle. My plane was torn to bits. I had a broken arm and some ribs too.

Reporter: (With a fake look of surprise.) What happened next?

Pilot: Luckily all the fuel was gone. There was a small fire burning in one of the engines but I knew I wasn't in danger. I unstrapped myself and crawled out. I was immediately surrounded.

Reporter: It must be terrifying to be taken prisoner by the Vietcong. Did you fear for your life?

Pilot: (Still smiling.) You bet. The minute I crawl out of that cockpit and see all those Vietcong and their AKs looking right at me. They look nervous you know. They were afraid. More afraid than I was maybe. I was still in shock and dazed from the crash. Those Vietcong in the jungles, especially the lower-ranking soldiers—they might not know about international rule of law when it comes to

POWs. They're liable to kill you right at the scene. I kept my eye on their trigger fingers.

Reporter: But they didn't…

Pilot: No. They asked me my name and rank and then took me to the head counter in Hanoi. I knew I was safe at least for the time being.

Henry couldn't make out where the interview had taken place. For all he knew it might have been the same Saigon base where Tom was stationed. The pilot looked extremely well, Henry remarked again. Well-groomed and fit even.

He took his morning shower, dressed and headed out back to work some repairs in the barn. The images of the interview revolved in his mind again and again. He recalled the reporter's preamble, about how statistically often aircrafts are shot down and crash while their pilots survive. "They often escape the jets before they actually crash," she had said. The pilot would hit his auto-eject button and be thrown out of harm's way and then glide gently down under the safety of his parachute.

✿ ✿ ✿

ACROSS town, Ann is cleaning out her closet. She is cleaning out her life. Everything that belonged to Tom went into black garbage bags. Tom's new pair of boots, his Air Force manuals that he would study from, the necklace he had bought her… Books and music they had shared, photos of them, these things that belonged to her but had no value anymore… they went in another black garbage bag. Mark, her new boyfriend, had long ago asked her to get rid of them, and it was about time she did.

Later that afternoon, Ann drove up to Marie's house. She drove the car hard up to the curb. She told herself she'd leave the engine running and so she did. She stepped out and grabbed the garbage bags from the back seat. She ran up to the door and rang the doorbell.

Marie came to the door and looked almost relieved to see her. "Ann! How nice of you to drop by. Please come in," she said stepping back.

But Ann stood her ground. "I'd love to, but I'm in such a hurry, you know? Listen, I'm sorry I couldn't make it the other day. But I wanted to give you these." She handed Marie the bags. "They were Tom's…" she added.

Marie took the bags she was handed. She seemed a little dazed and Ann felt for her. "I'm really sorry," Ann said resting a hand on Marie's shoulder. "I miss him too, and I'd love to stay. But my car is running, and I have so much to do. I am moving to Houston."

"Houston?" Marie echoed, looking down at the black of garbage bags she was handed.

"Yes, I think I might get a job there," Ann said. She paused, pursed her lips and seemed be looking Marie over. "Well," she said, stretching out her arms and moving in for a hug. "I've got to run!"

"Of course," Marie said, looking up, her hands still holding the bags and her arms at her side as Ann leaned over and squeezed her shoulders.

XI

TOM SOON LEARNED that for whatever reason, whenever he was away from the young village boy, he seemed weaker, less substantial, even less visible—even if only to himself, for no one else at the moment seemed able to see him. He discovered that if he came upon the villagers, alone and in a quiet, contemplative state, then he had a better chance of being noticed. They would turn their head, suddenly swat in the air, look up as if they heard a sound—but always they saw nothing and Tom remained consigned to invisibility. Late at night, with all the villagers asleep, Tom found that it was an easy matter to influence the villager's dreams. He seemed to have a strong link with the boy, Thamu, but he was just a boy and Tom thought he had better try with Thabo, the village chief. He visited him night upon night and though he thought at first it was all for nothing, he began to notice a change in the chief's behavior during the day. He visited Thamu often, asked again and again about the crash, if his nephew could remember anything else... And then one day, he told him, flat out. Tom felt strangely more materialized than ever as though present in the room. "Thamu, the spirit of this pilot has come to me in my dreams. His *peetyhoung* is among us. We must honor it and help it before it can be on its way. Otherwise, the entire village will suffer the wrath of the deities."

Now Tom was racing about the room, using every trick he had learned. He ran past the fire in the hearth, making the flames dance. He ran over to Thamu and blew in his eyes. He turned around and ran his body through Thabo's. He jumped to the lounging cat and startled it out the door. At the end of it all, consigned to defeat, he sat in the corner dazed and depleted of energy, when he noticed the boy, Thamu was for the first time looking right at him. Not through him, not behind him, but right at him.

"I see him, Uncle," the boy said. "I see the *peetyhoung*."

Thabo stood up. He was no longer the uncle, but the severe-faced chief. "You see him? Where?"

Thamu pointed to where Tom was sitting. Thabo saw nothing but turned in that direction, made a slight bow and clasped his hands and then opened them wide in the traditional greeting of the village. "Welcome visitor. We are children of peace; let there be peace between us. We do worship to the holy ones; let us honor the ancient fathers together."

Then he turned to Thamu. "You must address the spirit. We must learn what it needs so that there can be peace between us."

Thamu turned to Tom. Thabo seemed startled and unsettled by the experience; but Thamu was not afraid. He could see the *peetyhoung* and saw there was nothing to fear. He smiled at the *peetyhoung*; it was smiling back.

"You don't need to explain yourself to me again; I know who you are. My uncle's already told me everything." Thamu was saying. "You are honorary cousin. Member of family now."

"Thank you, *cousin*." Tom said amused at the idea of this adoption. He stood up, not sure whether the boy could hear him.

"I will take you home," he was saying.

"Home?" Tom echoed, wondering what Thamu could mean.

"We must go."

The footpath passed through a thick bush of thorny trees, bamboo and wild vines. The thickness of a grown man's arm. The underbrush covered in dead leaves, was wet and crawling with life. Insects, ants, beetles, termites, millipedes, snakes… some of them edible, some of them poisonous, some of them both… Thamu watched where he stepped as he went along and he wondered how it must be for the *peetyhoung* to be able to go about untouched, invisible, silent… the best of hunters.

Tom floating above, looked down at the pensive Thamu. This connection developing between the two of them was deepening. Tom often felt what Thamu was feeling. It was as if he could see his thoughts and access his memories. He would feel the same pangs of innocence the boy was feeling, his proud desires to redeem his mother, widowed for many years and relegated to the fringes of village life. They had been ostracized despite the chief's influence. There was nothing they could do. It was the way of the village. The boy's mind tells him it is because the other women think his mother will steal their husbands. The boy dreams of a palatial house that he will own atop one of the hills overlooking the village. He would install his mother there and those that wanted to see her, or get deer meat would have to make the long pilgrimage up the hill to her feet.

They came to an old tree on the side in a clearing surrounded on all sides by tall bamboo. It looked ancient and as though it had been blasted by lightning.

"This is the home of the deities," Thamu told him. He looked for Tom but couldn't find him anywhere. "Tom?"

Thamu calls out again and again, turning about him. All he heard was the sound of the wind pushing through the leaves. Thamu felt like he was the only living thing in this world. He waited and waited, but Tom didn't appear and when he decided he couldn't wait any longer, Thamu began the return trek to the village.

Tom was waiting for Thamu back at the hut. Thamu was relieved to see him, but disappointed by Tom's casual greeting. It was as though nothing had happened.

Of course, Tom sensed Thamu's disappointment. They were in each other's heads now. "What's the problem?"

"You are scaring me, Tom," Thamu told him.

"There is nothing to be afraid of. I was avoiding your friends."

"Why?"

"They don't like me, I don't think."

"It's important to respect the deities. I will bring you to see them. I will explain everything."

Tom shook his head. "No. Not now."

⇡ ⇡ ⇡

THE hut was small and dark. Even at midday the darkness lay about it. It had been that way for a long time and never had received any visitors or invited guests. No one had ever traversed that transom except Thamu and his mother. Thirteen years ago since Thamu's father passed away, Thamu went to live with his uncle's in his family's hut. He learned to become a man there as was custom in the village, and returned home to his mother seven years later.

"Why haven't you ever invited your friends?" Tom asked Thamu.

"It's not good manners to listen to someone's thinking," Thamu said, deflecting the question.

But sensing something troubling Thamu, Tom insisted. "That doesn't answer my question. Why?"

"I don't have friends," Thamu answered rather quickly. "They are strays. They are not my friends. Why should I invite them?"

"Ah, I see!" Tom said.

"What do you see?"

"*You* are the stray."

Thamu grew hot. "Why do you say that to me?"

"Because you say that to yourself," Tom answered.

"I don't understand."

"I mean when we speak of someone else, we are speaking of ourselves."

"I say it from anger."

"Your anger doesn't apply to others. You are angry with yourself."

"It doesn't matter, I am angry when I say it."

"You're angry because you let it get to your ego."

Thamu thought of his mother and the insults he bore at her expense from the village boys. "I don't know what you're saying." Thamu protested. He stamped his foot. "Why don't you go to hell!"

"I *am* in hell."

"I mean the true hell, where you burn from the inside

out."

And the moment Thamu said the words, Tom disappeared. He was gone for seven days, but for the following week, until Tom reappeared, Thamu didn't know if he would be gone forever, if he hadn't consigned his friend to the fires of hell.

"I am blind, mother," Thamu cried.

"What are you talking about, son?"

"My friend Tom—he's gone!"

"Who?" asked his mother.

But Thamu didn't answer. He went to bed, pulling the covers over his head and refused to leave it and wouldn't talk to anyone.

Everyone said he was sick. But no one could tell what it was. Mysterious illnesses were often fatal. The word got out and his 'friends' finally came to visit the hut. They flocked to the corner where Thamu lay on his cot. His mother told everyone that he was unable to swallow food. Some said, it was judgment for the deer meat charade— late judgment perhaps, but judgment finally arrived.

Thamu's spirit could find no peace those days. He returned each day to crash site seeking Tom. He'd spend all day there waiting for him, never venturing further than the creek just at the foot of the hill of the crash site. There Thamu tried to make the day useful and keep himself occupied. He hunted crab and fish, jumping from one rock to another. The creek was spotted with large moss-covered rocks. It turned the water into rapids like water in a pot coming to boil, frothy and foamy. The banks of the shore were filled with thick, green, stringy vines interwoven with each other, climbing over the plants and trees and stone and covering everything. Further up where the creek ran off from the river and its water were deep and still, Thamu put down his barbed fishing spear and bent down flat upon a rock. He gazed at first at the river bottom before dipping his head into the water. It was possible that Tom was hiding in the river, perhaps watching him. But Thamu saw nothing. He took his head out of the water and waded back to the shore. He looked up at the hill again and then the treetops. He listened to the jungle for a sign. Only Tom and the forest deity could see everything in the forest. But Thamu felt there was much he saw and felt as well. After all, he could see Tom while no one else could. Even Thabo had only seen Tom in a dream. And when Thamu described him to his uncle, the chief had turned white and called upon the ancient ones to bless the village. It was just as he had seen him in the dream. Then Thamu was able to answer Thabo questions and corroborate what Tom had told him in the dream. Things Thabo had not yet told anyone.

Even the snake that guarded the crash site was seen by the villagers only when it wanted to be seen. Thamu alone was able to see it crawling about the crash site and the mouth of the cave where Tom first made his home. The cobra appeared to be waiting for him that morning at the mouth of the cave. Thamu was hopeful and took it as a good sign. He sat and watched it all morning, but there had been no sign of Tom. Thamu tried speaking to the snake, but it ignored him, coiling about itself on the hot stone and going to sleep. Thamu waited and waited until he lost hope.

↟ ↟ ↟

LONG after Thamu was gone, Tom emerged from the cobra's mouth, emitted like smoke forming a cloud.

A moment later, Tom was standing on his feet before the cave in his green pilot's uniform. The cobra having performed its task was crawling back into the cave behind him. Tom's eyes were scanning the forest before him. It was deep night, but he was able to see it as though it was day. Everything alive in the jungle, including the plants and the water in the river, had a glow and luminescence. He stepped further off of the rock and leaping from tree to tree, flew above the forest until he landed at Sang La, the great river that fed all rivers and streams. He alighted on the branches above the calm, flowing water.

Tom could see the village fires in the distance and the smoke rising from the huts. He thought of Thamu and suddenly felt touched by the boy's devotion. He thought of home for the first time since all this happened with the same tenderness, of Ann and his family. He began thinking, that if he wished it hard enough, if he thought upon them hard enough, then he might suddenly find himself there. He shut his eyes…

A parliament of owls was just then flying overhead. The first to arrive took positions in the branches above him. The tree shook and Tom began falling from the branch, when a larger owl flew at him and tore at his cheek with its talons. Now Tom was falling as the other owls swirled around him, tearing at him where they could. Their beaks went for flesh but though they found none. Still, they tore at him as if they did. In pain, stunned, Tom flew off leaping again from tree to tree to the safety of his cave. All the while, the owls gave chase, tearing his uniform to bits with their talons. Finally at the cave, the last thread of his uniform picked off his naked body, Tom fell into the mouth of the cave, just as the cobra was coming out. The few foolish owls that alighted soon took to flight again.

The cobra rose up and grew far above their size. Quick on the ground, it chased them off the lip of the cave and into the air one by one. Only after the last sign of them was gone, did Tom's guardian return to its post within the darkness of the cave.

Tom never again appeared in his uniform. That day, he had also understood that there was no going back. The following morning he met with Thamu half-way on his daily pilgrimage to the site.

XII

DARK CLOUDS HUNG IN THE SKY that night after the American MIA team had come to inspect the crash site. It was about to rain again. There were no stars out, but there were many fireflies to be seen. Most of that day and night the rain had poured down as if the sky was leaking. But at night the rain made a sound that spread calm into the entire village along with feelings of serenity. Thamu laid down to sleep next to his wife with feelings of joy, happiness and a sense of calm. Thamu felt he had outwitted the Americans and the government officials even if only temporarily. It would be a mighty feat to withstand them. Thabo would have been proud.

Dee felt Thamu spoon up against her. It brought her feelings similar to the memories of relief from fear she had felt as a child when her parents finally came home. She understood that Thamu's business with these Americans could unsettle the entire village and their way of life. She leaned back against her husband, listened to the rain drops bringing a new day with them.

⚏ ⚏ ⚏

It was understood that everyone would be busy for the next weeks. The harvest had to be reaped and preserved. The rice fields needed to be sown again... There was too much to do and too much at stake for anyone to be idle. At the end of the month, the villagers called for the elder shaman to entreat the forest god to provide good crops for the year to come. The shaman came, offered sacrifices, slaughtered three chickens, performed the rites and called upon our ancestors. In return the village presented him with fresh eggs and three silver coins. These were placed on the ground at his feet.

After the shaman had slaughtered the chickens and poured their blood over the sacred stone, the villagers knelt down on the ground with their palms clasped together bowing three times. The villagers then prepared a feast in which all partook of the slaughtered chickens. The heads of the chickens, their feet, hearts and livers however were reserved for the shaman who would later make medicines from them.

On the first night of the sowing season, like during the harvest, everyone in the village celebrated. The sounds of drums could be heard throughout reaching deep into the forest. The whistle of the flute blew, and once the sounds of this music filled the air, the children were forbidden to play outside. It was said that if they were found, the spirits of their ancestors would come and take them away before their time. The ancestor spirits lived among the villagers after emerging from their place of burial. No one knew where the eldest ancestors were buried as they had died before the modern cemetery was created. They were said to be more peaceful enjoying a freedom that the others did not have – for those with a burial site were confined to return to it somehow. Like the ancestor spirits, the *peetyhoung* was a village familiar of sorts. *Peetyhoungs* were said to be the souls of those that suffered an untimely death and were not ready to enter their final resting place. They remained in this world, even if partially, to complete unfinished business in their lives. Tom was such a spirit. Thamu knew the stories of *peetyhoungs* even as a child, long before he had met Tom, though it was rare that anyone saw them. They were said to mostly come out at night, always in the guise of different animal forms: giant bats, owls, orangutans, wolves or even bamboo rats. At night people didn't go near these animals when they were sighted.

THAMU participated in the proceedings and performed his part as one among the villagers. He stood and watched as the shaman took his leave after all had been consumed and the forest deity appeased, and the old man began making his way back towards his home in the Eastern village. It was the last they would see of the shaman until the following year. They all took great pains in the parting, showering their blessing and good will upon the shaman. The villagers were always mindful that their annual parting might be the last and the following year might bring them a new shaman altogether. This would happen if the present shaman were to die. All the shamans were over fifty years of age and could get called up to heaven at any time. It was known throughout the tribe that all shamans lived double lives and that they already knew when their day would come to return to the sky though they never divulged to anyone when that might be.

Now the music began to die down and the older villagers and women began returning to their huts. The Feast of planting season that was held every year, before the seeds were put in the ground, to honor the forest and ancestral spirits was over. Thamu went at once to see Tom. This time he had more to discuss with him. Thamu knew the Americans would not give up so easily.

XIII

SOUTHEAST ASIA—the entire region had become a sore point for the United States. Very few people, even among the educated were able to see Laos, Vietnam or Cambodia for what they were. Nations, lands, people, rich with culture and history and their own perspectives, subject to the lashes and directions of their governments. They saw only an ideological enemy that the politicians in their fear-mongering had essentially fabricated. But Wagner had no such luxury of ignorance. He was forced to dig deeper, to get to know and understand these people. It was necessary if he was to do his job well.

And all this empathy if you wish to call it that, would not distract him from his job and his first duty which was to a fallen soldier and his family back home in America. He reminded himself, recollected his memories of his interviews with the family. It was these things that kept him true to his purpose and steeled his resolve to get Thamu's cooperation.

He had even visited Marie at her home in a small town in Iowa soon after being assigned his mission and before flying over to Laos. He left no stone unturned. They sat on the deck and looked through family albums.

She showed him pictures of Tom and herself when they were children still. In a picture Wagner remembers, they stood beside each other, her left arm draped across her brother's shoulders. Her smile showed her missing front teeth, and she had one eye clenched shut to block the sunlight. When Wagner pored over those old childhood photographs that day, the sense of waste, of futility and blind sorrow touched him profoundly. No one should die that way, alone and forgotten so far from home.

Something Wagner had learned about Tom, which surprised him, was Tom's apparent lack of interest in everything political, including the war. It was not unusual for conscripted service men, forced into the war, to be indifferent to the cause if not even, antipathetic to it. There were draft dodgers and there were anti-war protests—none of which anyone had forgotten. But it was unusual in Tom's case—a fighter pilot and an officer no less, with all that training and dedication to fly dangerous missions and not have a patriotic sentiment about it. He never forgot Marie's words to him: "Tom never had much interest in politics. In fact, he didn't seem to have an opinion on the war at all, which everyone seemed to have at the time. I'm sure you remember, there was a great debate about it with strong polemics on both sides as to whether the US should be fighting at all, whether the war was justified and so on. But Tom didn't seem to care one way or another." And when Wagner looked nonplussed at Marie, she added, "It was the adventure of it. The heroics. He wanted to experience new things, great things, perhaps leave Iowa and our small town."

Wagner had no idea at the time of the mess that he was about to embroil himself in. Of course he had read the briefings and he had an educated notion about Laos and its landlocked geography and isolated politics. Eighty percent of the land was mountainous and unsuitable for agriculture or for settlement. There were no highways and few waterways that provided access to Laos. Being landlocked there were no ports and the only means of transport into the country was by air—and that by helicopter for there were no runways or landing strips at the time except those secret airstrips the CIA had created for their own use and which no one knew about until much later. Even those CIA airstrips soon fell to neglect and were overgrown and reclaimed by the jungle shortly after the US ceased operations.

Now transport by air cost a fortune to operate. The planes got bigger with time which meant the runways had to be longer. The Laos government, or one should say, the "Lao People's Party" for the country had only one political party—could not sustain the cost and had no incentive to do so. Its people and economy were still relatively primitive—contact with outsiders was not encouraged and foreigners were not welcome. All this added to the difficulties that Wagner would encounter. Lately, he was growing more and more frustrated with all the different competing bureaucracies within the Laos government; but also with his own government and their apparent inability to clear the path for him.

Everyone on Wagner's team was convinced after their first meeting with the government authorities that money and only money would solve the problem. Enough money and they could pay everyone in the village, bribe enough officials, buy Thamu's compliance and pay for any work or excavation that needed to be done. Of course the Laos government and the defense minister himself, had no objection to this argument. And of course, his commanders back home had no idea what there might be on earth to possess this small, remote village or what a poor tribe living in the same remote jungle for hundreds of years might want with the remains of an American pilot. And Wagner knew that to enter into a dialog about Thamu's culture or his reluctance was inacceptable. It would be tantamount to inventing excuses. No one back home wanted to hear about *peetyhoungs* or the beliefs of these tribes and Wagner would be summarily dismissed.

The truth was both sides, the Americans and the Laotians, were unwilling to take the time to understand the tribe's position. The job was left to Wagner alone. It was not an easy task. Most cultures were rooted in traditions written in books or exemplified by a leader. These would be catalogued, recorded, preciously guarded. But the tribes' culture had no history. There was no beginning. It was an oral tradition that had passed from generation to generation. And if you asked any tribesman, he would tell you it had been so since the dawn of time. There was no law book or code of conduct that Wagner could appeal to or reference to sway the tribe and Thamu.

It didn't help that Marie was a congresswoman—one of the first women in the mid-west to be in congress and a little bit of a local celebrity. At first, Wagner thought this might come in handy, in pulling some strings so to speak and facilitating matters. In fact, all it did was add to the pressure, to the number of people he had to report to, the forms he had to fill out, and ultimately, how many people he might disappoint.

"I have a son, an only son," she had confided. "He has just turned thirty. Tom would have been fifty-four. Soon, it will be thirty years that he has gone missing. I will be sixty next year and though some would say that is still relatively young… I feel as old I can possibly imagine. When I think of my brother Tom, it's like a part of me has never left that place, that time. It awakens emotions and memories that may as well have been formed only yesterday. I don't feel much different than I did the day Tom left for Vietnam twenty-seven years ago."

"It must be terrible," Wagner interjected. "I will do everything I can to bring him home."

He had given his word. Wagner hated being put in that position.

XIV.

THE WINTER OF 1997 was coming to an end. It took two years before Wagner could get all the paperwork and requisite permissions and his team could return to claim the remains. They were now eighteen months behind schedule. As the flight from Bangkok, Thailand touched ground at the Laos airport, Wagner started panicking. After they passed through the terminal to the customs office, Wagner broke from the group and took for the exit. He felt he needed some breathing room. His team members watched him go off, none venturing after him, but all exchanging knowing looks with one another.

The hotel driver and tourist officer were standing by the customs office and jumped to attention once they noticed Wagner. They both ran over expecting to help the team with their luggage and equipment. The Lao officers were introducing themselves while Wagner's team was meeting up with him outside. Greetings and introductions were exchanged. Everyone shook hands. Wagner led the group, head down, terse in his speech and sweaty as a boxer. Soon they were all packed into the mini-bus and headed over to the Million Elephant Hotel.

May is a hot month in Laos; and the glare of the sun

hit the windows of the bus like a flame. Everyone's eyes shone back at him with that glare and looked to Wagner as if they were lit up with madness or evil. Thankfully, the minibus was air-conditioned and Wagner was soon feeling cooler and calmer. He envisioned a chilly spring morning and soon he was back home again away from all this maddening heat. Feeling sufficiently composed and reconciled now to his present, he opened his eyes and they fell directly upon the driver's ear. An ear so small, Wagner remarked to himself, that it could have belonged to a child. Was he from one of the tribes? Wagner wondered. He might have been. Like many who flocked to the cities seeking a better life, perhaps he had taken the trail that led out from the woods, the trail that disappeared and never circled back nor met with any other trail, to find himself in a new life, get integrated through some tribal connection already implanted in the city, follow training and land a job driving shuttle buses for tourists. It was the American dream, Wagner thought—or some paltry version of it. Wagner was curious if he was right in his assessment. That ear was too peculiar. But he decided he didn't feel like asking. If it was true, he thought, that the man was a tribesman, then perhaps he knew who Wagner was already and wouldn't want to talk to him. He knew this miniscule-eared driver spoke at least a little English. He had overheard him speaking to one of his staff at the airport. "Please go in," he remembered the driver saying. Perhaps that was the only phrase he knew in English. Wagner couldn't be sure... He suddenly wondered about ears and the capacity to hear, to enter into bilateral discussions and so reason and negotiate. He wondered about Thamu's ears now... Were they too small to hear the world Wagner knew? He needed to discover a way of persuading Thamu to cooperate with him. Otherwise, he was going to have to demand for his arrest.

↑ ↑ ↑

WAGNER wasn't honoring himself—this is how he'd put it. What's more—it meant a loss of control. He had sworn to himself, a personal and professional oath, that he would cease thinking about the case the minute they landed. All angles had been explored, every avenue to a solution mapped. He knew what must be done and thinking about it further was simply another delay, another futile attempt at escaping the inevitable. The matter had become an international incident. Political reputations were on the line. Failure to complete the mission was simply out of the question, even if only because the means to execute it successfully were so close at hand. Via force or otherwise. Failure would be an embarrassment.

But like the proverbial cup, Wagner's mind had already run over. They hadn't arrived at the hotel yet, but he felt his anxiety already swelling. His heart began racing when the bus pulled into the hotel entrance. Under the parking roof, his heart was pounding as though it wanted to be let out of his chest. He felt dizzy and weak suddenly. A cold sweat poured down him. The hotel porters opened the minibus doors to let everyone out, but Wagner couldn't trust his legs to move. When his team turned around for him, they saw him, panicked, with a tormented, pained look on his face and a hand clutching his chest. Wagner's team carried him out to the hotel lobby while the porters went to summon the doctor. They were all sure he was having a heart attack. A Vietnamese doctor soon arrived and by then, Wagner had already appeared to have recovered somewhat. His breathing and heart rate were falling and he was making motions to sit up. The doctor examined him briefly. It was an obvious prognosis. He took Wagner's pulse while counting on his watch. Then his doctor's bag came out. Three quick applications of the stethoscope and then a quick pull-down on the skin under his eyes to reveal his whites and the doctor was packing it up already.

The doctor looked around at the faces of Wagner's team and back at Wagner, and surmised Wagner was their superior. "This man is dehydrated and has succumbed to heat stroke," he announced. "In this heat, it is important to drink plenty of water and to keep the head cool. Fetch me some water," he told them. "I will tend to him." The doctor then bent down to help Wagner up. He leaned in to him as he did. "You've just had an anxiety attack," he whispered.

WAGNER was feeling much better by supper. He was telling his staff as they all dined together, that he was fully recovered, that he wasn't anxious about their meeting tomorrow with the minister of defense and his committee, and that he felt confident that he and his team would get the job done. He ate well, laughed with them and retired late.

XV.

THE TEAM MET IN THE DEFENSE minister's conference room. Saravong Savang and his entire delegation which they had met at their first meeting where there again. It was as though time had not passed in that room and stepping in Wagner felt that all those months in between had been a disjointed dream. He and his team were once again ushered in to their assigned seating opposite the minister and his delegation. Only when he was seated did Wagner notice a new face, one that had not been there at their first meeting. It was the chief of the Viangchan police. His name, Wagner would learn, was Chanetasith Virasane and he had a reputation for being a 'no nonsense kind of guy'. The minister had requested that he be present at their meeting.

Sitting opposite the minister, Wagner felt nervous, but was far from that sense of anxiety that overtaken him in the morning. Perhaps the doctor's original assessment had been correct after all—it had only been dehydration, a mild heat stroke, he told himself. He thought back to when they first had a meeting that the Laotian authorities, all the empty promises and hardline politics. There would "be no problem, absolutely no problem" the minister had first assured. The only thing "you, Mr. Wagner, our American friends" had to do was actually find the remains. Now, as he understood it, the remains had been moved from the crash site to an area in the jungle sacred to the tribe. Only one man knew for sure the location of the remains and he was refusing to speak. He wondered if this Thamu even understood the forces that he was conjuring upon his head. Failure, Wagner, already knew was not an option. The entire village, let alone one man, could not withstand the combined power and force that would be brought to bear. There was the Laotian government, the ministry of defense, police commissioners and more, to say nothing of the added pressure the US would be sure to apply as its collective patience waned.

↑ ↑ ↑

WAGNER was getting settled in his seat when the minister turned to the police chief. "And when you get there," he said quietly, but loud enough for everyone to hear. "Don't forget to try the bamboo-rat!" Everyone laughed and the police chief, a hard man, not used to showing his teeth, grimaced and nodded as though approving of the joke. Everyone knew the tribe people hunted or trapped the bamboo rat. They also hunted wild turkey and any birds they could trap or catch. But the bamboo rat was abundant and easy to snag. So it became a regular part of their diet and a general theme of jokes made at their expense. "And our Americans friends too!" the minister broke in. "They may like our bamboo rat, eh, eh?" And again everyone laughed as the minister laughed at his own joke.

"I'm told it tastes like chicken," Wagner said and the

laughter stopped. The police chief alone was smiling now and the room had gone silent.

A moment later, the minister was again showing his affable smile. He nodded to his secretary. "Delightful," he said. "It does taste like chicken, I am told!" Laughter ran through the room again. "Yes, yes..." the minister muttered. He cast a glance toward his assistant by the door. Seeing the signal, she left the room, shutting the door behind her, and everyone in the minister's delegation took up their papers and pens.

"Shall we begin?" the minister proposed looking Wagner squarely in the eye, but still holding that affable smile.

"We have today a special guest to present to our American friends," the minister began. "As a sign of our commitment to our joint cause of peace, to redeem the past of its war and pain and a token of our on-going friendship... The Laotian government will do what it must to see that our American friends find the answers they seek. I present Mr. Chantasith Virisane, the chief of police to assist our American friends in recovering the remains of their pilot as quickly possible. Mr. Chantasith has full jurisdiction and has been granted discretionary powers to act in this case. I believe he has some words he'd like to say."

The chief stood up, no trace of that smile left on his face.

"Thank you Minister. It is my honor to be asked here today to represent the Viangchan police in this matter. Our pledge and mandate from the ministry of defense is to provide support and security during the completion of this mission. We are committed gentlemen," he said, taking a pregnant pause to cast his no-nonsense glance about the room, "to ensuring the successful completion of this mission." He looked directly at Wagner. "It will be my honour sir, to personally escort you to the site of the location of the crash and suspected remains of the pilot."

Wagner listened, but only from the periphery. He was waiting for Mr. Chantasith to finish his speech and sit down. Until then, he felt all he could do was monitor his pulse and appear calm. Of course, he already knew what the minister was driving at, and before Mr. Chantasith was finished and took his seat, and Wagner could catch his breath, the police chief went on, laying down the groundwork that the minister had so carefully paved for him.

"We are aware that approximately eight hundred ammunition rounds have disappeared in the region after the liberation in the spring of 1973," the police chief said. Meanwhile, the minister and his affable smile were both on Wagner. The police chief went on: "These have never been recovered. To this day they are believed to rest with unknown criminal elements operating in the region. Their identities have never been identified but we have reason to assume that they are members of these mountain tribes and if they are not, they are at least being assisted and sheltered by them. There is no misunderstanding here. These men are enemies of the state. They are murdering criminals who terrorize the otherwise peaceful tribesmen and women. They are drug smugglers and corrupt the young of the villagers into transporting their opium. They control what everyone knows as the 'golden triangle' where opium is grown and harvested to be spread like pestilence through our people. This disease, is a cancer in the body of our proud nation. One day, an end will be put to all this. Today, we are here to show that these criminal gangs have no power. That truth and law, with the help of our American friends will prevail."

Wagner looked at the faces of this team next to him. He mustered a smile as if to assure them there was nothing to worry about when in reality all he was doing was attempting to suppress the sinking feeling that it was all slipping away from him, all his careful planning, all his research, all for naught.

"In light of these criminal elements and the threats they pose," the police chief went on with an approving nod from the minister, "we will be supplying ourselves with additional equipment and men. With the ministry's permission, we would require two additional helicopters to transport the required resources."

The minister waved his hand as though it were a worthless favor. "Of course. Granted." He turned to the aide on his right. "Make the necessary arrangements," he told him.

"Thank you, honorable minister."

The police chief sat down and resumed his stone glance.

Having the floor once again, the minister turned that famous affable smile on Wagner again. "You see, Mr. Wagner. You and your team will have all the help you need. The Laos government is here to help."

Wagner knew of former government army factions that had defected and taken refuge in the mountain, sometimes hiding among the tribes. From Wagner's understanding most of these soldiers had been American supporters or sympathizers during the war. They were called the Hmong. He looked at Chantasith and wondered how deep into this he was—if he knew that the minister intended to use these recovery missions as a means of ridding his mountains of dissenters or whether the police chief was another unwitting pawn.

The minister, his delegation, everyone was now waiting for Wagner's response. Wagner leaned forward in his chair. He would be guarded with his words. "We are delighted that the Laos government and its department of defense have taken this spirit of cooperation to heart. Our policy in this region has always been founded in the belief that only with transparency and trust between our two nations could a sustainable environment of stability be achieved in the region. We have encountered no criminal elements in reconnaissance of the area, but we thank the minister for his precautions and security measures on our behalf."

The minister flashed his smile.

"I think however, that the presence of police or of military may do more harm than good. It will frighten them further into silence and destroy the trust we have with the villagers."

The minister broke out laughing before Wagner could finish. His delegation laughed with him. "Trust," the minister repeated looking around. "*Trust* Mr. Wagner? You can't trust these mountain people. They are savage primitives. They have no loyalty."

"Our government has no desire to incite violence," Wagner told the minister.

"Oh, no! There will be no violence," the minister promised. "Will there, Mr. Chantasith?"

"No minister. We are here to keep the peace. My duty is to provide security and ensure the safe passage our American guests."

"Precisely," chimed the minister, affably satisfied. "You see, Mr. Wagner? It is understood. Violence is not something anyone wants. As minister, my first duty is to the welfare and protection of Laos and its citizens."

"Of course," Wagner said, though he remained unconvinced. "I have only one request: I'd like a small medical team to accompany us."

"A medical team?" the minister echoed. He thought about it and saw no reason to deny him the request. "Why of course, Mr. Wagner. I shall provide you with the finest field medic we have."

The meeting was over. It seemed there was nothing left to discuss. The machine had been set into inexorable motion. As Wagner and his team were leaving the room, he was struck by the finality of the proceedings. Indeed there was nothing left to discuss and nothing left to do. It seemed that all would depend on Thamu now. He would have to comply or the Laotian government's hand would be forced. The decision tree had been mapped out, Wagner, the minister, the chief of police were all pieces on a chessboard now.

♟ ♟ ♟

CHANTASITH took a short cut via the back door exit. He knew everyone who worked security on the grounds and was able to pass through with a glance or a nod. He was the first one out of the building and was already in his car driving off while Wagner and his team were exiting the front of the building. He caught sight of them, and stopped to study Wagner in particular. That American might be trouble, he thought. All his years of service had taught him to detect the problem cases from just a glance. He could tell from the way a man walked, the way he stood, the way he looked at you—if he was the sort to resist or to comply. Chantasith had made up his mind about Wagner. Driving back to the office with the glare of the sun on the windshield, he began cursing about the heat. A car drove past him. The driver had his head out the window to catch the wind. Chantasith cursed him too. He knew it was Wagner he was really cursing. He muttered curses under his breath all the way to the office.

↥ ↥ ↥

"I need a volunteer!" Chantasith announced entering the station.

"What kind of volunteer, sir?" asked one of the officers.

"I need a man to lead twenty armed policemen into the jungle with the American MIA team. We will have to deal with the hill tribes," he went on. "I need strong men. There might be some digging involved. We'll be looking for the remains of a pilot that crashed his airplane, twenty years ago."

"Why policemen?" asked another, younger officer.

"Because some hill tribe up there thinks the spirit of the dead pilot is his adopted brother or some stupidity. He is refusing to allow the Americans to remove the remains from its location. They fear it would anger the gods and bring disaster upon their villages."

"Pathetic!" said the young officer. A murmur went around the station, passing from policeman to policeman.

"I've already said it and it won't be the first nor the last lunatic you'll have to deal with," Chantasith repeated angrily. "So do I have a volunteer?"

His officers turned away from him, careful to avoid his eyes. They all scanned the room to see who'd get caught.

One female officer came in behind him.

"I would like to volunteer," she said.

But Chantasith wasn't amused. "No, we need a man for this job," he said.

The female officer stuck to her guns. "Under what article does it say that women aren't allowed to stand on the ground for any activities?"

"We don't have time for this," he yelled. "You know the views of the department, but it's the villagers I am concerned about. This situation is complicated enough without us instigating a war of the sexes with them."

The female officer snorted, but conceded.

"Very well, if no one will volunteer then I shall make my decision later today along with the list of officers who will accompany us. Those accompanying us and the MIA team will be reporting directly to the military air field tomorrow."

XVI

TWO HELICOPTERS were standing on the runway, ready for take-off. The engines were running, the top propellers were turning and gathering speed. Wagner could see the grass all around the field flattened by gusts as though a current of water was running through it and they were all under water already and just didn't know it. Wagner made for the first helicopter with his team trailing behind him. Chantasith led his team into the second. Both men stepped calmly, almost ceremoniously. They marched defiantly against the propellers, ignoring the lash of the winds as though in contest with each other, while their teams scrambled behind them, bent forward, holding on to their briefcases, attaché cases, their hairs as they climbed on board.

Everyone was soon seated and strapped in. The doors closed and the helicopter jerked before it lifted up. Airborne finally, the drone of the engines white-noising everything, Wagner finally found some peace gazing out to the landscape below. He tried to imagine what it would have been like for a young GI stationed to Vietnam all that time ago, and to be flying to his first assignment above enemy fire. Higher ground was always the advantage one thought. But Wagner didn't feel safe—quite the opposite.

Wagner felt vulnerable. Looking down was a tangled mass of jungle and shadow. There were a thousand places for an enemy to hide, while here he was, this loud blotch slowly crawling through a clear sky, visible and audible to everyone for miles around. There could be a thousand men down there and weapons all aimed on him for all he could tell. He wondered if Tom felt the same.

The helicopter touched ground in a rice field near the Eastern village. Villagers had already gathered, after first hearing and then seeing the helicopters come over the hills. They saw the men pour out of these great machine birds. They saw a group of foreigners and a second group of government men from the city. Both groups began setting up encampments on opposite sides of each other. The villagers looked at each other and their worry grew. Government men never came to the villages except when they wanted something. Now it was like they brought their entire homes with them and were moving in: Tents came out and went up. Tables, folding chairs, radio equipment, digging equipment, guns, ration boxes—these were all suddenly appearing like a new village spreading through the rice field. Keen observers they were able to detect Wagner and Chantasith as the chiefs of their respective clans. They saw Chantasith pointing and shouting to the government men and knew he was chief. They saw Wagner lean over and whisper to one of his team and nod assertively to others to set them to work and knew that he was their chief. The two chiefs did not talk to each other or look at each other. The villagers understood: that too did not bode well. One of the younger villagers broke from the group and headed back to the village to spread the news.

WAGNER had a smaller contingency and very little in equipment and supplies by comparison. The Americans had finished setting up camp before the Laotian team. Wagner thought he'd seize the opportunity to preempt Chantasith. He walked over to where he was standing, sitting on a stone by the bamboo groves bordering the field.

"I would like to speak to the villagers about our objectives here," Wagner announced.

Chantasith smiled and stood up slowly as though to suggest there was no hurry. "What would you like us to tell them?"

"There will be no need for *you* to address them. I would prefer to address them myself. The translator can then translate for me."

Chantasith pursed his lips. Wagner pressed on: "I want you to know that the US government is not here to interfere with this community or compromise its way of life in anyway. I needn't explain to you either, that we must avoid violence of any sort. We need cooperation from one person, a man by the name of Thamu. There is no need to involve the rest of the village as they know nothing about the remains. Only Thamu, if anyone, knows where those bones are buried. We know he has been taking care of the remains like holy relics in a shrine. It is a sensitive matter we understand, but one I am sure we can solve diplomatically."

Chantasith turned that crooked smile of his on Wagner again. "We will tell them that, Mr. Wagner. You can be sure of it."

"As I said, Mr. Virisane. *I* will do the talking."

"Of course."

Wagner began making his way to Thamu's village with

the translator and Chantasith following. After a few steps, Chantasith and his police escort took the lead. "Many dangers live in these hills," Chantasith explained. "Your safety is my highest priority. We don't know what animals, human or otherwise, might attack. I must insist," he said and soon Wagner and his men were taking up the rear.

They came to a hut on the edge of the village along the path connecting it to the rice field. A large hut, with firewood stacked high along its side wall. A small vegetable patch and garden graced the perimeter. Wagner hadn't really had the time to see the villages upon his last visit. He could see now how comfortable it really was, furnished with all the necessities for life and comfort.

Chantasith and his escorts turned and began walking toward the hut when an old man came out, shirtless and almost blind with age. Chantasith approached him and leaning into the old man, shouted loudly and roughly.

"This man here wants to talk to you," Chantasith shouted in his ear while pointing at Wagner.

The old man stepped away from Chantasith. He looked Chantasith up and down and frowned. Wagner thought he heard him grumble something.

Chantasith didn't like it.

A little girl came out of the hut and took the old man's hand in hers.

"You scream like a wet baby," the old man said. "Why are you screaming at me? I am not deaf. Are you stupid?"

The old man tried to fix his one good eye on Chantasith.

"We're off to a fine start," Wagner whispered to Liam.

Chantasith was chuckling to cover his embarrassment. "I'll forgive you, old man. You have no idea who you are talking to. That is why it is you who is stupid. But you had better watch your words from now on. I'll have my men here arrest you. Do you understand? You want to see your grand-daughter while you still have eyes in your head, don't you?" Chantasith asked and appeared a little calmer. "Now, this man will ask you some questions. It is important that you answer truthfully if you want to see these rice fields again."

The old man nodded.

"He will answer your questions," she said.

Chantasith stepped aside and Wagner and the translator approached. Wagner tried a smile and a soft tone, but the old man cared as little for him as he had Chantasith.

"I am looking for Thamu. Do you know who that is?"

The old man nodded.

"He knows," his grand-daughter confirmed. "We all know Thamu."

"Where is Thamu now?"

The girl shrugged her shoulders. Wagner asked the old man, "Have you seen Thamu today."

"No," he answered in a calm, low tone.

"Do you know where we can find him?"

"He is hunting in the forest," the child broke in.

Chantasith ran out of patience and stepped toward the old man suddenly. "Tell him where Thamu is!" he shouted. "We are not going to kill him. We just want him to bring us to the crash site. Do you understand me? Tell us where Thamu is!"

Wagner looked toward Chantasith with a consternation and disappointment that he didn't bother hiding.

"Where is his hut?" Chantasith continued. "Where is his wife?"

The old man motioned to his left. "At the end of the village," he said. "That way."

"Good!" Chantasith said. "We will find him ourselves."

The old man nodded. "It's my rice field," he said addressing Chantasith.

"What?" bellowed Chantasith, turning back.

"That's my rice field. You make your huts in my rice field," he explained.

"And so?"

The old man must have thought the statement self-explanatory for he said no more. Chantasith walked away.

They all marched off together to Thamu's hut, but found no one. The translator inquired with a neighbor who informed them that Thamu's wife would return home before night fall. All the women of the village did. Everyone returned home from the fields or the river or the rice fields at night fall. It was a stupid question to ask.

Thwarted at their first efforts, an exasperated Chantasith was already losing patience. It was Wagner that spoke up. "It is better to return to camp and wait for nightfall than to waste energy tramping about looking for the man. We will return here in the evening to find him sitting on his porch. Let's go."

���

BACK at camp, Chantasith's team of police volunteers had finished pitching their tent and already had a fire going. A pig was roasting on a spit, grease dripping down its sides. They were all standing about the roasting pig, mouths watering, swallowing back hunger… But they had spread tarps over the rice field and pitched their tents over it. The Americans had pitched their tents on the grass to the side of the field. Chantasith lost it once again. He threatened to shoot the idiot who decided to set camp in the middle of the rice field. Of course, it had been Chantasith who had said, "We'll set up camp right here." They scrambled all at once to take down the tents and move the camp. But, "It was too late," Chantasith told them. The crop was already damaged anyway and it would be a waste of time and energy.

Soon the pig was roasted and everyone was eating. Chantasith was again his affable self after having his belly filled. Wagner was sitting off to the side with the translator.

"It's delicious," Wagner said while chewing on a mouthful of meat. "Better than some of the barbecue, we have back home."

"Yes, very good, sir," agreed the translator.

"I've always been curious," Wagner said. "Where did you learn your English?"

"At Lao-American school, sir. It was the best in the country."

"Oh? When was that?" Wagner asked.

He learned how his translator had received his certification through night courses. He went straight there everyday after high school, he told him, for three years. He had hopes of winning a government sponsorhip to continue his education in Australia, but the war and the situation in Laos worsened. The left wing radicals had at that time moved in to many towns and taken cities across the country. The Royal Government was more concerned with winning battles at home than on foreign exchange programs. He graduated and got a job as a government translator and forgot about Australia.

"I've worked for the military, for the foreign ministry, even the tourism board," he told him.

"So you have been working in this job since?" Wagner asked.

"Twenty-six years today, though I missed almost three years in between," he said without explanation.

Wagner was curious as to the reason. "Why did you miss three years? Were you ill?"

"I was sent up to the Sumana learning camps in the north east after the liberation in 1975."

Wagner nodded.

"I only returned in 78." he added, setting his plate on the ground. "Many of my friends fled to Thailand. Some of them are now living in the United States. I decided to stay. I had parents and family. My in-laws too."

"But you are doing well now..."

"I have no complaints, sir. I love my job. I also teach English as a second language at night to civil servants. It is very gratifying."

OVER at the other side of the camp, Chantasith had also finished eating and was watching Wagner and his translator intently. He stood up and lit a cigarette, blowing a cloud of smoke out the side of his mouth. He began making his way over to Wagner.

"Gentlemen, night is falling. It is time to return to the village," Chantasith announced.

Wagner stood up. "Yes, I was just thinking about that. There's nothing we can do while it's dark," he said. He thought Chantasith and his men were too wound up. He remembered his encounter with Thamu the last time and didn't think it would go well if Chantasith were to barge in there and start barking out questions.

"Thamu will not be able to show us the burial site,"

Wagner added, "and certainly your men can't dig in the dark. We should return in the morning."

"Ah, but we may miss him and his wife in the morning again. We want simply to secure his location in order to plan our operations tomorrow. It may be a long hike and longer dig! My men are not used to laboring in this heat. You can stay here, if you prefer," Chantasith suggested. "As I said, we will not be questioning anyone, and so there really is no need for you or your translator to be there. Myself and a couple of policemen should be sufficient to get the job done."

"No, no, I'm coming," Wagner said. "We're both going," he added looking at the translator.

XVII

NIGHT HAD JUST FALLEN and the fog was already falling with it, rolling down the hills to settle on the village. The ground was wet, the grass and the rice were covered with drops of water, the size of a frog's eyeball it seemed to Thamu. He had taken a half dozen steps only and was already drenched from the waist down, dripping like he had just come up out of the river. He was watching the men at the camp from his vantage point, deep in the forest. They had settled right at the foot of the trail that led to Thamu's village and he saw that he'd have to cut through the camp or go around the hill if he wanted to return. Squatting on a ledge, in the shadow of the brush, Thamu saw policemen standing in line for their exercises; jumping up, banding sideways up front, bending backwards, repeatedly. An officer walked to and fro before them, shouting orders. It was a strange dance to be performing Thamu thought. When Thamu saw Wagner, he stood up. He forgot everything he had taught himself about being a hunter. He recognized Wagner. There was no doubt it was the same man that had questioned him about the *peetyhoung*. They were back.

And Thamu stood up, perhaps feeling threatened, like the leopard will rise on its hind legs when confronted with a foe. For the first time in his life, Thamu no longer felt like the hunter stalking his prey, the king of his jungle— No, he was the one hunted now. Thamu had become the prey. Sensing the predator, Thamu took a slow, step back and disappeared into the jungle behind him.

🐾 🐾 🐾

CHANTASITH was determined to resolve these 'stupidities' as soon as possible. If he was to keep order and the respect of his men, he would have to show everyone who was running the show here. He was not about to be challenged by a low savage from the hills. He would assert his authority one way or another. Every second that he was defied was a further embarrassment. And this American, this Wagner and his team were only getting in his way. They were foreigners after all and shouldn't be here. Chantasith couldn't understand in fact the need for their presence. They could have stayed home, let Chantasith and his men do their work. They could retrieve the remains a lot sooner without the need for all this translation and oversight and then some ministry puppet could have their sacred pilot's bones delivered to them. The foreigners only added to the problem. They brought no knowledge or expertise and were there only to interfere. It made him angry to have to listen to these Americans giving orders about something they knew nothing about. They weren't Laoloum nor Laotian and knew nothing about the situation. He had visited these hills as a child with his own father, during the liberation wars. He had seen these pathetic peasants squatting outside their bamboo huts and understood even as a boy: they were little better than animals. You could not reason with them in the way you couldn't reason with a dog. If you want the ox to pull the cart then you needed a stick. It was the only thing it understood and it was pointless to argue with it. His father had known it and had made sure Chantasith grew up to know it too.

Now, it was the Americans' turn to learn it.

Chantasith told his unit to remain at the campground until he returned and took only a handful of men and his lieutenant with him. He had a scowl on his face and no one seemed willing to argue. A minute later they were off, Chantasith stamping at the fore, Wagner, the translator, the lieutenant and everyone else trailed behind in silence.

The village huts came into view again as they turned the corner into the clearing past the bamboo groves. Once they passed the old man's hut, they could tell that the villagers had been waiting for them. Their appearance caused a commotion that seemed to set all those that were talking silent, and all those that were still into feverish motion. Some of them ran into their huts, others darted down a path as if to spread the news or to flee in mortal terror. Chantasith stopped everyone he could on their way to Thamu's hut. He grabbed the first runner by the arm: "Have you seen Thamu?" "Where is Thamu?"

He wasn't in his hut. No one knew where he was. Everyone shrugged and Chantasith grew hotter. He was losing face and patience. He marched headlong toward Thamu's hut.

To his left, trying to keep up, Wagner was scanning the crowd for Thamu and already fearing the worst. Off in the shadows a woman was watching him intently. Wagner hadn't noticed, but the translator had seen her creep from the shadows behind a hut. He had been observing her watching Wagner and saw her disappear again behind the hut as they drew nearer.

The translator touched Wagner on the arm. Wagner leaned in.

"I saw a young woman observing you intently the moment we entered the village. It was as though she knew you."

"Which woman?" Wagner asked.

"I'm afraid she's disappeared. She was right there," the translator indicated pointing to the hut she had disappeared behind.

Wagner moved quickly, but not quickly enough. He reached out and swept the translator's arm down, but Chantasith had already seen it. He stopped.

"What's that? You see something over there?"

The translator looked to the ground. "He says he had seen a woman watching us," Wagner explained. "But she's disappeared. It was nothing."

"Maybe it was nothing... Maybe it was this Thamu's wife... Or maybe," Chantasith said a little louder and looking around him, "She likes American men. Hollywood men, eh, Mr. Wagner?"

His police escort chuckled and snorted. Chantasith motioned them towards him. "They were pointing at that hut," he told them. "Let's go have a look."

Chantasith's men put their hands on their holsters and began moving toward the hut. Wagner moved to follow but Chantasith stopped him.

"Mr. Wagner, for your security…"

"Excuse me, if there is someone there with information about our pilot, then I wish to interview them."

"Of course, Mr. Wagner. But first, let my men secure

the danger. We don't know who might be hiding in that hut."

"Forgive me, Mr. Virisane, but the only danger I perceive here is from your overzealous men who seem too ready to reach for their guns. Now if you'll excuse me…"

But Chantasith wasn't letting him go. "No, you excuse me please Mr. Wagner. You are foreigner in my country and you think you know the dangers better than me?"

"I sense no danger from these people."

"Of course you don't, Mr. Wagner!" Chantasith said laughing. "But these people are savages, I assure you. They do not respect the law. They are illiterate all of them."

Wagner stepped closer. "And do *you* respect the law. Mr. Virisane? Article two of your constitution asserts the principle of equality among all its peoples, the ethnic peoples especially. All Laoloum citizens deserving the same respect and rights under the law. So, like I said before, if you'll excuse me…"

Wagner had won the argument much to Chantasith's chagrin. He had to let him go. In any case, his men were already coming out. "Just an old couple in there," they announced to Chantasith. "No one else."

"All the same," Wagner said. "I think I'd like to ask them some questions." He motioned for his translator to follow. Thamu's wife wouldn't betray her husband's whereabouts if he didn't want to be found. It was most likely, Wagner thought, that he wouldn't have told her anything at all for her own protection. He might as well try his luck here.

"Very well, Mr. Wagner. You ask your questions," Chantasith said with a twisted nose. He called his men over once Wagner and the translator had turned their backs.

"I think we should take Thamu's wife and hold her prisoner," he whispered to one of his senior men. "It will send a clear message that we are not playing game. Once we have her, we will them that we are holding her for questioning until her husband is willing to come forward and comply with the law."

"Hadn't we better wait?" his lieutenant suggested.

Chantasith lost his temper again. "Wait for what?" he shouted. "Do you want to spend another night in this swamp because one naked savage won't speak the truth? We will make him speak," Chantasith promised, gritting his teeth. "All men must hold to the truth! We go now, while the Americans are unable to interfere, and they will see how we get to truth in Laos."

Chantasith stormed off for Thamu's hut up the path, his lieutenant and escort following anxiously behind. Chantasith was a man on the rise. It wasn't every day that a police chief was invited to the Ministry of Defense. The word had spread quickly through the police station and then to all other stations across Laos. Chantasith was 'going places' as the Americans often said, and everyone wanted to go with him. It wasn't just the lieutenant—everyone on the assignment was eager to please, eager to show Chantasith that they could be depended upon; that he'd need them at his side as he made his way up in the world.

Meanwhile, Wagner and the translator were inside the hut facing the consternated couple. They were elderly and frightened for their only daughter. She had gotten mixed up with Thamu. They knew Thamu and his deer meat and that proud mother of his would one day bring trouble to them all. Now, two very strange-looking and stranger-smelling men were standing inside their hut speaking gibberish in it was most certainly a devil's tongue. One had a nose and ears that were white like milk. His face looked hot like embers and, to the elder man of the hut, looked as though he must faint or melt—he had never seen anyone so red and white at the same time before.

"Hello, my name is Wagner," he had said and then pointed to the other man who looked like those men from the city. This other man spoke Laoloum and every time the man with milk ears spoke in his devil's tongue, the second man seemed to understand his wishes and described it to them. "We are friends," he said. "He is called Wagner. He is come from far away beyond the hills and beyond the ocean even. He is from America."

The old man seemed unimpressed. The couple invited them to sit. The woman motioned to a bamboo cushion on the floor and the old man watched bemusedly as Wagner tried to cross his legs one over the other on the floor. He must have the bones of a hundred year old man, he thought.

"He must be sick," he told his wife. She looked at Wagner and frowned. Wagner saw her pouting at him with motherly concern and decided to start.

"We would like to ask you," he said nodding to his translator, "who that young woman outside your hut was?"

"Oh!" said the man; and he looked to his wife.

"We saw a young woman outside your hut," the translator repeated. "It seemed she wanted to talk to us. That's why we are here."

"Yaya—she's our only daughter," the woman said.

"She disappeared when we approached. Do you know where she would have gone?"

The old man shrugged his shoulders.

"Do you know where Thamu is?"

His wife looked to her husband. "We don't know where she is," he said.

Wagner knew they were hiding something. He turned to his translator: "Tell them she is not any kind of trouble. That we are here to ask her help only."

The translator did as Wagner asked. "He says they don't know where Yaya went," he told Wagner.

"Ask him again if he knows where Thamu is. Ask him if they've seen him today."

The old man seemed to study the question the translator asked him. "Thamu is not here," the man told the translator."Thamu lives up the path. He is a good man. Visit him you'll see."

"Tell him we would like very much to visit him, but can't find him. He is not in his hut."

Wagner could see the old man shrug his shoulders again. His wife was already losing interest and seemed to be smiling unconsciously at him.

"Okay," Wagner said, patting his translator on the shoulder. "Just one more question." Wagner turned to the father. He spoke to the translator while looking the man in the eyes. "Tell him, that I don't need to bother asking if he loves his daughter. Tell him, that I am a reasonable man and the last thing we want is an incident. Tell him," Wagner ordered the translator.

The translator spoke and after a pause. Wagner asked, "Tell him to confirm that he understands."

The old man held up his hands and nodded to Wagner.

"Now tell him, that there is a man outside visiting Thamu's hut right now. That we know Thamu is not there, but that the police commissioner sent from the capital, a man by the name of Chantasith, is not so reasonable. Tell him."

The old man nodded again.

"He will send his men out to find your daughter. Tell him."

The old man nodded again. His wife seemed alert again.

"For her own sake, it is better if I find her and speak to her than if the police commissioner does."

The father spoke: "There is a cave she goes to. She sees Thamu there. The cave is on the other side of the hill range."

"That is all we know," added the mother. "Tears were welling up in her eyes."

⚊ ⚊ ⚊

CHANTASITH was a determined man. He wasn't about to allow anything to get in his way. He felt for the first time, a true sense of power and he knew, he *felt* it—nothing could stop him. He had the entire Ministry of Defense, the entire government behind him. If he failed, it would be his own fault. He wasn't about to be defeated by a peasant hill-savage. Their defiance was an insult, not only against him, but against the entire Laotian people's government. He was enraged just thinking about their cheek at even contemplating defiance. He stamped all the way up to Thamu's hut, his escort keeping pace behind him, and then reaching it, did not bother waiting to knock but broke the door in with his shoulder.

Chantasith burst through the hut's front door shattering the bamboo cane all over the hut. He wasn't expecting to find this Thamu he had heard so much about so he wasn't disappointed when all he made out was a woman's figure at the foot of the bed. She was sitting on the floor with her knees up to her chest, trembling with fear. Chantasith smiled when he saw her panic. She had been waiting. She knew they were coming for her husband, for her.

Chantasith walked over and his lieutenant and the escort followed, pouring into the hut to stand along its walls. Chantasith bent down and pulled the woman up to her feet.

"Where is your husband?" he asked, shaking her. "Where is he?"

"I don't know," she cried.

Chantasith noticed she was missing an eye and laughed secretly. Not just a savage, but an outcast, he thought. It made him angrier still, that this pariah of all creatures would defy him. He shook her again, leaned back, and struck her twice in the side of her head. "Tell me where your husband is or you'll be a corpse! Do you hear me? I swear it on my blood!"

She broke down and sobbed. "I don't know," she cried. "'He left the village three days ago, and told everyone that he would be gone for a while and not to bother searching for him." Her knees threaten to buckle but Chantasith held her tight. "Stand up straight," he ordered her.

Chantasith took up a step back to look at her better. Thamu's wife stood there uncertain, her head turned to the side, too afraid to raise her eyes.

"I think you're lying," he told her and unholstered his gun and then put the barrel to her head right above her ear. "I said, I think you're lying."

"No! No!" she cried.

"Do you know it is a capital offense to interfere with a federal investigation?"

Her hands went up to cover her face. "I am not lying! I

am telling you the truth. He is not here and I don't know where he is. No one knows where he is."

Chantasith cocked the gun and pressed the barrel harder against her head.

One of the junior officers in the retinue lost his cool and stepped forward. "Please sir," he pleaded, "I don't think she's lying. I believe her."

Chantasith spun around and turned his gun on the officer. "You *think*? Is that what you said? Wait outside! " he ordered and then turning to his lieutenant. "Take his gun. Our colleague needs to take a walk and think about policing and his loyalties. He won't need his gun where he's going."

The lieutenant took the officer's gun and escorted him outside the hut. The remaining three officers stood frozen. Chantasith spun back around and returned his attention to Thamu's wife. "What's your name?" he asked her.

"Nang-Dee," she said.

"You are Thamu's wife?" Chantasith asked moving in closer.

Dee nodded still afraid to raise her eyes.

Chantasith was now leaning in close, smelling her neck, her hair. "Why would this Thamu marry a one-eyed pariah like you?" he said and licked her neck. Dee jumped, startled by the sensation of his tongue on her neck. Chantasith grabbed her and pushed her against the wall. She began wailing, "Please! No, no!"

Chantasith laughed. "Shut up!" and struck her again on the mouth this time. Her wailing fell to a whimper. "That's better," Chantasith said. "I think I must know why this Thamu married you. Perhaps you have a golden cunt…" he said, laughing, pushing her up against the wall. He turned to address his team. "What do you think about that boys? A cunt of gold! In all my years at the station, I never heard of such a thing," he said, pulling up her skirt. His hand ran up her thigh and found the tuft of hair. Chantasith licked his lips while he cupped her vagina and pressed in with his fingers.

The officers who had started twitching, now all had their eyes turned on the lieutenant who had just again re-entered the hut. Looking around, he read the distress in their faces immediately and then saw Chantasith at the other end, pressing himself it seemed against the woman.

"Mr. Commissioner," the lieutenant said softly, and cleared his throat. "I believe the Americans are done interviewing the elderly couple and are on their way here."

Chantasith heard his lieutenant and pulled back from Thamu's wife. He struck her again, pushing her forcefully against the wall. "If you don't tell your husband to come back here tomorrow, I will come and take you with me in the helicopter. You hear?" he shouted, his spittle peppering her as he did. "I'll burn this whole village down if I need to. He can't hide from me!"

And with that, Chantasith let her go and left Thamu's hut with his team behind him.

XVIII

YAYA WAS RUNNING UP the foot path as quickly as she could. She couldn't tell for sure if those policemen had followed her. She was too frightened to stop and look back. Two crows flew past her in the open sky along the path, cawing as they did. She took it for a bad omen and the next moment, had stumbled on a root in the path and tumbled to the ground, hitting her chin on stone. The fall stunned her but she was up again the next moment, bleeding from her chin but alive and alone. She continued up the path through the jungle. She walked now, much calmer after taking the hit to her chin. She was no longer afraid of being followed. It was like Thamu had told her: Fear is the best hunter; it silently overtakes us from within. He had showed her the cave where he sometimes hid and went to speak with his ancestors and the *peetyhoung*. Even the forest deities spoke to him there, he said. It was there that Thamu had taught her about the pleasures of love-making. He told her he had never shown another person his secret cave. She was the only one.

There was a difficult part of the way one had to navigate, across a ledge on the mountain. Then, one had to pass a dense jungle to find the mouth of the cave hidden bamboo shoots one had to push aside. Thamu had taught her how to get there and how to step so as to leave no trail to the cave. She had followed his instructions again. She called out to him at the mouth of the cave. "Thamu!" she whispered leaning in. "Thamu!"

Thamu came out from the mouth of the cave. "Yaya!" he said surprised. "Yaya, you shouldn't have come here," he said. "Why have you come?"

"I've come to tell you something," she said. "I've come to warn you."

Thamu shook his head, but conceded. "I'm listening."

"There are strange men in the village. They came today and made camp on rice field. They are asking for you by name. They have been to your hut. I remember one of them. The American who was here before. They have many policemen with them. I'm afraid Thamu."

"I know," Thamu said simply. "I have seen them too. Tell me Yaya, did they see you?"

"I don't think so."

"You weren't followed?"

"I made sure, Thamu."

Thamu hugged her and taking her hand, led her into the cave.

INSIDE the cave again, Yaya noticed how much things had changed. Thamu had lain down bamboo mats in the corner. The stone wall at the other corner of the cave was black with smoke from the fire Thamu had been burning. The whole placed smelled of dry meat and smoke. Thamu had a wild hare on a spit over the fire. Off the corner, almost hidded by the darkness, Yaya also saw old military crates. After her eyes had adjusted to dim light, she saw they were loaded with weapons and ammunition. Thamu had a rifle out. It looked like he had been cleaning it, priming it for use.

"Did you see my wife, my mother, before you came here?"

"No, but I saw them headed to your hut."

"Saw them? Who did you see?"

"Policemen, four of them. Before I fled, I saw the Americans go into my parent's hut and the police into yours.

"You didn't tell your parents about the cave or where you were going?"

"No, I've told no one... Thamu, what is that for?" she said pointing to the crate of ammunition. "Where did you get it?"

"I found it in the woods. It was left behind from the big war. The *peetyhoung* led me to it."

Thamu meant the Liberation war of 1975. After the war ended, many men simply abandoned their posts and returned home. Soon after many seized on the guns. Some used them for hunting big game. Others would sell them to foreigners.

"What do you need it for?" she asked him.

Thamu looked worried. "I don't know," he said. "It was the *peetyhoung* said I should find it and bring it here. He must have some purpose for it."

☥ ☥ ☥

BACK at the camp, after another frustrated effort, Chantasith was slowly going mad with the indignation of it. What little patience and self-restraint he possessed had finally snapped.

Wagner knew nothing of what had happened in

Thamu's hut. When Wagner asked, Chantasith had simply said that she knew nothing, which Wagner believed, even anticipated she'd say.

"We can't waste waiting on Thamu to return," Chantasith was telling him. "What if he never returns? We'll be out of supplies in two days and all these men cost money, you understand?"

Wagner nodded. "Of course. It is my objective to resolve this situation as quickly as possible."

"Your methods haven't worked," Chantasith said bluntly. "You wanted to talk to these people and interview the entire village perhaps. We have tried your way and still we know nothing. We will try my way, now."

Wagner didn't want to find out what Chantasith's way might be. "You're wrong," he said. "We've made progress."

Chantasith snorted. "Progress? What progress do you think you've made? You think you are convincing these savages to trust you?"

"I hope so," Wagner replied. "But that's not what I mean. I mean, we know where Thamu is."

Chantasith had stopped. His eyebrows were up and his eyes open wide, perhaps in surprise or expectation. And here Wagner hesitated. Did he want to share what he knew with Chantasith? Wagner thought about it again. It was better to trust Chantasith. He felt he could control him and that by showing trust and including him in all decisions, it might finally assuage him.

"He's in a cave. Apparently northwest of here on the other side of the mountain range. All we have to do is get a topographical map of the place. I'm assuming your government has charted the territory assiduously given all the conflicts that have been waged here."

Chantasith wasn't biting. In his head, he was already

plotting how he might find the cave on his own. "You'll be surprised, Mr. Wagner, at how inadequate the government of Laos has been in documenting its geography. And besides, how do you know he is there? The old couple told you? They will tell you whatever they think you want to here. 'Yes, he's hiding in a cave. He's up in a tree. He's over the mountain and in some magic valley.' It is a game they play with foreigners."

"No, I believe they were telling me the truth," Wagner insisted.

"If you say so, Mr. Wagner… His wife however, said nothing about a cave to me so—" And here a thought arose in Chantasith that hadn't occurred to him before. Had she lied to him? Did she know about the cave, but refused to tell him? The thought drove him over the edge.

"This is more than just about your pilot remains," Chantasith said. "These villagers are outlaws. They are interfering with a federal investigation. I have a mandate from the Minister of Defense and they are lying to me, withholding information and harboring a fugitive."

"A fugitive?" Wagner echoed. "How is he a fugitive? He is not even a criminal."

"He is a criminal," Chantasith said grinding his teeth. "He was a criminal the minute he refused to cooperate with us. Now, with much thanks to you and your team, I know he is hiding in a cave. That officially makes him a fugitive!" Chantasith said, raising his voice despite the control he was attempting to keep.

Wagner took a breath and tried to size up the situation. He was an expert at facilitating, negotiating—he still felt he could control Chantasith.

"I understand your position," Wagner began. "You are perfectly justified in declaring him a fugitive. And I appreciate your zeal in the application of the law. I am also losing patience. I am only afraid that if you proceed with a manhunt, we may soon forget the reason why we came here in the first place. I am concerned you see, that his status as a criminal fugitive may take priority, or eclipse, the retrieval of the pilot's remains. Do you understand my position? I'm sure the Ministry of Defense shares it."

Chantasith appeared somewhat mollified. "I understand. But let me ask you: Is it a grave matter to interfere with a federal investigation in your country?"

"It is," Wagner conceded.

"Then you understand *my* position. I am police commissioner and cannot allow the law to be defied in my presence before my own policemen. But do not fear, Mr. Wagner. You Americans think too much. You cannot find the remains without first finding the fugitive. I will find the fugitive and then you shall have your remains."

Wagner cleared his throat. "I must insist, I—"

But Chantasith's veins were already popping on his neck. "I must insist, Mr. Wagner," he interrupted him. "This man is now a criminal and a fugitive. His actions are a crime against the government. It is an internal matter now."

"And the remains?" Wagner reminded him. "Will the minister be happy if Thamu is harmed and we lose the remains? I will make sure the minister is not. My government will make sure."

But it was a feeble threat to a man seized by pride and ambition. "For your own security and of your team… This is my highest priority. No one would be happy if another foreigner lost his life here. You understand? This man's gone into hiding. Who knows what he might not be planning? He might be plotting to kill you right now.

I remind you Mr. Wagner: You don't understand these people. You think you do, but you don't. This savage and his *peetyhoung*—why he'll eat you alive if his spirit tells him to, and feel all innocent while he does it. They are a superstitious lot and I'm sure he knows you've come to defile the remains of his *peetyhoung*. For understand me now—this is the problem and the reason for his silence: You are defiling holy ground and committing a thousand and one atrocities against their gods—and I wouldn't be surprised if they aren't preparing to kill you and everyone in your American team, just like that," Chantasith said, snapping his fingers.

"And how do you know all this?" Wagner asked. "How can you be sure what he is thinking and what he will do?"

"I know my people well," Chantasith said and sneered. "With respect, you are a foreigner. What do you know of them?"

And Wagner saw the opportunity to impress Chantasith, perhaps even win him over. "I have learned that this tribe is named Khmu. They migrated from the south in the fourteenth century to northern Laos." Wagner had studied what little he could find. Kun Cheng, the king set a border that ran across the foot of the mountain range after a revolt broke out. This essentially drove the Khmu into the mountains and away from the fertile lowlands. The Khmu's army tried to break through but were driven far up the hills and mountains where their cavalry, horses and elephants, could no longer pass and so perished. They have remained here ever since, and so were known collectively as hill tribes. However, many of the Khmu were captured and taken prisoner. This prisoners were kept as slaves.

"*Ka* the word you use to denote the Khmu means 'slave' as I'm sure you well know, " Wagner went on. The

Laotians call the Khmu peoples, 'Ka' or slave even today; and the Khmu tribe had been excluded from the Laotian constitution and forced to live outside the protection of the law and with no rights whatsoever. At the turn of the 19th century, when the French colonized Laos in their Indochina expansion, the Khmu were registered as citizens of Laos for the first time. Still they were referred to as "Ka" by the general public. This prejudice has haunted them since Laos was formed.

"It must be very painful for the Khmu to be called 'ka'…" Wagner said and looked at Chantasith for a sign of sympathy. Instead Chantasith looked bored.

"I hear it was only in the 40's when Laos joined the Vietcong campaign against French colonialism, and the Khmu themselves joined the liberation army, that they were recognized as equal citizens for the first time in their own country," Wagner said. "But I understand there is still much prejudice against them."

"Yes, I understand you have a similar situation in your America, with the—blacks, how you say?"

"African Americans."

"Yes, of course."

"And the Indians."

"American Indians, yes."

"And the Mexicans."

Wagner said nothing. "You see," Chantasith concluded. "I can read history books, too."

"I agree, my country perhaps may have done worse—"

Chantasith snorted.

"My point is that, given the prejudices and the history, it might be easy to understand why Thamu or a person of this village would be running scared."

"My American friend," Chantasith broke in with a

crooked, pained smile. "It is getting late and I have much to prepare for tomorrow. I would love to discuss history with you all night, but I must take my leave. I intend to set off first thing in the morning."

Chantasith turned to go, but Wagner stepped in front of him. "Set off? Where?"

"For our fugitive, of course."

"But we don't know where he is."

"You've said it yourself, Mr. Wagner. He is in cave."

"But we don't know which cave nor where this cave is."

"Then we will check each cave one at a time if we have to. Tomorrow my men and I will go out looking for this cave. We will recruit some of the villagers for help. I suspect, as I am sure you do, Mr. Wagner," he said with a wink, "that we will find your relics in the same cave we find our fugitive in. Do you agree?"

Wagner knew he couldn't keep him much longer. He had to take what he could get and he seized his opportunity. "This is why I intend to accompany you. Please notify me before you set out."

"Of course, Mr. Wagner," he said as he began pulling away. "Be ready at dawn. We'll set out at first light."

XIX

BOTH MEN HAD RETURNED to their respective sides of the camp after their impromptu talk. Both were holding meetings in their tents. Wagner was briefing his team on the schedule for what he feared would be a difficult day tomorrow. He hesitated mentioning his conversation with Chantasith and in the end kept the details to himself. They were to be up at dawn and to be prepared for what might turn out to be a long hike into the hills and jungle. "The police chief probably thinks we don't have it in us," he said, thinking he had divined Chantasith's strategy. "But we'll show him. If he and his team can trek that jungle, so can we."

But at the other end of the camp, Chantasith was having his own meeting and it involved the village and the villagers more than it did caves in the hills.

"We will be leaving camp at five A.M. sharp," he told his lieutenant. "I want you to prepare two teams and make sure they are ready to move at five. Is that understood?"

"Five A.M." the lieutenant repeated.

"I want you to call the ministry and have them send the helicopter again."

"A helicopter, sir? May I ask what for?"

"We may be looking for caves. We may wish to

transport prisoners."

The lieutenant cleared his throat. "Excuse me, sir. We have no prisoners."

"That is only because you and the men aren't doing their jobs," Chantasith growled. "Now, do as I say. Make sure you find out who the pilot on duty is and you talk to him directly. Tell him to return tomorrow, but to land on the field about two kilometers south of the village. We saw it on our way here, and if the pilot follows the same flight path, he will see it. Do you understand? He is not to come to the camp nor near the village.

"I remember the field," the lieutenant said. "I can get the coordinates from the surveyor's map to the pilot. There will be no mistake."

"Perfect. Now, first go prepare the men for tomorrow and then radio the ministry for the helicopter. Remember talk to the pilot directly. Make sure he understands or it's you I'll hold responsible!"

"Understood," the lieutenant said.

"Good! Now go gather the men and report back to me when you're done."

The lieutenant turned to leave. Chantasith raised his hand. His voice was calm and he said, almost like an afterthought, "I almost forgot…" he began, delighted with his skill at acting. "Who is the most junior officer on the team?"

"A young man. Saivongsa. Just married."

"How long on the force?" Chantasith asked, more pleased than ever at his performance.

"Two months, sir," the lieutenant said. He shuffled on his feet. He knew he had taken a risk by bringing on an inexperienced officer. The lieutenant began explaining himself, "He volunteered, sir. He has—"

Chantasith interrupted him. "That's fine… fine," he broke in waving the topic away. "I want him on sentry duty tonight. Post him outside that idiot's hut. Tell him, I want him guarding the door. No one enters or leaves that hut tonight."

"Yes, sir," the lieutenant said and left quickly. He knew Chantasith and seen him get this way before. He was on a war path, and it was best that he leave before Chantasith gave him more to do.

Inside his tent, Chantasith was reclining in his chair, his elbows on the arm rest, his hands crossed before his face, trying to conceal the grin pulling at the corners of his mouth. "*I* am the police chief," he told himself. "*Me*. The police *chief*. It's up to *me* to solve this problem. *I* have the power and so I have the right." He was thinking of Wagner and the presumption of these foreigners who thought they could come here and tell him how to do his job. He was the police chief. He was in charge and that meant not only that the decision was his and his alone to make, but that it was up to *him* to take those decisions. He was thinking of Thamu's wife as he told himself this. Reminded himself, he felt, that it was a responsibility, a duty for him to take matters into his hands. He was captain of the ship and it was up to him alone to set its course. "I am the police chief," he whispered, to himself alone in his tent. The image of Thamu's wife was fixed in his mind—of her breasts rising and falling with her breathing, the smell of her when he pressed against her, and the feel of her thighs. "I am the captain," he whispered.

XX

THE CAMP WAS QUIET. Everyone was asleep except for Chantasith. He had been up drinking and studying the hill formations on the surveyor's maps for the likeliest candidate for caves. Now he was creeping out of his tent and crossing the camp to his men's tents. He cast a long look at Wagner's tent at the other end of the camp. But Wagner's men had retired to their tents after being given instructions long ago. Wagner himself had been sleeping well, not to say obliviously, for some hours now.

Emboldened, Chantasith stood up from his crouch and walked proudly, defiantly to the nearest tent. Reaching it, he drew his gun and leaning in, put the barrel to one of his men's head. He was still asleep, even with the gun to his temple, Chantasith thought in disgust. He tapped it gently and leaned in further.

"You wake up slowly, put your uniform on and come with me or I will blow your head off right now."

But the man was disoriented and looked like he might scream or struggle before he came to his senses. Chantasith reached in with his other hand and put it over his mouth.

"It's the chief," he said into his ear. "Shut up and put your uniform on. Quietly now... Do it!"

They crept along the edge of the camp across to the other side of the field and onto the path that led to the village. The village soon came into the view, then Thamu's house. There was Saivongsa at his post: sitting on a stone by the front wall of the hut. Asleep. Chantasith looked at the policeman he had pulled from sleep and put a finger to his lips. Stepping quietly, almost tiptoeing, Chantasith went right up to Saivongsa and kicked him. "Get up! Get up, you bumbling fool!" he whispered, frothing at the mouth and red in the face with the restraint he was showing. He boxed him in the ear. "I was able to come right up to you! You don't think if I were a barefoot savage, accustomed to hunting in the jungle that I wouldn't be able to get past some soap stinking, snoring city boy? I could dance in and out. Get up! Get up!" Chantasith bent down and picked the man up by his collars. "On your feet! By God, if I learn he's been here while you slept, I'll shoot you myself."

Saivongsa could smell the alcohol on Chantasith's breath.

"Now," Chantasith said, turning about to the second officer. "Let's go see what's going on inside. You lead the way," he said, pushing Saivongsa ahead of him towards the hut door.

Saivongsa reached the door and Chantasith told him with a head a movement to open it. "Quietly," he said.

Saivongsa stepped in, Chantasith was right behind him. "Shut the door," he said to the second officer. "Make sure no one comes in."

Chantasith took out his gun. "Keep moving," he told Saivongsa. "To the back."

It took a moment, but soon their eyes were accustomed to the darkness in the hut. Chantasith could see her now, asleep on her bamboo mat, covered in a grey blanket.

Chantasith pulled on Saivongsa's arm. "Take this," he said, handing him a rag. "And gag the bitch's mouth with it. Do it!" Chantasith ordered.

Saivongsa was young but he knew that police work could sometimes get ugly. He always knew that day would come. He was new here and didn't really know much of what was going on. He had to trust the chief. It didn't really matter anyway: he had already gagged her when Chantasith began tying her hands behind her head.

"Don't kick! Or I'll tie your legs too!" he told her. "You remember me, don't you?" he said, leaning into her. "Yes, I know you do. I remember you," he said laughing. His hand was already running up her thighs. She squirmed under his touch, but that only excited Chantasith more.

"Where is your husband?" Chantasith was asking her. His mouth was on her neck. He was panting heavily.

"Maybe you don't have a husband at all… What kind of man would marry this one-eyed outcast? What do you think Saivongsa?" he asked, without turning around.

"This wouldn't happen if your husband was here." His hand had forced his way up her thighs, through her underwear.

"Not much of a husband to leave his wife alone at night, eh Saivongsa? Not much of a man."

Saivongsa stood there in shock, dumbfounded. He wanted to speak, but was uncertain. He wondered about the other officer—if he was a party to this.

Meanwhile, Chantasith began undoing his pants. "We will show you how a real man treats a woman."

Chantasith tore off her dress. "I want your husband to know. You tell him when he sees your dress, when he sees you—tell him you finally met a real man."

Chantasith unholstered his gun and put it in her

mouth as he penetrated her. Soon he was moaning while Saivongsa watched on mortified. He could see her face now in the dim light. Her eyes were open. She had a vacant look on her face and seemed like a dead piece of meat rocking on the mat as Chantasith humped away at her.

"You like that, don't you?" Chantasith said, finally exhausted. He took the gun out of her mouth and stood up. "Your turn," he said turning to Saivongsa.

Saivongsa was still in shock. He heard the chief, but was still processing it as though he had heard the words in a dream and was still in the process of recalling the dream. His eyes were on Thamu's wife. She showed no reaction and was staring blankly into the air above her.

"Your turn!"

"No… sir. I don't want to. I mean sir, I can't. I am a married man."

Chantasith had his gun pointed at him in a moment. "Do it or you die!" he barked. He stepped closer and cocking his gun, put it to his temple. "This is how this works. Either you do it or I shoot you. I report that I caught you in the act of raping this poor woman. When you were caught you reached for your gun and I shot you dead. Your poor wife will die thinking she married a rapist. No one will ever know the truth."

Chantasith stepped behind him, still holding the gun to his head. "Do it, you moron!" he seethed and began pushing him toward her. "I said you do it, or you die."

Saivongsa approached the mat.

"On top of her," Chantasith commanded.

Saivongsa looked to her for some sign of life, some expression. He leaned down and lay on top of her.

"I can't," Saivongsa protested again.

Chantasith was looking at his limp penis. "No, I guess you can't!" he said and started laughing. His gun came down and Chantasith was leaning back, clutching his midriff with the force of the laughter.

"I ask for men and they give me boys!" he announced.

At that moment Thamu's wife turned to Saivongsa. She held his eyes. "Shoot me," she whispered. "Don't tell my husband what they've done to me. Shoot me, but don't tell him. I don't want him to suffer. I know you understand."

Saivongsa was seized with pity for her, but Chantasith had stopped laughing. "Guard! Come in here," he shouted and the second officer came into the hut. He came in just in time to see Saivongsa roll off of Thamu's wife behind Chantasith. Chantasith had made sure of it.

"I will deal with that later," he told him. "We are taking her with us. Perhaps her husband will show some courage once he knows she suffers for his cowardice. Bring her!"

XXI

IT WAS MORNING. 4:30 am and time to rise by the signal of the alarm Wagner had set the night before. He had showered, shaved and dressed in ten minutes. At a quarter to, he was exiting his tent after going to the latrine, and noticed that Liam was preparing coffee. Wagner approached and Liam handed him a cup.

"Just like you take it," he said. "The color of caramel and just about as sweet."

"Thanks. What's going on over there?" he asked him.

Wagner had noticed that Chantasith had gathered his men at the other end of the camp and was addressing them.

"Don't know… he was already talking up a storm when I came out to set the kettle and he hasn't stopped since. The man's been on a tear. I thought he'd boil over, before the kettle did. Was it something you said to him last night? He doesn't look happy."

"No, I don't think so," Wagner answered.

"Well, the smaller the man, the longer the speech, I guess."

"All bark no bite, you think?"

Wagner studied him for an answer.

"No," Liam said, correcting him. "I don't think so."

"Nor do I. And it's his bite that concerns me. I wonder what he's telling them up there. Is the translator up, yet?"

Wagner could see Chantasith at the other end of the camp addressing his men.

"We have posted a guard outside the fugitive's hut," Chantasith was saying and everyone remarked the change in language. No longer a witness, the man was now a 'fugitive'. Some of the men were suddenly excited and a stir travelled among the group as they looked to each other. "But we can't wait for this *fugitive* to return home or decide to reappear. It is clear now that his absence is not accidental, but a deliberate act of avoidance. In refusing to provide testimony to this special mission from the Ministry of Defense, he is interfering with the investigation and is now officially wanted by the government for questioning. Our duty gentlemen, is clear."

The policemen stood about mostly confused. Some wondered if there had been a development, while others had never understood the mission at all. All they knew is that they were there to collect some thirty-year old bones, which was hardly a job for a policeman and that since their arrival, no progress had been made.

"Since he is a fugitive," Chantasith went on. "And we have reason to suspect that some of the villagers have knowledge of his whereabouts—they must have—the entire village and these villagers can be considered to be harboring the fugitive. This too is a crime and we are authorized under the law to seize and detain if we need to.

"I have sent a team ahead to the village with your

lieutenant. He has been given special orders as will you. We know that the fugitive is hiding in a cave. Your colleague Saivongsa here, managed to extract the information from the fugitive's wife. You should learn from his example and his initiative." Chantasith put his hands together and began clapping them slowly. A sly grin he couldn't entirely conceal, threatened to break out over his face. The men in attendance followed suit, all turning to Saivongsa who stood off to the side mortified, and clapped. Those nearest him were able to congratulate him more intimately. Saivongsa endured the slaps on the back, the pats on the shoulder and the elbows to his sides. It was a nightmare, he felt sure.

Wagner heard the applause coming from Chantasith's men and wondered what they could be celebrating. He turned to Liam.

"Get me the translator. Quickly!"

He returned his gaze to the other end of the camp. He noticed half his men weren't accounted for. He couldn't see his lieutenant either.

The applause ended and Chantasith went on: "This woman refuses to tell us the precise location of the caves, however. We are holding her for questioning, but at present have not been able to get a precise location from her. We know these caves are off to the south over the hill ridge. Today, we find this cave."

XXII

THE MORNING SUN was before them, shining in their eyes. Wagner had found his translator in his tent, sick to his stomach. He began to wonder if Chantasith hadn't slipped him anything. He was about to ask Liam, but was afraid of sounding paranoid. Especially after his anxiety attack in the hotel lobby. When Chantasith showed up with his men at five AM sharp as promised, Wagner was forced to leave without him. "I will lend you one of my policemen," Chantasith offered. He seemed jovial and Wagner was suddenly hopeful that perhaps it was really all nothing but paranoia.

"I suppose that will have to do." Wagner said. "In case we meet Thamu, I will need a translator."

Chantasith smiled and was agreeable. "Of course, Mr. Wagner."

Chantasith called Saivongsa over to his side.

"I know you speak some English. You will act as translator," he told him.

Saivongsa still bewildered, still in shock, could do nothing but nod his head robotically.

"I gave you an order, officer!" Chantasith growled.

Saivongsa was momentarily brought out of his dream to show obedience to Chantasith's authority. It was a perfect control tactic. Chantasith had perfected it over the years with prisoners, witnesses, his men, even his own wife. Beat the man, then make him thank you for the beating, then you own him.

"Yes *sir*," Saivongsa conceded and slipped back into his protective shell again.

"This is an opportunity for a young man like yourself," Chantasith was saying. "I shouldn't have to remind you. Think of your young *wife* and your future *family*," he told him with emphasis, and then turning to the American team, "There! I have found your translator," Chantasith told Wagner. "Let's go. Time is wasting!"

Chantasith set off along the edge of the rice field toward the path, his men following him in file behind him.

Wagner quickened his step and met up with Chantasith at the head of the line. "Where is your lieutenant?" Wagner asked. "Is he out sick as well? Where are the rest of your men?"

"They are at the village." Chantasith said flatly.

"At the village?"

Wagner stepped back and gritted his teeth. He wasn't afraid to show his disappointment and frustration. "I thought we had agreed that we were going to explore the hills for caves and signs of the witness together."

"Yes. Of course we are. This is part of the search. Many of the villagers must know about these caves. They can give us information. How do you say? Narrow our search."

"And so what exactly are your men doing at the village?"

"We shall see," Chantasith chimed.

They started up along the path to the village and Wagner could do nothing but follow. Looking around, he was suddenly aware that something dreadful had gone wrong. He could tell from the looks on Chantasith's men's faces. Some were excited; some were worried. The young officer Chantasith had assigned to him as translator avoided all eye contact with him every time Wagner looked over. He looked like a scolded child, or a victim of some trauma. It seemed to him like he had something to hide, whether out of shame, from his own wrong doing or a something he was covering up for his team. Wagner couldn't tell which.

Along their way, he noticed Chantasith called Saivongsa up to his side again. He couldn't hear what Chantasith was telling him, but he could well imagine.

"You will translate," Chantasith was telling him. "You will tell me everything he asks, everything he learns. You will tell me everything you translate for him. Do you understand?"

Reaching the old man's hut again—the first landmark they had encountered upon landing there—Chantasith stopped and turned about to address his men.

"I want all of you to pay attention to the villagers," he said. "Any one of them might have information on where our fugitive is hiding," he told them.

At that moment, a young boy came running up the path. He was obviously distraught. He started when he saw them coming up the path toward the village and was about to dart into the fields when he saw Wagner. He ran toward him, shouting and waving his hands.

Wagner looked the boy over. He was drenched in sweat. Every nerve in his body seemed to be throbbing under his skin. "Easy son," Wagner said and put a hand on the boy's shoulder. "Just a minute…" Wagner called the translator over. "I want to know what it is this child is telling me. Ask him: why are you crying? Why are you running?"

Saivongsa nodded meekly and turned to the boy. "Why are you crying and running?" he asked him.

The boy broke out in a torrent of speech. He stamped his feet and pulled at his hair while he spoke.

"What does he say?" Wagner asked the translator.

"He says they put a gun to his sister's head. He says they will kill her if she doesn't tell them where Thamu is now."

The child was sobbing while Wagner consulted with the translator. "Who are *they*?" Wagner asked the translator, but Chantasith had already walked over.

"And you know where Thamu is?" Chantasith asked him, bending down to meet him at eye level.

The boy shook his head and Chantasith stood up again.

"Of course you don't!" Chantasith said laughing, and then sarcastically: "No one knows anything!"

Wagner stepped in. "If you don't mind… I wasn't finished speaking with this child…" He turned to Saivongsa. "Ask him who his sister is."

"He says, he is Toy. Yaya's younger brother," Saivongsa answered.

Wagner looked over at Chantasith.

"Tell him to show me," he told Saivongsa. "Tell him to take me to his sister."

A minute later they were at the village and Wagner learned that Chantasith's men had already gone into every hut. Six villagers—all adult men—were tied to poles stuck into the ground. They had gone in armed and belligerent. If the villagers weren't frightened before, they were terrified now. It would be harder and harder to secure their cooperation and Wagner figured Chantasith knew it. He began wondering if bloodshed wasn't really what he was after.

Wagner's team was speechless. Liam and the others were rubbing their heads, looking to the ground and probably avoiding eye contact with him. This was getting out of control and Wagner felt he was to blame. His team would feel it too. Not just the blame, but they would also feel the embarrassment for him. It was *his* lapse.

To boot, Yaya was nowhere to be found. The men had been tied, some of them beaten by the looks of it and all they got from them was that they didn't know where Thamu was. All they knew was that Thamu went hunting every morning and always returned home in time for noon; but that he had gone out hunting the yesterday, before the team arrived and never returned. In effect, they had learned nothing.

"You said you would wait for me before doing anything."

"Before going to look for the caves," Chantasith corrected him with a smile. "I said, I would wait for you before setting out with my men to investigate the caves, that we would do it together. I have not gone to the caves, Mr. Wagner."

Wagner was finally understanding how unscrupulous Chantasith could be. "I see you're playing word games with me."

"Word games?" Chantasith said, feigning ignorance.

"You'd make a good politician in my country," Wagner continued.

"Me?" Chantasith broke out into a hearty laugh. "No, I am a simple policeman, that is all."

"Is that so? Then tell me, Mr. Virisane did the minister order this action against the villagers?"

"The minister is a very busy man as you know, Mr.

Wagner. He has given me authority in this matter."

"I think I'd like to talk to the minister myself."

"I have already spoken to him."

"All the same. I think I'd like to talk to him myself."

"Of course, Mr. Wagner," Chantasith said with a sneer. "You do what you need to do."

Wagner looked at his watch. It was getting to mid-morning. The sun was already getting hot as it came up from behind the high east mountains. Wagner stood there considering. He'd want to call the ambassador as well, he thought. But for now, he thought the best he could do was come to the villagers' defense and win their trust and favor that way.

"If you're done interrogating those men, then I'd like to try," he told Chantasith.

"Be my guest. But you'll find nothing."

"Then what was the point to all this?" Wagner asked, opening his hands and arms to take in the village scene, with its prisoners, frightened population, and all these policemen trampling about.

"At least now they understand that Thamu is not their friend. That this would have never happened if he had simply answered our summons. That if he cared about them at all, he would already have returned. Instead, he chooses to make them suffer. I am confident that if anyone knows anything, they will come forward soon. And that if anyone were to see him, they would report it or bring him in. It is important to separate the criminal from his network," Chantasith concluded. "He cannot survive alone in the jungle for long. Even if he could, it's the being alone that will get him. A man with friends can suffer any disgrace. With friends to help him, he might live out there all his life."

How cunning of him, Wagner thought. He would have thought the psychological insight to have been out of his reach.

"So you're saying you're done with them then?"

"Yes, Mr. Wagner."

"Then I may untie them after I am done."

Chantasith raised an eyebrow and then smiled. "Yes, Mr. Wagner. You can be their hero, their savior. Be my guest!" Chantasith said chuckling as he walked away.

"What they don't tell me, they will tell you. Is that what you think Mr. Wagner?" Chantasith was thinking as he walked away. "I shall have to disappoint you then. There will be nothing left for you."

Like a beaten dog, Saivongsa was about to follow Chantasith. He no longer knew his place it seemed. Wagner stopped him. "You stay with me," he said. "I will need your help in interrogating the men."

Saivongsa stopped and stood there awaiting further instructions while Wagner called Liam and the rest of his team to his side. Together they approached the prisoners. Wagner stood before them with Saivongsa at his side.

"Tell them there is nothing to be afraid of," Wagner told Saivongsa. "Tell them that Liam here," he added putting his hand on Liam's shoulder, "will be untying them. Explain to them that we are not here to harm or arrest anyone. That all we want are the American pilot's remains and that we will be leaving the moment we have them. That we are looking for Thamu who knows where the remains might be found."

Liam went to each of the prisoners in turn and freed them. Moments later, they were all released and standing about holding their waists and massaging their wrists around which the cords had been tied. Wagner told

Saivongsa to ask if any of them knew where Thamu or Yaya was. All of them shook their heads. One man broke down. He began crying. Under Wagner's direction, Saivongsa asked him why he cried.

"He says that Thamu is a good man. He has done no wrong. He says they are a peaceful people and that they have done no wrong," Saivongsa translated.

"Tell him we know that. We want to help Thamu. Tell them the police chief is angry because Thamu has run away. But we want only the remains. Then ask them again if they know where he is."

They received the same response. Everyone shook their heads or shrugged their shoulders.

"Tell them that it is better for Thamu if we and not the police chief finds him."

Still the same response.

"Okay, tell them they are free to return to their huts."

After he was done setting the prisoners free, Wagner realized Saivongsa was nowhere to be found. In fact, Chantasith had left the village with all his men. Wagner wondered now if he hadn't set off for the caves without him or if he had returned to camp. Either way, Wagner was in a hurry to return to camp and try to reach someone in the capital. There were no phones out here, no cell reception. All they had was a shortwave radio that he could send messages on. He'd have to go through an operator who would have to transcribe what he said and then take it to the ambassador for a response.

XXIII

CHANTASITH AND SAIVONGSA were leading Thamu's wife up the path through the rice fields south of the village where Chantasith had arranged for the helicopter to be. She was muzzled and they had tied her hands at the wrists. Chantasith had removed her blindfold so that she could walk the path without stumbling.

The air was clearing up after the dawn and the mists hanging over the mountain had already been burned up by the morning sun.

When the path took a turn after they had passed the rice fields and the village was no longer in view, Chantasith stopped.

"This will do," he said. "I want to give you a little going-away gift," he added looking at her.

"You wait here," he told Saivongsa, and then took her behind the shrubs. This time Chantasith searched for her eyes as he lay on top of her. "Look at me!" he said. And grabbing her jaw turned her head to his. She lay there with her legs open, her eyes staring past him. There was no sign of life in her as she began to rock and shake under Chantasith's thrusting.

Chantasith ejaculated inside her and then got up quickly. "I think I've grown tired of you," he said, pulling up his pants. "I like a woman who is a little more passionate," he added laughing.

He made his way to the path again and to Saivongsa.

"We'll give her a couple of minutes," he told him. "I was rough on her. Go guard her. Make sure she doesn't try escaping."

Chantasith lit a cigarette and took a hall while he stared peacefully and contentedly at the view from the mountain path. It was shaping up to be a great day.

Saivongsa went into the brush and saw her on the ground, slumped against a tree, her dress open.

He approached her slowly. "I am sorry," he said.

He knelt down and went to cover her nakedness, when she suddenly came to life it seemed. She grabbed him by the wrist, looking him dead in the eyes.

"Kill me," she said. "Please… kill me."

Saivongsa fell back in horror. "I—I can't do that."

"My husband loves me very much. This will bring great shame to him and my family. You must kill me," she pleaded.

Saivongsa was mortified. "I am sorry." he stammered. It was all he could say.

Chantasith had finished his cigarette and was now calling.

"We have to go. Please stand up," he said trying to help her up.

"My husband will be shamed and have much guilt," she repeated.

"No one will know," Saivongsa told her to appease her and suddenly realized the monstrosity of what he had said. He hated himself. He wanted to kill Chantasith and then kill himself.

Now Chantasith appeared. "What's taking so long?" he boomed.

Saivongsa turned around and looked Chantasith in the eyes.

"I thought you were you having another go at it," Chantasith said winking and taking out his gun. "But now I see you have a problem. Let's go," he said, pointing the gun at them. "The helicopter is waiting."

After another bend in the path, a clearing appeared to their right, and there in the middle of it was the helicopter.

"Alright, let's go. The two of you—get in, take a seat and not a word!"

They climbed aboard the helicopter as told. Chantasith with his gun on them, climbed in last and closed the latch door behind him.

"Let's go!" he cried to the pilot. "Get her up."

The pilot switched on the engines and the propellers started turning. "Where are we going. There's a proper town south of here, with a police station and a jail. We are taking the witness there for holding."

The helicopter lurched, swung to the left and then was on its way. Dee was studying the door and the latch that Chantasith had pulled on. Now in mid-air Chantasith stood up and made his way to the cockpit to take the seat next to the pilot.

Dee saw her opportunity and rushed to the door. She grabbed at the latch, pulling it first one way then another. Finally, the door flew open, pushed back by the force of the wind.

Chantasith turned around. Saivongsa went to grab her, but before anything could be done, Dee had already leapt to her death.

Chantasith and Saivongsa leaned out the side of the helicopter. They saw only the winding rivers the rocky mountains tops and their green slopes. All they could hear was the beating sound of the helicopter's propellers. Chantasith closed the sliding door.

"Take us back," he ordered the pilot. "Turn around and take us back!"

They landed on the same spot where they had taken off only minutes ago.

"You'll return to the city. We don't need you now," Chantasith told the pilot.

"I have to enter a flight log?"

"Of course. Write that you were transporting food and supplies for us," Chantasith said and then reminded the pilot. "Tell anyone about this and you'll be a corpse."

↟ ↟ ↟

THINGS were slowly returning to normal at the village. The women were in their huts, cleaning, cooking, taking counsel among themselves. The men were out working the fields, hunting, carting wood. A group had gathered outside Thamu's hut. They were standing about, rubbing their wounds. Privately, the villagers had begun worrying about Thamu. In some it seemed that worry had given over to anger. Some felt he was already dead, others that he ran away... Now, they learned that Dee was also missing. Had she run off to join Thamu and leave the village to the mercy of these police and military men?

"My daughter-in-law has disappeared," Thamu's mother was saying again. "These men have taken her."

"Are you sure she has not run off to join Thamu?"

And the old lady appeared stumped. She was silent for a while. "It is not like her," she added after a moment. "She would not leave without a sign, without telling me—someone. She's taken nothing with her. No change of clothing. How do you explain that?"

The village men looked at each other, nodding their heads and grumbling. It seemed that they were the ones stumped now. Then one of them had an idea. "What if—" he began, "What if Thamu came and took her?"

Yes, that was plausible, the men agreed. He might have come down stealthily and made off his wife.

"For her safety," one of the men said.

"Yes, to protect her," another added.

"Fools!" Thamu's mother raised her arms in despair. "Stupid men!" she said, shaking her head. "Return to your wives and make yourselves useful for once. Go!"

She grabbed the broom at her door and began sweeping the road at their feet as though to sweep them away.

It was difficult for the villagers to agree on what the exact reason of Thamu's disappearance was or what his motives might be. Until they did, they felt they couldn't reach a consensus on what to do about it.

Even Saivongsa had begun hating Thamu for placing all of them in this situation. If the man would just hand over those bleeding bones none of this would have happened! His wife would be alive and well. There would have been no rape. The village would be at peace... It enraged him! At first, he had felt a sort of sympathy for the man. He knew Thamu, like everyone else in the village felt threatened by the government. To have such a police and military presence suddenly dropped on them must have sent waves of shock through the entire region. When the men were ranting and laughing about how his backward superstition was going to get Thamu killed, he had felt a sort of kinship with him. Who is to say which beliefs were right or wrong? But this Thamu, was at least standing up for them—he was standing up alone against all of them. Now, he lost all interest in the man. Up to the moment, but he had been following his orders reluctantly. Now, he would do so with alacrity. The sooner they caught Thamu, the sooner all this would be over. He felt his own life was at risk. He knew too much about Chantasith and what had happened. He had been a witness to it all, even if Chantasith had tried to make him an accomplice. Chantasith would eventually want to get rid of him somehow.

Perhaps if he had gotten word to the American sooner, all this could have been avoided. Now, looking at Chantasith's back, following him on their return to the camp from the helicopter landing site, he was thinking it was too late.

XXIV.

IT WAS NOON and the sun had long reached its high point. Everyone was sweating and trying to move as little as possible. Wagner's men were sitting in the shade of bamboo on the edge of the camp. The Laotian policemen seemed to be handling the heat better. The Americans who weren't used it seemed frustrated. Wagner in particular look annoyed to the Laotians. It wasn't the heat that had Wagner hot under his collar however. He perspired like everyone else, but had long forgotten about it or was oblivious to it.

Chantasith was nowhere to be found and he wanted some answers before speaking to the Ambassador. His men were all off to the side, dazed not by the heat, Wagner was sure, but amazed at how quickly everything had slipped out of control. For the first time, Wagner felt powerless. Chantasith had the guns and if he didn't fear using them, even if only to intimidate, then there was nothing Wagner could do. To control the situation, Wagner had to control Chantasith. He had always known this—but he was realizing now, that Chantasith might be uncontrollable. He could feel that anxiety welling up within him again. He wanted to run off, disappear… Damn it, if this wasn't really *his* problem, why should *he* care? And each time that anxiety loomed, Wagner took comfort in the call he had scheduled with the ambassador. The embassy had people that could help. The ambassador had connections to high-level Laotian government and could resolve this situation and get Chantasith under control with just a couple of phone calls, Wagner felt sure.

He had telegraphed the embassy immediately upon his return to camp and after being unable to find Chantasith anywhere. One of the junior officers was in charge of the communications equipment. Wagner had waved him over. "Set up the equipment. I need to send a message to the embassy." Once the machine was ready, Wagner recited to his communications officer: "Chief of police stop Laotian stop appointed by minister of defense stop name Chantasith stop entered village without orders stop evidence of imprisonment and beatings stop Chantasith present whereabouts unknown stop query request to remove him from field operations.

The operator had responded with one word: 'hold'. They waited twelve minutes. Finally the ticker started going off again. The communications officer read it back to Wagner: "Ambassador requests conference with Wagner stop time sixteen hundred stop shortwave band eight three."

Wagner got the shortwave radio out is hard shell casing and set it on the bureau. "Fire her up," he told his officer.

"You know this shortwave radio is not secure," his officer told him.

"What do you mean?"

"Anyone can listen in."

Wagner shrugged it off. Nothing they were about to discuss was exactly classified. "That doesn't matter. The police chief is out of control and something needs to be done about this."

The officer nodded as though he agreed there was

nothing else to do. "Where do you think he is?"

"Probably hunting Thamu. I thought I heard a helicopter earlier…."

"Yep. Single prop. Probably the same one they brought us in on."

Wagner stood around watching the officer get to work, when feeling useless, he felt the anxiety encroach. "Well, I think I'll see if I can't get a break from this heat," he said. "I'll need you around at sixteen hundred, in case we have difficulties."

"Yes, sir. I'll be here."

Alone, Wagner felt defeated. He felt that anxiety welling up again. He wanted to lie down and give up—at least for today. Instead, he returned to his tent to pore over his files and prepare his notes for his call with the ambassador. Many of his own staff had retired themselves. Some sat on the rocks that lined the water troughs running through the fields, others were in the shade of the bamboo grove— everyone seeking respite from the noonday sun.

🛆 🛆 🛆

IT was in the late afternoon by the time Chantasith and Saivongsa re-entered camp. They had 'talked' along the way. This is what Chantasith told Saivongsa as he lead him through a circuitous path through the hills on their way back to the camp. "We're going to have a talk along the way." Then Chantasith asked Saivongsa for his gun and for a moment Saivongsa was sure Chantasith was going to shoot him dead with his own gun and leave him there to rot in the jungle. There was a tense moment when

Saivongsa didn't know if he should give Chantasith his gun or shoot him in self-defense. All the while, Chantasith smiled at him with a grin that seemed malevolent.

"What's your problem, officer? Follow your orders. Your chief of police is requesting your gun!"

Saivongsa put his hand on the holster and stepped back, shaking his head slowly looking at Chantasith like a rabbit frozen by a floodlight.

Chantasith let out a hearty laugh. "I am not going to kill you!" But then he looked at him again with that malevolent grin. "Do you know how to hunt a hunter, my young friend? You become the prey. Take out your gun and fire two shots in each direction. Let this Thamu know we're here."

Saivongsa looked at him tentatively.

"Then we'll climb up to that ridge. If he's anywhere in the area, he'll hear the shots and come investigate. We'll have the high ground; we'll see him coming. Take your gun out officer! Follow your orders."

They waited in silence for thirty minutes. No Thamu appeared and Chantasith took it as evidence that Thamu was nowhere on this hill side. "He would have showed," Chantasith stated simply. They climbed down from the ridge, walked across the valley to the other range and did the same. "He would have showed," Chantasith declared when Thamu failed to appear again. On and on it went, with Chantasith ordering Saivongsa up and down the vantage points, while Chantasith sat and waited for the Thamu that never showed. Saivongsa was beaten, psychologically and physically. Chantasith knew it. "You're a good officer," he said patting him on the shoulder as they were now finally heading back for the camp. "I tell you what. Your request to be transferred out of this assignment has been denied. But don't worry about things you can't control. You just follow orders."

It wasn't until some steps later that Saivongsa processed what he had heard. "Why? If I may ask, sir, why has my request for transfer been denied?"

Chantasith smiled again, patting him on the shoulder as they walked. "I'm doing it for your own good. You're like a son to me," Chantasith said. "I don't want to see you spoil your career over this."

"I'd prefer to just transfer, please. I'll deal with the consequences—"

"There will be questions if you were to request a transfer. The department, even the men on the field, your brothers in duty, everyone will need to know why you are abandoning them in the middle of your assignment, your *first* assignment. When you are unable to answer—because of course there is no answer a man can give—you will be ruined. They will deem you mentally unstable. Your career will be over. I can't let that happen to you. Ah, there's the camp!"

Saivongsa saw the camp on the rice fields like so many pieces on a chess board and he felt like there was no escape. He was a cornered pawn. Word was given as soon as Chantasith was sighted coming up the path and all his men stood to attention one by one. Liam made a bee-line for Wagner's tent.

Standing before the tent, there was no door to knock at of course, Liam cleared his throat and called out in a loud voice. "Excuse me sir. The police chief has returned."

There was a slight rustling sound and then Wagner answered from within. "Thank you. Let me know if he leaves the camp again."

Liam stood there for a while uncertain. He found it

odd that Wagner had not come out of the tent to address him. "Will that be all, sir?"

"Yes, thank you Liam."

Inside his tent, on his cot Wagner sat finishing his report. He'd wait to hear from the ambassador before dealing with Chantasith.

↑↑↑

NOW Chantasith has all his men lined up. Saivongsa was at the end of the line, still dazed. Liam watched from a distance as Chantasith began pacing up and down, ranting and raving. Liam would have liked to know what they were saying, but the translator was still holed up in his tent, sick. Liam was fairly sure by now, that Chantasith had something to do with it.

Chantasith noticed Liam standing by the bamboo groves watching them intently. He wondered where Wagner was, but was glad not to see him. He needed to get this over with before Wagner or his men got wind of it.

"Today my friends, I have learned something. It is nothing new, this thing I have learned. It is something, I always knew; but somehow forgot. It is something, my father had told me, and his father before him. It is something you yourselves already know. Perhaps some of you were burning inside to tell me, to remind me…" and here Chantasith smiled warmly as though they were good children and they pleased him, "…but were afraid to, or didn't know how. The truth I have forgotten colleagues, is that we must take care of our own. Our American friends are looking after their own interests and we must do the same. I have faltered and failed you as your police chief, I admit. But no more! Today, one of the villagers, a key witness in our investigation, has escaped. She could not have done this alone. Look to the men next to you. Do you think any of them would have betrayed us? No! If not one of us, then who else?" Chantasith paused for effect. "So it stands to reason, and I am quite certain, this could not have been accomplished without the help of our American friends."

A murmur spread through the ranks. Some of the men were already nodding their heads as if it was something they had known all along. Chantasith took it all in with a look of gratification. Then, he put his arms up.

"Yes, I know. But we must remain professional and true to our duty. Let us look at the situation. We arrived here three days ago. Since arriving we learned nothing. Both our key witnesses are gone. Both witness we could have had in our custody, if not for the Americans. I don't know what their plan is, and I tell you frankly, I don't care. I am here to do my job and get back home. We all have families to return to and this game of summer camp is getting old."

There was a general consensus on that point, and here Chantasith got almost everyone—everyone but Saivongsa who persisted in his daze— agreeing that camp life was uncomfortable and that Wagner was to blame. The rank and file were all nodding up and down the line. Saivongsa was still silent. He was realizing how deep Chantasith's deception ran and how far he could go. He felt trapped— it was a dangerous game and one Chantasith appeared adept at, while he didn't seem to be made for it. Was he a coward? He secretly wished that the other policemen knew Chantasith as well as he did. He wondered if there was anyone at the ministry he could talk to, before more people were hurt. Was it cowardice to do nothing? The idea of his cowardice plagued him. He thought of his wife. How could he face her? But again, didn't he have a responsibility to keep safe? His instincts told him to limit his contact with the Americans and the other policemen, to keep Chantasith's dirty secret to himself. It was wise, he knew.... But he also knew it wasn't wisdom that was informing his decision. It was fear. Chantasith had humiliated him. No, perhaps he wasn't as smart nor as courageous as he thought, and it was only fear that kept him from coming forward and reporting Chantasith.

"And if we allow this Wagner to continue interfering in the discharge of our duties, we'll be rotting here for months!"

Chantasith paused again, basking in his newfound powers of oratory. The murmur had grown into a grumble.

"Don't worry, men. If I still have your confidence..."

And all the men here let out a resounding cheer.

"I think I may have a way of atoning for my mistakes. I have a solution and a plan that will get us all home. Tomorrow morning, the witness's mother will gather all the male adult villagers in her hut..."

Over at the other end of the camp, Wagner was getting up from his cot. It was time for the call with the ambassador. Wagner gathered his papers up into the manila folder and walked into the command tent. His communications officer was bent over the radio.

"We're all set," he said. "The channel is open. We just have to wait for them to get on at the other end."

Wagner nodded and took a seat on one of the equipment crates. A moment later, the static turned to crackling and then there was a voice.

The communications officer was about to speak, but Wagner was already on his feet and snatched the microphone away. He was impatient to get this over with. Besides he remembered his communications training well enough and now had no need for the communications officer. Everyone had heard the 'rogers', the 'over-and-outs', the 'five by five' for 'loud and clear'. A 'Charlie' was anyone listening. Commanding officer was 'sunray'. He had already run over code for the alphabet in his head. Alpha, bravo, charlie, delta, echo, foxtrot…

Wagner leaned in to the microphone. "Niner-zulu, this is Sunray in Bauviny. Come in. Over."

"Copy that Sunray. This is sierra two zero bravo. Reading you loud and clear. Standby for CO personnel. Out."

"Copy that niner-zulu."

Wagner covered the microphone with his hand and turned to his officer. "I can take it from here," he said dismissing him. "I'll call you should I need anything."

Soon, the radio was crackling again and moments later, Wagner heard the ambassador's voice. The ambassador sounded positive—Wagner might even say, cheerful. It made it somewhat more difficult to have to break the news to him that things might be spiraling out of control.

"This is sierra two zero bravo. Radio check. How do you read? Over."

"This is Sunray. Lima Charlie, Sierra two zero bravo. Reading you loud and clear."

"Good, good… How are you Wagner?"

"Well, sir, thank you. I'm sorry to take up your time… We have a situation here on site with the Laotian commanding officer."

"Military?"

"Civilian. Police. But appointed by the Minister of Defense."

"Roger that," the ambassador replied. "What's the situation report for your location?"

That was an official request and Wagner knew his communication would be transcribed for official records. He opened his manila folder and took out his summary notes.

There was a moment of silence after Wagner had finished delivering his report. Then the ambassador's voice came through the radio speaker."

"Copy that, Sunray. Moving you over to secure channel. Sending you COMSEC frequency. Over."

The ambassador requested they move their conversation to an encrypted channel. Generally, these frequencies were reserved for priority communications and emergencies. Any critical operations in the area would require that these dedicated channels remain open. Wagner hadn't expected the embassy to have such a strong reaction and he didn't know what to make of it. He took a moment to process the development.

The ambassador pressed on. "I say again. Sending you COMSEC frequency. Over."

"Roger that. Ready to copy. Over."

Wagner took up a pencil to take down the frequency keys. At the same time, he called out for his communications officer. "Get Liam and return here ASAP. We're switching to COMSEC and I want you both on the call."

By the time the communications officer located Liam and returned with him, Wagner had already switched over to the secure channel. He had the ambassador on at the other end.

"Alright," began the ambassador. "I'm going to dispense with any communications protocol. Tell me again what happened. Any casualties? Serious incidents?"

Wagner didn't know yet about Thamu's wife. "Nothing reported," he answered. "The man is taking the law into his own hands however. I'm concerned that we shall have *incidents* very soon if something isn't done."

"Go on," the ambassador urged.

"Chantasith disappeared from the village earlier today. He's gone rogue. We were supposed to set out this morning together for the hills. He had entered the village overnight. By O-seven hundred hours, he had already well over a dozen villagers tied up and beaten."

"I see…And why were you setting out for the hills?"

"We heard the subject is hiding somewhere in a cave on the hillside."

"Is the information reliable?"

It was obvious to Wagner now, that the ambassador as well, had no care for the villagers. "I think so," Wagner replied, a little disappointed. "He's nowhere in the village. He's got nowhere else to go. It seems natural that he would have taken shelter somewhere in the outlying area."

The ambassador let out a long breath. "Yes. In that case, someone from the village must be helping him. Bringing him supplies and information."

"Yes, that's usually the case," Wagner agreed. "Of course everyone from Chantasith to his communications officer thought of that.

"What about his wife?"

"She claims ignorance of everything."

"Hard to believe."

"I agree, wives are hardly credible witnesses in most cases, but I believe her. There's another woman who's disappeared after questioning. We believe she may know where he is. Unfortunately, she too, has disappeared."

"I see… It's been a half a week… Is there *any* progress?"

Wagner looked at Liam, then his communications officer and then back to the microphone again.

"We've been here three days. Since then, we've managed to alienate the witness and all the villagers…."

"But this chief of police…" the ambassador broke-in, growing more impatient by degrees.

"Chantasith…" Wagner reminded him.

"Yes, Chantasith—perhaps he's learned something?"

"I don't know—I…"

"Okay, Wagner… I need you to listen to me…."

"Yes, sir, of course."

"I'm not saying we condone their methods… but perhaps dealing with the Laotians is best left to the Laotians. It might give us the results we need. You've been in Laos a week now. You've been in Vinay for three, four days—whatever it is—and by your own admission, you're further from your objective than when you began."

Wagner was red in the face. "But Mr. Ambassador, this—"

"Listen Wagner, we have another problem. The pilot's sister, the congresswoman has been poking her nose into this. My office is sending weekly situation reports to Washington on her request. She's raising a big stink over there about how our government abandons its fallen soldiers and that sort of thing. It's indifference or incompetence, she says."

Wagner was thinking it was probably both.

"You know how these politicians get," the ambassador was saying. "It's not only a personal crusade; it's now a platform. She's announced an official state visit to Laos.

Of course, she can't do that and we've refused her. Safety concerns, security issues…. We gave her the usual reasons. And of course we can't stop her. We can only refuse her visit an official state sanction. She's coming anyway. She'll be here in forty-eight hours, probably with a retinue of reporters. I was hoping you'd have some answers for me."

"I'm sorry, sir. If you could put in a call to the defense minister and get his police chief out the way, I'm sure my team and I will have moved on Thamu before the congresswoman arrives. I—"

The ambassador interrupted. "Thamu?"

"The witness, sir."

"Yes, of course."

"Listen Wagner. We're going to hold off on involving the minister for now."

"I don't understand…"

"Our only priority here is to find the remains before Marie's arrival. I don't know how involved we can get on what is really an internal Laotian matter. The villagers I mean…"

Wagner was beginning to understand just how hopeless the situation was. "I see… but Mr. Ambassador, with Marie on the ground and the police chief gone amok, I mean it's hardly safe… I won't be able to ensure her safety.

"Wagner, listen to me. Not only do I agree, I also sympathize. But do you think there's anything I could do about it? You think I could stop her if I wanted to? My advice to you is to wrap this up before she arrives… as soon as possible. Keep a close eye on this Chantasith fellow. Let's let him have his run of the field for these forty-eight hours. Despite his draconian methods, he might lead us to our man, to Thamu. All this might have blown over by time she's arrived."

"Sir, I fear that violence may break out. Perhaps I have not stated the situation clearly. I'm not sure the chief is in control of himself or his men."

"Of course Mr. Wagner, of course... No, I hear you loud and clear. Do what you can from your end in the meantime. Wagner, this is an internal affair after all. We don't have the power to interfere. As far as Marie's security is concerned, I'm sure this police chief, no matter how much of a mad dog he might be, is not stupid enough to endanger a foreign dignitary. She'll probably have a detail with her anyway. In fact, I'm sure she will."

Wagner was shaking his head. This was not at all what he had hoped for. The ambassador had effectively tied his hands.

"Yes, sir. These are official orders, sir?"

"Copy that. They are your official orders."

"Yes, sir. Roger that."

"You'll report back here on this channel same time tomorrow for your Sitrep."

Wagner nodded. "Yes sir. Copy that. Wagner out."

XXV.

WAGNER HAD FINISHED his call with the ambassador. Chantasith was done with his rallying speech. He had called his lieutenant to his side and given him orders to go to the village and arrange for the gathering of the villagers tomorrow morning. Meanwhile, the translator was still recovering in his tent, so neither Liam nor any of the Americans had any idea what was brewing.

Meanwhile Wagner was in his tent pondering what Marie's arrival meant. He was now exhausted from wrestling with his anxiety. His nerves were racked and he had come out the other side it seemed. Suddenly, he felt numb. It was a great release, even if it only lasted for a second—he travelled to this place within himself it seemed, where suddenly none of this mattered. He didn't care—not about Thamu, the remains, the villagers or anything. He felt no responsibility and in this place there was no anxiety. It wasn't his responsibility he reminded himself now. He was just a man among many. A cog in a big machine. All he could do was his best. The result was out of his hands. Fate, nature, God, chance—whatever you want to call it—would determine the outcome. He had only to do what he could. If he did that, there would no anxiety, and his responsibility if any would have been fulfilled.

Feeling buoyed by the realization, he called Liam in to his tent.

"I've spoken with the ambassador. Not only will he not help us, he tells me that Marie, the dead pilot's sister, a congresswoman now, is on her way here."

Liam raised his brow. "Is that wise? I mean given the situation."

"I'm sure she'll remain in the capital. It'll be an afternoon field trip. Let's not worry about that. It's out of our hands," Wagner said, and he had to admit, it felt good just to say it.

"What about the police chief? Are you going to tell him?"

"Don't know yet. It might calm him down; it might enrage him further... I think I'll have to find the right moment."

"Well, tonight might not be the right time."

That got Wagner's attention. "What do you mean? Has something happened?"

"It's just that he was up there earlier before all his men, ranting under a hot collar to his men. It was an old shit show."

Wagner was relieved. He didn't want to confront Chantasith anymore today. "I'll deal with it in the morning," he told Liam. "Any idea what it was about? The shit show, I mean."

"I have no idea, sir. I think just general frustration. Shouting at his men, trying to motivate them.... that sort of thing."

"I see... And they're all at camp?"

"Looks like it. Getting ready for supper."

"And the translator... How is he?"

"Still recovering, sir."

"Very well then, Liam. I think that'll be all."

Liam made a motion to go and then stopped. "Will you not be joining us tonight for supper, sir?"

"I think I'll be turning in early today, Liam. I'll be in my tent should you need me. Please keep me informed of any movements in the camp tonight. I want to know if anyone leaves it tonight. Clear?"

"Of course, sir. As you wish."

"In fact, let's start keeping watch. Rotate the men for sentry duty. Four hour rotations."

"Very well. I'll take the first watch myself."

"Thanks Liam."

"Of course, sir."

↟ ↟ ↟

WAGNER was having a fitful sleep, turning over and over in his cot. He was dreaming and dreaming so vividly that he was half-awake and aware of his body twisted atop the cot, while the rest of him was alive somewhere in a dream. There is a figure leading him. It took Wagner awhile before he recognized who it was. Tom, the dead pilot was leading him in silence through a network of civilian underground bunkers. The bunkers were like catacombs, littered with the dead, mangled bodies of not only insurgent soldiers but civilians, women and children. Tom was showing him the results of the American air strikes in Laos.

Wagner had of course read up on American activities in Laos as part of his prep for the mission. The US had been secretly bombing Laos for over seven years, until Nixon finally admitted there was a definite and aggressive preemptive war being waged in Laos against communist insurgents. The official American position became that they were cooperating with the Laotian government to deter a Vietnamese invasion of Laos. They had to curb the spread of communism in the region they said. But there was no invasion. Declassified intelligence reported that all the Vietnamese did was take their supply route through Laotian land to avoid American air strikes. The US government knew this, but decided to publicize the fact as evidence of a Vietnamese invasion. The US continued on its campaign of bombing Laos. They had to destroy all supply routes and cut off all reinforcements that might finds its way into Vietnam whether by air, land or water. And that meant controlling Laos.

"It's a mistake" Tom said, turning to him.

Wagner didn't understand. "What's a mistake? Why are you showing me this?"

"I told you it's a mistake," Tom repeated. He was wearing his full pilot's uniform. "They gave us the wrong coordinates. We shouldn't have come here in the first place."

"It's not your fault," Wagner said.

Tom turned to him. "You shouldn't have come here either."

"It's too late for that now," Wagner said. "We're here to take you home."

Tom smiled at him. It was a wistful smile, like the one an adult gives a child.

"I can't go," Tom said. "Listen."

And at that moment, a terrible wail went up in the cavernous bunkers. Rivulets of blood began running down the walls of the bunkers, like rainwater seeps down cave walls.

Somewhere inside the bunker a child was crying. Bodies were strewn about on the ground to their left. The corpses were mangled, blown apart. Limbs lay scattered everywhere, separated from the stumps that were once bodies. Some of the bodies were still smoking from the explosion. Around them, stray dogs sniffed around the perimeter, licking their chops, attracted by the smell of roasting flesh, but afraid of the fire and still shell-shocked from the bombs. Off in a corner, some of the dogs had already fallen on an arm. Some others on one of their own killed in the bombing. Now some of the more adventurous dogs ventured in. Wagner watched with horror as one of them caught the nearest corpse with its teeth and began dragging it back to perimeter away from the fire, leaving a trail of guts and blood on the ground until Tom ran over to kick it away.

"Every one of these bunkers are filled with bodies like these," Tom was now telling him. "Listen," he said again. Wagner heard the cries of pain and wails of the dying coming from everywhere.

"And now, *look!*"

Wagner scanned the area again. He saw the mangled corpses, the salivating dogs, the naked savagery…

"You don't see it," Tom said.

"See what?" Wagner asked.

"The uniforms," Tom told him.

"I don't see any uniforms…What do you mean?"

"Exactly!"

And only then did Wagner understand the point Tom was trying to make. There were no uniforms. All the casualties were civilian.

The next moment, they were exiting the bunker. The smoke and the stench of burning bodies was getting too thick. They took two steps when a jet flew over them. They could hear the roar of its engines though they couldn't see the plane. Seconds later, an explosion erupted some hundred yards away.

Wagner and Tom scrambled to safety behind a rock. Beneath them in the valley, Wagner saw the bush in the distance rustling like something was moving through them. Looking closer, he saw the procession. Hundreds of people crawling on their bellies, trying to reach safety. Wagner knew they would find no place to hide. It was a matter of minutes, hours maybe before they were killed. The jets would empty their deadly payloads on the hillside and fly back to the Thai or South Vietnamese airbases for refueling and refitting. They would be back tomorrow if the job didn't get done the first time.

Wagner was shaking. "This doesn't scare you, Tom?"

Tom smiled. A plane was just flying overhead at north to northwest. Tom pointed at it. "Afraid? You see that plane? That's me up there, piloting that plane. It's my first mission. I can't see anything from up there. I reach my coordinates and drop the payload. What do I have to be afraid of?"

"We must help those people," Wagner said, pointing to the line of refugees.

"We can't," Tom said. "There's nothing we can do while those planes rain bombs from the sky. Only the mountains can save them now. Look!"

In his dreams Wagner sees the long line of refugees, crawling on their bellies across the jungle to the mountain side. There the mountains opened like a mouth to swallow the villagers. Down into the earth they went and Wagner could see them all, living within the stomach of the mountain, cozily and happy. At the center of it all was Thamu, enthroned, adorned and worshipped.

XXVI

WAGNER WOKE UP in the morning later than was usual. It was uncharacteristic of him—to sleep in like that. In fact, lately he'd be up before the alarm went off. Perhaps it was the dream or the insomnia of late, but this morning it was the alarm that woke him up. He could have stayed in his cot all morning, under those Laotian army issue blankets. He didn't care what they felt or smelled like. He felt he needed it. His head was groggy and it took him awhile to get on his feet. That odd dream he had of Tom—so vivid that it made him think there might be something to this *'peetyhoung'* business—had taken a lot out of him. He felt like he had really been in those bunkers. His ears were ringing from the shell shock. It was going to be a rough day, he was thinking while he shaved over the basin. Chantasith was going to be hard to handle today, he felt. And he had yet to think about Marie's arrival. That was going to complicate everything. No, he wasn't relishing the day ahead of him. He felt like those villagers, crawling through the bush on their way into the belly of the mountain. He felt like he was already under that mountain. He wished it could hide him… The dream returned to him again, with all its detail—more like the memory of something that happened than the trace of a dream—and it occurred to him: The mountain that sheltered the villagers then was the same mountain that sheltered the villagers today. Tom was showing him where every villager hid. He had shown him where *Thamu* was hiding.

Suddenly, Wagner was wildly excited. It was just a dream, of course, and Wagner wasn't a man of superstition. Still, the subconscious had a way of speaking to us through dream—and the eyes and ears are always recording and the mind always spinning so that it makes connections before we ourselves are aware of them.

Minutes later, he was shaved and dressed and standing before his tent. He watched as Chantasith's police troops marched out of camp towards the village. Something was brewing. Chantasith had grown angry, even violent lately. It was suddenly clear to Wagner, clear beyond a doubt—Chantasith was out of control. Meanwhile, the ambassador had tied his hands. "There's an old saying in my town," the ambassador had explained. "If you want to get a rooster out of the hen house, you throw in a weasel."

Wagner had little doubt that Chantasith would set fire to the hillside if he had to, and flush all living creatures out of it—but it was those creatures and the other villagers, if not Thamu himself that the ambassador had forgotten to add to his equation.

Liam had seen Wagner come out of his tent and was now walking toward him with two cups of coffee, one black, the other creamy. He handed the creamy cup of coffee to Wagner. "Cream and sugar—just the way you like it," he said.

"Thanks. What's going on over there?"

Liam turned around. "Don't know. Like I told you last night: He's planning something. They were all up and standing to order early this morning."

The two of them were standing before Wagner's tent, gazing out beyond the rolling hill to the west that was beginning to appear, brightening by degrees from the reflection of the morning sun.

"I see," Wagner said. "And the translator? How is he?"

"Recovered I think," Liam answered. "He had some breakfast today."

Wagner nodded. "At least that," he thought. He had his translator back. "Call him over," Wagner told Liam.

Liam returned with the translator a minute later. "Feeling better?" Wagner asked him. The translator nodded. "From now on, you eat only with us." The translator nodded again and Wagner continued. "I want you to go over to the other side of the camp and ask for Chantasith. Tell them I want to talk to him."

Liam interceded. "But sir... He's not there. I mean, we saw him leave. You and I, just a minute ago, we—"

"I know," Wagner said. "You're going to go over and poke your head in every tent. If anyone asks you, tell them you are looking for Chantasith, that you need to see him immediately—that you are looking for him. Do you understand? Then I want you to report back to me on what you see in those tents: people and equipment."

"Yes, sir." The translator sped off, eager to show his worth again.

Alone, Liam turned to Wagner, "I never imagined the police chief would behave this way. I don't know what point he's trying to make."

Embarrassment, Wagner thought. That's the point. Thamu had embarrassed all of them. One man was defying the will of two governments. One man had outwitted a team of policemen and a foreign delegation. None of that really mattered when compared to the fact that Thamu was defying Chantasith. Chantasith had his own superiors to report to—and knowing the sort of man he was, the continual embarrassment was too much to bear.

"How do you think the police chief will take to the news of a woman coming here to solve his problem for him?" Wagner asked.

Liam looked over, a smile breaking over his face. They both chuckled.

"Who knows?" Wagner added. "It might be love at first sight, the way it was with us."

They were having a good laugh over it when the translator returned, a little flush. He was clearly not fully recovered.

"They're all gone," he said. "Not a single policeman left. Just the cook and the helper."

Wagner smile was slowly fading. "What about the equipment?" he asked.

"They've taken it all."

"Guns? Ammo?" Wagner asked, now walking toward Chantasith's side of the grounds.

"Gone," the translator confirmed. "They've taken it with them."

"Alright…" Wagner said turning to Liam. "I want you both to set out to the village. Find out what's going on. Report back in 40."

Liam turned back. "If you don't mind my asking, sir… What will you be doing?"

"I'll be having breakfast," Wagner answered.

Liam and translator looked at each other and set off after Chantasith in silence. Wagner was watching the water boil, trying to remember more of his dream—details that might help place the mouth of that mountain.

DEEP inside that mouth, in the belly of the mountain as Wagner had dreamt it, sat Thamu visibly agitated. Yaya had just finished telling him what she had seen happen in the village. For days now, she had been reporting to Thamu all she saw, bringing him not only news, but nourishment and those little comforts she could smuggle without suspicion.

She had just finished recounting how Dee had disappeared, how the police had pointed their guns at her, how her very own father and many other men of the village had been tied to poles and questioned all afternoon. Some of them beaten. Thamu wanted to return to the village at once to put an end to it.

"No Thamu!" Yaya pleaded with him. "If you return to the village, you will have to tell these men where the *peetyhoung* rests."

"But I will not break the sacred bond."

"I know you won't. And so they will kill you."

"If they must and it is the Spirit's will, then so be it."

"But they will not stop there," Yaya then said and broke down crying. "They will not stop until they have the *peetyhoung*. They will not believe that you are the only to know. They will kill everyone, one by one until they find it."

"What am I to do?" Thamu asked, shaking his head. "I don't know what to do… I wish Thabo was here."

Yaya took Thamu's hands. "You must stay here!" she insisted. "It is safer for everyone. Right now everyone is free to come and go. We can hunt, gather fruits and berries. The women are safe… But if you surrender yourself without the *peetyhoung*, all that will be over."

Yaya went on piling argument upon argument and

slowly convincing Thamu it was better for everyone to remain where he was. The police and Americans had no knowledge of the region. They would never find the caves. They didn't know the ways of the mountain or the jungle. They would get tired and go home soon. "How long could they last?" she asked him. They would run out of food soon, she reminded him. These were city men... how could they navigate the narrow dirt paths through the bush and the mountains? "They came in a giant helicopter for goodness sake!" she reminded him, and Thamu laughed.

Thamu knew better than anyone how difficult it was to move from one part of the jungle to another. He had spent his boyhood hunting in its shadows. Walking was the only option for the police officers. Helicopters wouldn't be able to take them beyond the rice fields where the land was flat enough for a landing. Up here it was all jagged walls of rocks, trees and bamboo sprouting among thick, wild and thorny vines climbing and hooking over everything—tree to tree, stone to stone—the entire jungle was hidden from aerial view by a thick canopy as dense as moss. That's why Thamu had retreated to the jungle. He would know long before they even got close to him, if a crowd of men were moving through his jungle. The birds would take flight, animals would call, the entire world would give signal for those with eyes to see and ears to hear.

And the cave was just as comfortable as one could imagine it could be. With Yaya's help they had covered the cold, stone floor with bamboo and even laid down sleeping mats. Off to the side, a cooking area had been improvised and improved with time that suddenly had grown convenient. A stone fireplace they had made with a steel transom for hanging a pot also served as a spit for roasting the wild fowl Thamu sometimes trapped. Yaya in the meantime, sat on a stool he had fashioned out of a stone and some driftwood he found by the river. Her knees were bent sharply as the stool was low. Her skirt parted down the side exposing her legs and thighs. It was all very comfortable indeed, Thamu thought. He resisted his desire for Yaya. Instead, he put his own hand over hers.

"Tell me again, Yaya," he asked her. "What happened with Dee."

And Yaya told Thamu again, explaining to him everything she saw, everything she could remember.

î î î

CHANTASITH'S voice was already growing louder in the distance. It boomed across the valley. He was shouting, apparently irate. Liam and the translator hurried on up the path hoping to get closer. They turned on a bend and then suddenly saw the backs of a group of policemen ahead in the distance. The policemen's footprints were still fresh on the damp ground beneath him. Liam crouched and then pulled the translator into the bush with him. "We'll have to get closer," he said. "And we can't stay on the path." They could still hear Chantasith. "What's he saying?" Liam asked the translator. "Just threats. He will have everyone's badge and their pensions if they refuse to follow orders… that sort of thing."

They soon arrived at the village and Liam could see that Chantasith had already sent a team ahead with his lieutenant. There was little they could do while Chantasith remained in the center of that crowd. Soon, however Liam got his break when Chantasith pulled his lieutenant to the side. Liam grabbed the translator. "Let's go," he said.

"We're going to creep up next to them, behind that hut. Remember as much as you can, because I am going to want to know everything they spoke about."

Chantasith's voice came louder now. It appeared nonsensical, as he obviously began to curse.

"I tell you, this guy deserves a bullet in the head," he was telling his lieutenant. It makes me sick to think of the man hours we've put into this—and all because of some foreigners who came here decades ago to kill us in the first place."

Liam could see Chantasith's jaw muscles flexing. He was grinding his teeth.

"Make sure you find that idiotic lunatic," Chantasith was saying. "You had better bet there's someone in this village who knows exactly where he is."

"We'll turn them against each other. Just like you planned," the lieutenant was saying.

"Fine. Let's get to it, then. Are you ready?"

They could see the lieutenant take out a notepad and go over the main points with Chantasith.

"I don't know why I needed to write it down," the lieutenant was complaining. "I mean, it's simple enough."

"Just say it exactly like we wrote it, nothing more nothing less," Chantasith growled. "And yes, they are simple enough orders. You and the men should be able to remember them and follow through. In case, you don't," Chantasith sneered, "we'll finally know the cause of all this bungling is illiteracy. Now, repeat it to me, just like I told you."

The lieutenant did as he was told without further complaint or questions. He knew better than to press Chantasith when he was in a mood, which was clearly the case. Left alone, Chantasith was now staring out to the rice field outside the tent, searching his feelings and trying to connect himself to something. He thought of his wife and then of Dee and grew aroused. He was surprised how little remorse he had over the suicide. But it had been her choice after all.

Off in the background, behind the old hut, Liam and the translator were walking backwards, crouching. They reached the back of the hut and then made a dart for the cover of the jungle. Back on the path, Liam turned to the translator. "Tell me everything," he told him.

↟ ↟ ↟

CLOUDS obscured the sun and though it was a cold, dark morning, both Liam and the translator were sweating by the time they reached Wagner. Wagner stood patiently waiting until they caught their breath.

"Easy boys," he said. "Easy. Catch your breath... You look like racehorses who just finished the derby. What's the hurry?"

"Chantasith has told the villagers to find Thamu," Liam began. "He has offered a prize."

Wagner was dumbfounded. He had effectively put a price on Thamu's capture. It had become a bounty hunt.

"We thought you needed to know..." Liam was saying, still winding down on his breathing. "Apparently all the adult men in the village have gone off to find Thamu."

The translator looked uneasy. "Do you know? What the villagers told him? How they reacted?" he asked them.

Liam looked the translator in the eyes, and then Wagner. "We left before we could find out. What's your point?"

"Forgive me. You are not sure. I think, because you believe we are afraid of him, the villagers will go and look for Thamu."

"And you are not afraid?" Wagner asked.

"I think no one is afraid," the translator went on in near perfect English. "Do not worry, even if the men know where Thamu is, they will not betray him. He is like family. All village is big family, you know? They will tell him to go take hiding further off. Nothing more."

Wagner chuckled. "The amount he's offered is a handsome sum? I've seen families go to war over smaller inheritances."

"I am not saying they will not bring Thamu home. I am saying the men in the village are smarter than you think. Another thing, I heard…" the translator turned to Liam. "I hadn't mentioned it before, because I am not sure. But… I think Thamu's wife has gone missing."

"Missing? What do you mean?" Wagner asked.

"No one knows where she is. She was missing all day yesterday and this morning they learned she had not returned. Her cot was not slept in and the hut was empty. All the village is whispering about it."

"Perhaps she's run off to join Thamu," Liam said.

"I don't think so," the translator said.

"No. Nor do I," Wagner said.

Liam was the one now to voice his reservations. "What do you mean? Where do you think she is?"

"That we don't know. But wasn't she in Chantasith—I mean, the police chief's custody yesterday? And now no one knows where she is?"

"What can we do now, sir?"

"I will confront Chantasith about it," Wagner said, with a sudden burst of confidence. "I will confront him and learn the truth about it from him. In the meantime, there's something we can do. Come into my tent," Wagner ordered. He was thinking of the dream he had, and the terrain around the cave. "I want us to look at some maps."

XXVII

CHANTASITH WATCHED THE VILLAGE men leaving the village in a long file up the path toward the hills. He set his own men after them to make sure the villagers 'behaved honorably in this contest'. He thought his idea was brilliant and he was quite pleased with himself as he watched the village men setting out for Thamu with alacrity. Of course, everyone loved Thamu; and it would be hard to betray one of their own. But Chantasith was confident that the sum of money was sufficient to stir whatever group of malcontents there might be to revolt and finally into surrendering Thamu.

Among the villagers filing out to seek Thamu's hiding place was Yaya's father and her brother-in-law. They too had set out, but of course, with actual knowledge of where Thamu was hiding. It had been no secret in Yaya's household, of the growing love affair between these two, and now with Yaya's constant disappearing in the mornings they knew she had taken to visiting him. At the tables, in hushed tones at their bedside Yaya had whispered to her mother, sometimes her father, about Thamu and his situation. They all agreed, he was brave and doing the right thing. Now the old man, wise in the world, already new that the 'right' thing often wasn't the wise thing, and more often than not, was the dangerous thing. He could weather his fear for Thamu's safety, but now he was afraid for his daughter. He did not trust this city police chief. Ever since Dee had disappeared the old man had not slept well. Everyone in the village was speculating on what really had happened to her. And now that it seemed the police chief wanted Thamu for himself—that the Americans, it seemed, were no longer in control—and that no one cared about the remains anymore, but only to capture Thamu—was in the old man's mind signs of trouble and of a fight they could not win. Together with his son-in-law, he set out to warn his daughter and Thamu. Of course, they could not defy the spirits nor the will of the *peetyhoung*—and the old man found solace in that at least. The deities were on their side and so long as they did the will of Nature, the deities would remove all obstacles from their path and bring the village and the villagers through to the other side of this conflict safely. To defy them would be suicide. It was the villagers' duty to support Thamu then. For they knew, if Thamu failed in pleasing the Deities, their wrath would be set loose upon the village.

Yaya's father reached the mouth of the cave and called out for her. A moment later Yaya and Thamu emerged. The men greeted each other warmly. Thamu appeared contrite, as he was feeling guilty of all the suffering going on in the village in his name. "My deepest soul goes to the villagers and the safety and bounty of the crop," he told them. Yaya's father put a hand on his shoulder. "We know, Thamu. You are good man and we are here to help you. You honor our village and the spirit of our chief Thabo."

Thamu then asked if there was any news of his family, and of Dee.

"The Americans protect your family," Yaya's father assures him. "The top man," he said meaning Wagner, "visits your mother often. They bring her supplies and make gifts. They have given her blankets and candles, a mosquito net and other things for the hut…"

Thamu was smiling.

"And Dee?"

The old man shook his head slowly. His son-in-law shrugged his shoulders. "No one knows."

"This morning the police ordered everyone into the hills. They have offered a prize to the first person to bring you or information leading to your capture."

The old man stopped. Thamu was shaking and sweating now.

"Perhaps you need to consider moving from here?" he suggested.

"I fear for what they may do the village if I were to disappear," Thamu confessed.

"You cannot give yourself to them without surrendering the *peetyhoung*," the older man reminded him.

"They will torture you until you die or give up the *peetyhoung*," Yaya rejoined.

"So there is no reason for you to remain," Yaya's brother-in-law added.

Thamu's eyes fell upon the ground and his mind seemed to be far off. He was wondering what Thabo would have done.

↟ ↟ ↟

BACK at the camp, Wagner had finished plotting their hike to the mountain he had selected. The topography, the location and orientation all seemed to fit what he had seen in his dream. Wagner told him he had received a tip from one of the villagers, and no one pressed him for details. They had plotted the course together, leaning heavily on the translator's advice, who though not from the region, was at least Laotian and provided much information they would not have otherwise known. Possibility of traversing, impasses, how much bush they might have to cut through…. Then Liam had gone to pack supplies while everyone prepared and met before Wagner's tent. The plan was to set out for the cave, but to drop in on the village first. Wagner wanted to see things for himself and talk to Chantasith who he imagined—given his portly stature and general disposition—would not be accompanying his men on the trek through the jungle.

Wagner had not been wrong in his assessment. Sure enough, there was Chantasith sitting in the shade of a parasol sipping on watermelon juice. There were some older women to be seen, sitting in front of their huts or tending gardens, but otherwise the village was deserted.

"They've all gone looking for Thamu," Liam said.

Wagner wasted no time. "There's Chantasith. You fellas wait here. I have sense I'll get more out of him if he's less defensive, and he's bound to be less defensive if I go it alone."

Liam nodded. "We'll give you some room. We'll wait for you up by the path at the north edge." Liam turned to the translator. "Come on. Let's go."

Wagner waited until Liam and the translator were out of sight, before he let out a deep breath. He could see Chantasith and knew Chantasith had seen them. He was ignoring them—no longer even acknowledging their presence. Wagner began walking toward him. He reached Chantasith, the lounge chair, the parasol and the melonade. He had Saivongsa with him. Chantasith took another sip.

"Mr. Chantasith. Good morning."

"Ah, Mr. Wagner," Chantasith almost sang. "How nice to see you! Out on a stroll with your team? You Americans are so adventurous." The sarcasm was dripping off him.

"It seems the village is off on an adventure of its own," Wagner rejoined, pretending to look around. "It's empty. So is the camp…"

Chantasith was chuckling. "You are right, Mr. Wagner. You are clever man. I could not have put it better myself." He looked him in the eyes. "Everyone loves a good adventure, don't they? I have given them a game to play."

"And what game is that?"

"How do you call it? Peekaboo? Hiding and go seek?"

"Hide and seek."

"Yes. This Thamu is hiding. So we are seeking. It is a game. Nothing more."

"I've been told a cash prize has been offered to anyone capturing the witness."

"What game is not made better with a prize? Mr. Wagner you disappoint me. I thought you knew that."

"I always thought it was the people you played with that made the game better or worse."

Chantasith took another sip of his melonade. "No, Mr. Wagner," he said quite flatly. "It's the prize."

Wagner was almost amused. "And who authorized the prize?"

"I did," Chantasith replied with satisfaction.

"Did you get the defense minister's permission to do this?"

"I don't need anyone's permission!" Chantasith scoffed.

"Then who will pay the reward?"

Chantasith laughed. "Pay? No one is going to be paid! Once we have that idiot fugitive in our hands, we are done. Perhaps I will send them a thank you note," Chantasith laughed.

"I see."

"Oh, don't be so tender-hearted Mr. Wagner! They are lucky I do not arrest the lot of them for assisting the fugitive and for not cooperating with an official government investigation in the first place."

"Investigation?"

"Why of course! The investigation into the whereabouts of your dead pilot."

"I would classify it as a recovery mission."

Chantasith shrugged his shoulders. "You classify it as whatever you like."

"Thank you, Mr. Chantasith. I'm afraid it is my duty to do so. Another item I need clarification on for my report to the embassy. I understand the *witness*'s wife has disappeared…" Wagner paused to see if Chantasith would bite. The young officer with him, who appeared catatonic was blinking now, blinking more than usual. But Chantasith was as stoic as ever. "What do you know about it?"

Chantasith pursed his lips. "Disappeared you say? I have not heard such a thing… She has joined her fugitive husband then. Thank you for bringing this information to us. We will deal with her later."

"I see. So don't know anything about it?" Wagner looked at Saivongsa who was careful not to make eye contact and then back at Chantasith.

That seemed to get under Chantasith's skin finally. He stood up from his lounge chair and stepped toward Wagner. "Mr. Wagner, did I not just tell you a moment ago, that I had not heard of it? Has someone filed a missing person's report that I don't know of? What are you implying?"

"Last I heard she was being held by your men for 'questioning' I believe were your words."

"Yes, and we let her go after she told us nothing."

"And that was the last you saw her? Do you remember what time it was, she was released?"

Chantasith let out a laugh. "You leave the investigating to the professionals, Mr. Wagner. I appreciate your enthusiasm, but really... these matters don't concern you."

Chantasith turned to go.

"One more thing, Mr. Chantasith: I've been informed by the United States ambassador that the dead pilot's sister will be making an official visit to Laos. I expect she will be meeting with your defense minister and probably touring the village."

Chantasith was annoyed. "More Americans? A woman Mr. Wagner? You think this is a place for an American woman?" He grew hotter with each question. "You think the defense minister has time to sit down with a crying relative? Do you not think this arrogance of you Americans blinds you?"

"Not just a woman, Mr. Chantasith. A congresswoman. There will be a retinue of people with her. I suspect much international press as well." Wagner paused again for effect. "I think it would be best—for the two of us—if we began cooperating."

"I see. Mr. Wagner, I am a policeman in my heart. I leave the politics and the uh... 'cooperating' as you call it, to the politicians. I don't know what a congresswoman is, so I know that here in Laos it means nothing."

"I understand she will be wanting to meet with Thamu's

wife," Wagner began. He saw Chantasith flinch and after Chantasith ignored the comment, Wagner knew he was lying about not knowing Dee's whereabouts. "She believes she can convince Thamu's wife to convince him. Woman to woman," Wagner added.

Again, Chantasith showed unusual restraint. Wagner felt confirmed.

"I tell you something else, Mr. Wagner," Chantasith said leaning in to him—and Wagner knew he had hit a nerve. "There is no point in this sister coming here. It will all be over before she arrives." Chantasith turned to go. "Enjoy the games, Mr. Wagner. I tell you what, if you or one of your team find the rat, I will pay you the prize money personally—and I will take your congresswoman dancing!" he added with mockery. "Won't we?" he asked, turning to Saivongsa.

Saivongsa was beyond reach. Chantasith let out a hateful laugh. "Refill my glass," he told Saivongsa.

Like a beaten dog, Saivongsa shuffled over and took Chantasith's cup. It was all a dream.

♟ ♟ ♟

WAGNER and Liam were well on their way along the north path to the mountain ridges they had scoped. They were walking a narrow path in single file. The translator was some paces ahead. Liam followed and Wagner brought up the rear. He was thinking there was little else he could do except find Thamu before Chantasith did or at least keep Thamu safe until Marie's arrival. Though he wasn't sure how he felt about it, he knew that Marie's visit would escalate matters in the Laotian government and at the embassy and hopefully flush Chantasith and his men out. Worse was the very real danger that this bounty hunt would result in bloodshed. With all of Chantasith's men storming into caves, 'guns a-blazing'—it would probably be to Chantasith's immeasurable delight if the 'fugitive' was found dead, the remains never found, the case closed and the Americans left disappointed.

Liam noticed Wagner's pensiveness. He slowed down in his step and when Wagner caught up, he asked him, "Learn anything from Chantasith?"

"Not really."

"The wife?"

"Says he didn't know she was missing. He was lying. And there's something else," Wagner added. "There's a junior officer that knows more than he's letting on."

"What are you going to do?"

"We'll find Thamu," Wagner repeated. "Once we find him, there will be no more cause for all this calamity. It'll be an end to all this inconvenience and suffering."

Wagner picked up the pace. He could see the mountain they would have to circle in the distance. The opposite side of that mountain with the river trailing in its northwest valley was where Wagner thought he would get lucky.

⇡ ⇡ ⇡

BACK at the village and alone, Chantasith was slowly losing it. He was fuming and even the thought of Thamu's capture—which he believed imminent—could not appease him. The nerve of these Americans! The gall these men had to send their wives over here to beg and plead for them! It turned his stomach. And the presumption—*that* was too much to bear! To think they could all just come here and tell him what to do.

He could no longer find pleasure either in his melonade, nor the shade… and the lounge chair suddenly seemed incongruent to the surroundings.

It wasn't long after, Yaya's mother came out of her hut to dust her blankets and Chantasith realized he hadn't seen the old man all day. He was furious. He charged over and grabbed the old woman by the arm so forcibly it snapped her head back.

"Where is your husband, old woman?"

"He is out with the rest of the men looking for Thamu, just as you told us to."

"Why would a man of his age go hunting for Thamu? Can you tell me?"

"For the money, of course."

Chantasith laughed. "For the money she says! He expects to win with all men of the village, younger and faster than he could hope to be, also looking?" He shook her again. "A man his age? Trudging through the wastes and the jungle? No… I tell you what. A man his age doesn't leave the fireside unless he knows exactly where he is going. And so your husband knows exactly where Thamu is. Come here."

Chantasith grabbed the old woman by the crook of the arm and pulled her away to the side of her hut. He put in her view of the square where the poles had been set up and where they had tied the men the day before. "Your husband is cheating," he whispered in her ear. "The Americans don't like cheaters in their games. Cheaters go in the penalty box," he said pointing at the poles. "When do you expect him back?" he asked her.

But she just stood there staring vacantly at the poles.

"When?" Chantasith repeated.

The old woman was shaking. "I don't know, he hasn't told me anything," She told him.

"Don't lie, old woman!" he seethed. "I am a married man too. I can't leave the house without my wife asking me when to expect me back."

The woman was wry. She had seen the years come and go. "Maybe she needs to get your best friend out of bed before you're back."

"I see," Chantasith grunted. "You dirty hill-dwellers think you are so smart, but you will see." Chantasith began dragging the old woman off to the poles. "You think I will give you special treatment because you are some elderly witch in your village. A criminal is a criminal. You will learn. Everyone will learn."

Chantasith's grip on the woman was tighter than even he would have wanted, and he was bruising her though he didn't know it. Inside, he was boiling over with rage. He stood the old woman up against one of the poles and took her arms and began tying them behind her.

XXVIII

ALL this chaos and trouble at the village, and all that worry at home, the nights his wife tossed and turned and could not sleep, was getting to him. He knew an end had to come of it, before tensions erupted and something terrible happened. For the moment, the police felt safe, going about terrorizing everyone at the village. But the policemen did not know that the men of the village had gathered after Dee's disappearance to decide if they should act and what measures to take. They did not understand that it was the only the elders of the village—their words and counsel—that persuaded the men to wait. Some of the villagers had been speaking of revenge even then. It was their village, their jungle—how easy it would be for three or four of them to attack them in the night. Then they would understand and go home. As time wore on and if the crimes committed on one side persisted, then he knew that even the elders would slowly began leaning towards retaliation.

No one knew as well as he. For Yaya's father was one of those elders—and he himself was thinking 'enough is enough'. All this uncertainty and fear for his daughter was a growing strain. Everyone in the village had someone to fear for. He was walking through the woods pensively. He thought he had been careful to walk a circle and so return to the mouth of the cave. He had left his daughter with Thamu alone to part in privacy, and now he had gotten lost. The bush had grown thick; he had been forced to take some detours, had been turned around and now he was lost. Suddenly, the ground was damp and soft and everywhere he stepped, he seemed to be sinking through mud. He spun about, trying to get his bearings... if only there was something he might recognize... when he noticed the leaves at his feet moving about them. They were too wet and too heavy for the wind to be ruffling them he thought. A long chain all about him, began pulsing as if something was trying to get up from out of the ground. The old man peered in closer. His eyes weren't so good anymore and the animal's camouflage was almost perfect. Then he saw its eyes, and then the outline of the flat head of an anaconda. It was the size of his leg! He stepped back and saw another anaconda behind him, larger than the last. This one could wrap itself around him and easily crush the bones out of him. He was circled—he had stumbled into a nest of anacondas. They were known to hunt near ravines where deer and other animals would come to drink. Today, perhaps they would feast on old man flesh, he thought. He was caught. He couldn't escape forward, nor backward. He knew if he made a move, they would grab him. They heard with their bellies, through the vibrations on the ground. Every boy in the village knew this. The more he moved, the closer they would circle in. If he made a run for it, they would surely catch him. And if they hooked him, there was no way he had the strength to pull them off his body. Careful, not to move, he cried out for help. Once, and one of the anacondas twitched. A second time, and the second anaconda began slithering toward him. Now, the old man felt doomed. He covered his mouth with both his hands to mask the sound of his breathing. There was nothing he could do now except watch. The anaconda behind him was now crawling away, but the one in front of him was moving towards him, its head flat against the leaves, coming closer and closer, its tongue darting in and out quickly. The old man closed his eyes and called upon his ancestors and his deities to help him. Suddenly, he heard a gunshot, and opening his eyes saw the anaconda falling back away from him, its head exploded, cold blood spraying out of its head to hit him in the face.

"Are you ok?" said Yaya.

Still shaking the old man took his daughter in his hands. Thamu grabbed the dead snake by the tail and pulled it away. "Big one," he said, smiling.

"Thank you," the old man said. "I thought my day had come."

Yaya pointed to the other snake, now making a run for it.

"Let it go," Thamu said. "The gunshot has scared it off."

"Yes, and probably attracted many a different type of snake," Yaya's father said. "We have to get out of here. We don't know who's about when half the town and all the policemen are out looking for you. Someone might have heard the gunshot."

He began pulling his daughter away.

"Go down that way," Thamu said pointing. "You'll hit a foot path. Turn left, you will see the path you came up on after a hundred or so paces. Yaya knows. I must go and cover the entrance to the cave."

Yaya, her father and Thamu parted, promising to meet again, before any decision in the village was made. Thamu darted off to cover the entrance to the cave with the bamboo and leaves, he had set aside. Then he returned to the spot where he had killed the snake, climbed a tree and waited.

↑ ↑ ↑

IT made for difficult walking trekking through the Laotian jungle and the translator, not personally invested in this search mission, had already given up hope and begun complaining.

"It's impossible to see anything in this jungle," he said, sitting down on a stump. "Why there might be a villager and a thousand ghosts behind that tree and a hungry tiger waiting to devour us behind them!"

Liam and Wagner looked at each other and smiled, but kept walking.

"Then you'd better keep up," Wagner said with a wink. "I hear that's how wild cats hunt. They prey on the weakest. They might follow a group for days, wait for the slowest one to fall far enough behind and then pick him off. I'd hurry if I were you."

Wagner and Liam were still chuckling when Wagner suddenly grew excited. "Look!" he told Liam. "Fresh prints!"

Liam ran up and followed Wagner's finger to the spot on the ground it was pointing to. There in the dirt were two sets of fresh foot prints that Yaya and her father had made earlier that morning.

"What do you think?" Wagner asked him.

"One of them looks smaller. A child's?"

"Or a woman's…"

"What would one of the women be doing so far out

here?"

"Exactly," Wagner agreed. "Let's find out."

Wagner doubled his pace up the path, making sure to keep sight of the tracks Yaya and her father had unwittingly made.

"Better keep up!" Wagner shouted to the translator.

Then at that very moment, as they clambered up the path, the sound of a gunshot rang through the air. All three, stood to attention. They were silent, motionless... waiting. Seconds passed... they waited for more sounds, more gunshots. There was nothing. Liam was looking over at Wagner expectantly.

"Where?"

"North by northwest?"

The three of them hurtled themselves through the jungle in direction of the gunshot's origin. Fifteen minutes later, all of three of them were standing about with their hands on their knees trying to catch their breaths.

"I don't see anything," Liam was saying.

"They're gone," the translator added. "Whoever that was."

Down the hillside beneath them, obscured by the thick canopy of leaves, were Yaya and her father walking down the very same path Wagner had just been charging up minutes ago. Yaya's father noticed the new set of prints. Three of them by his count. He told his daughter they had better hurry.

Up high sitting on a branch of a giant, old rubber tree, just yards away from Wagner, sat Thamu chewing on tree leaves, watching it all.

XXIX

IT WAS LATE AFTERNOON and many of the policemen along with the villagers were already returning—some of them, mostly the policemen—afraid to be caught in the jungle after sundown. There would be no way of making their way back, no light by which to see, and they would have to spend a sleepless night in the jungle. Chantasith saw them as they began emerging out of the jungle and down the path toward the village. The men seemed jovial. They were all having a good time in general it appeared. His policemen had broken ranks to the point that they were now mixing with the villagers as though their field trip had been a bonding experience. Chantasith was enraged. "They had better not have returned empty-handed," he muttered his under his breath. "God help me!"

The returning villagers and policemen were making their way when they saw the old woman tied to the pole. The policemen then saw Chantasith barreling down on them. All of them now, wondered if the safer idea had not been to stay in the jungle after all. One of the village men ran over to Yaya's mother's side.

Chantasith watched, even further enraged. "God help him if he unties her," he muttered. "I'll have him shot. I swear it!" Two dogs took off barking, suddenly running out past him to greet the returning villagers it seemed with wagging tails and hanging tongues. Everyone saw them run up the path, then past the villagers. Chantasith watched as the dogs stood, waiting at the edge of village wagging their tales. A second later, they began to bark and to nip at each other. It was the old man and his daughter, Yaya. The dogs whined and then ran up to the two of them, licking their hands and chasing each other in circles around their feet.

Chantasith drew his gun. He pointed it at the old man, right past through the crowd of returning villagers and policemen. About twenty arms went up. Then, Yaya seeing her mother ran to her. Together she and the other began untying the old woman. Chantasith's arm swung to the left, then back forward again. The veins on his neck were pulsing and his finger was twitching on the trigger.

Saivongsa who had been watching the proceedings with growing disgust for himself, suddenly stepped in between Yaya and Chantasith's gun with his arms outspread. "No!" he cried.

Chantasith turned crimson with fury. "Boy! Step aside or I'll shoot you for insubordination!"

"No!" he said again.

Yaya was trying to comfort her mother. Chantasith and Saivongsa were staring each other down. The other policemen watched in shock. Wagner, Liam and the translator were just then returning from the fruitless search to stumble upon this scene. After the gunshot, they made their way back to the path with some difficulty but could not find the tracks back to the cave. Thamu had covered Yaya and her father's tracks and then hidden the entrance to the cave so well, that Wagner and his team passed within twenty feet of it without ever knowing. They were now returning to camp empty-handed and the first thing Wagner saw was Chantasith pointing a gun at one of his officers. He appeared to be protecting some villagers.

"Stop!" Wagner cried.

Seeing the American, Yaya ran over to him. Pleading with him, she pulled at his shirt, trying to pull him toward her mother. She was babbling between sobs. Of course Wagner couldn't understand a thing.

"What's she saying?" he asked the translator.

"She is saying, 'they want to kill us, you must protect us.'"

Wagner nodded and looked Yaya in the eye as he gently pushed her off. "Tell her not to worry," he told the translator, and then turned to Liam. "Liam, go untie the woman."

Liam began walking, but Chantasith had understood. He shouted to his lieutenant in broken English so that everyone, Liam and Wagner included would understand. "Take out your gun! Shoot anyone goes near the prisoner!"

Liam stopped and looked back at Wagner. Wagner smiled and nodded as if to say 'it's okay' and Liam began turning back around. Wagner was standing there still. In his mind, he had already decided that he would walk over and untie the woman himself. It was a done deal—in a sense it had already happened. He wasn't afraid—he felt no danger. It was impossible that anyone would fire upon him…. No, he was looking for that old anxiety within him that use to plague his waking moments. It had been days now—he had not felt it. He had almost forgotten about it. He was suddenly free of it and was just realizing it. What had it been? he wondered as he began walking. What was it that had set him free of its bonds? All at once, he knew the answer. He smiled at Liam again as he passed him on his way to the woman. It was 'action'. He had no other means of describing it. Before he'd sit and he'd worry about a decision and possible outcomes. He'd run down the decision tree, inspect the leaves minutely—but now he acted. He let his 'gut' make the decision and then used his thoughts to implement it. There was no worry, nothing to ponder, just freedom and liberation in the act. It was as if action set the spirit free. And he knew this was what he was doing: setting himself free as he began untying the old woman.

Chantasith's lieutenant looked at him, Chantasith looked back. The lieutenant lowered his gun.

A moment later, Wagner had the woman untied and Yaya and her family were reunited. It was a clear moral defeat for Chantasith. Wagner knew he would not take the blow passively. He was already calling his men over to him as Wagner was calling Liam. "Take them to their hut. Or wherever they wish to go. Consider yourself their chaperone, body-guard, personal attaché—I don't care what you call it, but don't let them out of your sight. Also: we're pulling out of the campsite and setting up here in the village until Marie arrives. We need to provide security for these people."

Chantasith was now marching over toward Wagner. Wagner could see him making a beeline for him out of the corner of his eye. He chose to deflect Chantasith's aggression by tending to the old woman.

"This man knows the whereabouts of your witness," he said, seething with rage and pointing at Yaya's father.

Wagner looked over to old man and then at Chantasith.

"That may be," he said. "But is that a reason to kill him?" Wagner looked Chantasith in the eye. "Were you going to shoot my lieutenant, Mr. Chantasith?"

Chantasith snorted. "I have done what I can to assist you Americans. But you cannot be helped! Do as you like!"

"My wife has done nothing wrong," Yaya's father now spoke up. "What business is this? What kind of man are you?" he asked Chantasith.

"I am doing my job," Chantasith growled.

"Then do it well!" the old man retorted. "Tying up an innocent woman is a mistake in any job."

"And where were you today then, old man?" Chantasith returned. "Where were you?"

"Why I went out looking for Thamu, just like you asked us to."

"I'm sure you did," Chantasith answered sardonically. "And so where is he?"

"We couldn't find him."

"You couldn't find him?" Chantasith laughed. "Of course you know the cave he's hiding in…"

"There are many caves. We know or think he's been in one of them. But since you and the Americans have arrived, he keeps moving. Now we've lost track of him."

Chantasith was staring at the old man, trying to burn a hole through him with his eyes. Suddenly. Chantasith wasn't sure whether or not he believed him.

"If Thamu doesn't want to be found, then no one can find him," Yaya's father went on. "Even as a boy, he was already the best hunter in the village."

"Then how do you suggest we find him old man?"

Yaya's father stared back Chantasith. The old man was no fool. "Maybe if we bring him his wife, and ask her to call out for him, he will come out."

Chantasith would have killed the old man with his stare if he could. He turned away and glanced at Wagner who had been observing intently. "You're all criminals as far as I'm concerned," Chantasith sneered and stormed off.

ʎ ʎ ʎ

MOST of the village men had returned now carrying the spoils of their day in the hills. Of course none of them had any knowledge of Thamu's whereabouts, but all were carrying fruits, nuts and even some animals pelts from the set traps they had visited along their way. Those that arrived first had already fallen to eating and drinking. The police men were having a good time in general, some of them even now mixing with the villagers as though their field trip had been a bonding experience. Chantasith was enraged. He gathered his lieutenant and three of his most senior men and told them to finish eating and meet him back at the camp in fifteen minutes.

With Chantasith gone, everyone seemed to relax a little. The women came out of their huts and then soon the children were running about their fathers' legs. Yaya and her family were reunited, Thamu and the *peetyhoung* were safe, the 'angry bear' as the villagers had taken to calling Chantasith, was gone and it seemed that the village had won a victory or at least the right to celebrate that night even if their victory might be short-lived. They had won this ledge, this ridge, this territory and could rest a moment in it. It was still a mystery to most of the villagers why anyone, especially the Americans would want to disturb the *peetyhoung*. Did they not love their ancestors in America? It seemed like cruel torture to the villagers that anyone would want to separate the *peetyhoung* from his remains in the belly of the mountain. Everyone knew that at the heart of the mountain, deep at the center of that rock was the gate to the spirit world. If the bones were to be removed, the *peetyhoung* would no longer be able to travel between this world and the other. He would be imprisoned on one side or the other depending on when they moved his remains. If they took his remains while he was on this side, and took it too far, he would not be able to make it back to the mountain and return to the spirit world. If they took his remains away while he was in the spirit world, there would nothing for him to return to. He would arrive at the gate and find no door for him to step through and come into this world.

Some of the men of the village had gathered in the center of the village—a rudimentary square lined by huts and stone markers. Wagner noticed them. A serious look went around the circle of faces and Wagner thought he had best address the villagers while everyone was gathered. He motioned for his translator. A moment later, the translator was calling for everyone's attention and Wagner and Liam were joining him in the center of the square.

"You will translate the words exactly as I say them, after each pause," Wagner told the translator. "It is very important that you do so. Do you understand? It is more important that you remain true to my translation than for you to attempt to frame my words in a way they are accustomed to."

The translator assured him he did, and Wagner began.

"My friends," he began. "Let me start first by apologizing for all the confusion and the pain our visit has caused. It was never our intention that anyone be inconvenienced, much less hurt. We Americans, are visitors not only in your village, but also in your country. We feel very saddened by all the suffering our visit has caused. We did not know there would be trouble. We never wished harm to Thamu or to anyone else."

Wagner was scanning the crowd as he spoke. He noticed the men were smiling, in fact, most of the villagers were smiling at him as if this was a stage show. And perhaps it was to them, Wagner thought. This was no different to them than a typhoon storm passing through their village and they suffered it with the same equanimity as they would an act of God. They didn't understand and they didn't need to understand it. It seemed to Wagner that they were just happy that he was there to share it with them while the police—not so much. Wagner pressed on.

"We understand now, that since we've arrived, a number of injustices have been perpetrated. We are terribly sorry for these last wrongs especially. We understand now that the behavior of your police is not in the spirit of our mission. We will be setting up camp here, with your permission of course, in the center square. Our men will be on guard duty throughout the night. There will always be a man posted as a lookout."

The villagers were looking about at each other and all nodding up and down to one another as if in agreement.

"I also want you to know that you can come to us if you have anything you'd like to say."

Wagner stopped, hoping, perhaps just trying... but no one spoke up.

"Or if you need anything... Finally, I understand that some among you, may possibly be in contact with Thamu. Or may possibly be able to get into contact with him. Perhaps Thamu is listening right now. I have a message, I would like to give him. From myself, personally to him.

"And this is my message to Thamu: Do not be afraid. We know you are trying to do what is right as you understand it. Very soon Tom's—the *peetyhoung*—his sister will be arriving from the United States. She is coming from very far away. Her only wish, and that of her family's, of Tom's family, is to be able to say goodbye to their beloved son one last time and then set him to rest. This is something they never had a chance to do. I am sure you understand. We wish only to speak to you. Myself and Tom's sister. We understand the police have been acting dishonorably. We will stay in the village and help as much as we can, until Marie arrives. You will hear and see the big engine in the sky on the day she comes. We hope you keep safe until then."

↑ ↑ ↑

WHILE Wagner and his team were moving camp from the rice field to the town square, Chantasith and four of his policemen were at the edge of the forest. They were standing there for the cover of darkness it provided, and speaking in whispers. Chantasith was giving orders.

"These villagers have made fools of you men," he was saying. "And now the Americans are going to bring in a woman—a woman!—to do the job they can't. And the job you, and you, and you, and you can't do!" Chantasith said, thrusting his pointing finger at each man's chest in turn. "I don't know how you men will be able to show your faces around the station when everyone hears of this... this... this fiasco!"

Chantasith walked back and forth around his men while they stood to attention. "This is what we are going to do," he finally said. "I am going to give you boys another chance to redeem yourselves. We will set out every morning—the five of us—and comb every tree and bush in this jungle until we find him. We will find him before this American witch arrives. Anyone asks you, you tell them we've gone hunting while we await orders from the minister. I will inform the Americans myself—that since they will not accept our help, my officers and I will be taking some much needed time off. 'R and R' as the Americans call it."

The four policemen listened, the backs and necks straight, their eyes staring outward. Chantasith had chosen these men particularly—and he had a particular reason. All four of these men had done military service. Like Chantasith, they had come to the police force from the military and the Ministry of Defense. Chantasith knew he could count on them to follow orders unquestioningly. And if any of the policemen knew how to move through the jungle or spot an enemy in the trees, it was these four men. All of them had served duty along the border and the interior jungles looking for revolutionary guerilla units.

Chantasith told his men to sleep well tonight and prepare for the big day ahead. Watching the men disappear into their tents, all four of them without a word to each other, he felt pleased, even confident. It was as if the Americans had played into his hands. He couldn't have planned it better himself, he thought. It was a stroke of genius was what it was. Genius to rival the greatest of the generals in history, he felt. He had stolen the American's victory and made it his own. And now he would storm the castle with his band of heroes.

XXX

IT WAS A LOT EASIER said than done—this business of transporting the camp. Night had fallen, they were just now pitching the tent. They had yet to set up the communications bureau, wire the batteries for the lighting and the radio equipment, set up the latrine... Wagner was contemplating calling it a night and having his men sleep under the open sky. They could resume work in the morning. Then suddenly the translator was calling him.

"Excuse Mr. Wagner," he called.

Wagner was annoyed by the interruption. "What is it?" he shouted back.

"There's a child wants to talk to you. Her father is with her."

Wagner put down the tent pole he was attempting to assemble. He had a vice-wrench in his other hand.

"What girl?"

"Over there," the translator said, pointing to the area behind him. "At the edge of the square over—"

The translator had turned around to point to them, but couldn't seem to find them. "Sir, they were just there."

"What did they want?"

The translator began approaching Wagner.

"You know what they wanted?" Wagner repeated.

"Please sir," the translator said leaning in and whispering. "She said her Aunt got raped and that they have taken her away to the city in the flying machine. She wanted us to help them bring her back."

"Rape?! How did she know the woman got raped?"

"I don't know sir."

"Who is her aunt?"

"I'm sorry, sir. I thought it best to find you right away so that you might hear the details yourself."

"Wagner threw the vice-wrench down." He muttered some profanity under his breath. "Alright men, he called. That's it for tonight. You can keep working or sleep out in the open and take it up in the morning. It's your choice…. Liam, you're on first post duty. Rotation every four hours." Then Wagner turned to the translator.

"Ok, come with me. Let's see if we can't find this girl. How many aunts can't there be?"

"Sir!" the translator interjected almost shocked. "Every woman is everyone else's aunt in this village!"

Wagner was smiling. "It's called sarcasm…"

The translator laughed. "Okay, sarcasm. You try to say something by saying the opposite. I know sarcasm." The translator cleared his throat. The police chief is a nice guy. How do you say: hell of a guy?"

Now Wagner was laughing as well. "That's right. A good example." Suddenly, he was serious. "You believe the little girl?"

"I think so. It's is hard not to. She's a little girl."

"Who was the man with her? You said it was her father…"

"I assumed…"

"Don't assume," Wagner said. He paused. "What was he saying?"

"He didn't say anything. He was just holding her hand."

Wagner was wondering why an adult would have a child tell the translator about her aunt and how she understood what rape was.

"The little girl said her aunt was raped?"

"That's correct, sir. She—"

Wagner interrupted him. "How would a child know about rape? How did she describe it?"

"She said the man mounted her aunt—it is how they speak here," the translator explained. "That her aunt was crying. She said they beat her, they mounted her and took her away."

"There's more to this story," Wagner said. "Let's go find them."

They did their rounds of the village. A couple of times the translator thought he saw the girl, other times it was the man he thought he saw. Each time they approached, it turned out not to be the case. It had already been getting dark and it had been difficult to see them clearly in the dim light, the translator complained. And then they all looked very much alike. Wagner had to agree. The gene pool wasn't exactly a cornucopia. The men all wore their hair the same, and the women as well. If it wasn't for the ritual scars of some and the different jewelry they wore to mark their status, it would be hard to tell them apart from a distance.

Finally, they had to give up. The night had fallen. Villagers were starting to turn in and most of the children were indoors already. "We'll try and find them in the morning," Wagner told the translator. "It's no use in this darkness."

↑ ↑ ↑

LIAM was at his post at the edge of the square, his back to the village and his front to the dark jungle, the path and the rice fields behind them where Chantasith and his team still kept camp. "I'll relieve you myself," Wagner told him. He looked at his watch. "At O two hundred hours."

"Any word sir, on when the congresswoman is scheduled to arrive?" Liam had asked him.

"No ETA as of yet."

The question reminded Wagner that he hadn't had much time yet to really digest her arrival at the village and what that would mean. He would have to be blunt with her and tell it to her directly the first chance he had. Wagner rubbed his head as he took actual stock of the situation. At the moment there was one accusation of rape, two accusations of kidnapping, several beatings witnessed and a police chief that was not cooperating—that was to say—possibly the cause of it. He could not guarantee her safety.

All these thoughts and more were swimming in his head as he fell to sleep, and his last thought before drifted was wondering again how it was that there was no anxiety rising out of this tumult of thought.

Wagner was fast asleep in his sleeping bag on the flattened, trodden ground of the village square. Suddenly, he had the sense that a stranger was next to him. A man much larger and taller than he, the way he, at six-foot-two must appear to the villagers. He could feel this presence and then the scent of tobacco smoke and opium poppy that Wagner had seen the villagers smoke in the evenings. He sat up in his sleeping bag.

There, just next to him was a man taller than the tent leaning up against a lamp post. Before Wagner could open his mouth, the man along with the lamp post and even the street corner it had all been standing on, disappeared.

Perhaps it was taking his eyes awhile to adjust, he thought. He searched the darkness for the man, the lamp post, the street corner. All he could see were fireflies at the edge of the woods. Everywhere he looked, was darkness ceding to thicker darkness. It was impossible to see at all. Suddenly, he felt a coldness where his anxiety used to be. He remembered the warmth of the sleeping bag and wanted to be in its embrace again. He lay back down and then reaching for the zipper and the bottom by his feet, his hand touched something soft, warm, with hair. He was sure it was a head. He was on his feet the next second scrambling to turn on the camp lights. Now, the area was flooded with light. Calmly, Wagner returned to the scene. He found his sleeping bag all askew and at is foot—no, not a head, but a bird's nest the size of a football. Wagner looked closer. No, it wasn't a bird's nest at all. It was a football with little birds with human heads nesting in it. No, no… not a football. It was a bomb. A Phantom F-14 air to ground collateral bomb. It's casing had been torn open as if frozen at the exact time of explosion. Inside the bomb, the center of ignition erupting were hatchlings, their open beaks turned to the sky in anguish of hunger. Wagner turned away. He saw worms crawling over the earth. He bent down to pick them up and began dropping them into the hatchlings waiting beaks. Wagner was smiling, pleased with this little communion of his with nature, nesting and caring when he felt a cold breath on his neck. He spun about and there in the distance at the edge of the village, behind a statue of Liam, was Dee—the witness's wife naked, bleeding from her head. She made a motion for him to follow her and then disappeared into a grove of banana trees. Wagner darted after her. He found her, crouched over a termite den. "I'm inside," she said. "Help me get out."

"No, no…" Wagner reassured her. "You're here with me. You're already out."

The woman turned slowly and she looked sadly at Wagner for a long time.

"Help me get out," she repeated.

"How? How do I help you get out?" Wagner asked her.

"I will show you. But someone must take my place, while I am gone."

"Who?"

"You know who," she said.

"Me?" Wagner said, not so much as a question but a confession.

"No, not you…" Dee told him. "If you stay here then I can't show you what I need to show you."

"I will kill the termites," Wagner suggested, "and free you."

"No!" she cried. "Never! You mustn't."

Wagner was confused.

"It's not their fault," she reminded him. "There is a young officer. He is a good man. He will take my place."

And suddenly Saivongsa appeared out of the night, sleepwalking. His eyes were closed and he came in silence as if still dreaming. He reached the termite den, crouched down and thrust his head into it.

"There," Dee said, "it's done."

Wagner stood still, amazed at the spectacle and not sure what to do.

"They will eat the brains out of his head," he told her.

Dee walked over to Wagner and took his hand. "It is better that way," she said. "You eat the fruit when it is ripe or it will rot on the tree."

Wagner looked at her as if trying to understand. "I understand," he said, looking at her naked body. It had been some time now on the road and Wagner hadn't been with a woman all these weeks. Her breasts were full, her hips smooth. Wagner was surprised at how beautiful she was.

Dee noticed him observing her and was smiling at him by the time his eyes had finished the tour and met her glance. She leaned in and pressed herself to him.

"Let's go," she said. "We must hurry."

A moment later she was running ahead of him, now clothed in the black and red striped traditional dress of her tribe. Her hair had grown longer and though dressed, she seemed wilder as she ran down the path springing over rocks and fallen trunks with the agility of an animal.

Wagner set off after her. Tall trees obscured the sky and he had trouble seeing. Dee was running quickly and it seemed the path could be trusted. Dry leaves matted the ground and not a root or a twig it seemed, was there to trip one up.

"Faster!" Dee cried.

Wagner tried to keep up. "Where are we going?"

"Hurry," she replied. "We're almost there."

Not long after—and a good thing it was, for Wagner was out of breath—Dee came to a dead stop. Wagner slowed his pace. As he drew nearer, he noticed she was standing before a tree, reciting words. Wagner drew closer to hear. The moment he was at her side, the trunk of a tree opened up like an eye and Tom appeared, cradling something in his arms. A sinuous branch or tree root wrapped itself around his waist and held him aloft. The eye opened wider and the tree deposited Tom gently before them. Wagner could now see that it was the bomb Tom was cradling, with the hatchlings still within all of them crying for succor.

The wind started blowing stronger. Wagner thought he caught the odor of charred flesh, of animals being burned alive. He almost choked. He turned away to breathe better and that's when he noticed they were surrounded by a pack of wolves. Their coats were a deep, rich black and their eyes glowed red like embers. Fangs sprouted out of their jaws and covered the snout almost like a rib cage. It was horrifying.

It seemed at least, that the wolves were under Tom's command. He gestured to them and they all heeled, sitting back on their haunches. Their growls receded and the flesh on their snouts fell to cover what little of the fangs they could.

"The wolves guard the *peetyhoung*," Dee said. "You are able to come here, because I brought you."

"I'm not sure, but I think I've been here before," Wagner said. "I seem to remember having met you," Wagner added turning to Tom.

"Yes," Tom said. "In the belly of the mountain."

The wolves howled. Wagner shuddered.

"You needn't worry," Tom promised him. "Thirty years ago, they chased me, hunted me, would have torn me to shreds with their fangs. I made peace with them and now we are all friends."

Wagner turned around and saw that the wolves had become puppies. Big, floppy-eared puppies.

"How did you make peace with them?" Wagner asked.

"Watch," Tom said. He held up the bomb, and all the wolves were on their hind legs at once, licking their chops, excited, their ears flattened and their tails stiff. He threw the bomb in the air and it dropped in the midst of the pack. There was an explosion and then rivers of blood came pouring out. The wolves fell at once to drinking. A minute later they were drunk, rolling on their backs and sides in a circle around the bomb.

Wagner felt a hand on his shoulder and turned around to see Liam.

"How did you get here?" he asked him.

"Drink," Liam said.

"What?"

"Drink... Sir? Sir?"

Wagner was having trouble seeing suddenly. The light had changed somehow. The air as well. Gone were the rivers of blood, the wolves, Dee... He was seeing the inside of his tent. Outside Liam was calling him.

"Urgent phone call for you, sir.... Sorry to disturb you..."

"Just a moment," Wagner said, smacking his lips. His mouth was dry; he felt thirsty and parched. "I'll be there in a second."

XXXI

WAGNER found Liam waiting for him just outside his tent.

"It's the congresswoman," Liam said. "They've patched her in through the embassy frequency. She's on an AF Transport calling in. The signal's a little choppy."

Wagner looked around. They had finished setting up camp in the town square and we're walking to the com station—also set up. "What time is it?" Wagner asked.

"It is ten past nine, sir."

Wagner was taken aback. He had never slept in before.

"I must have forgotten to set the alarm," he said.

"We didn't feel like waking you. We rotated sentry duty among ourselves. There was nothing to report."

Wagner shook his head. "Thanks Liam. I owe you one."

They reached the comm station. Liam handed Wagner the headset. Wagner cleared his throat, put on the gear and flicked the switch from 'standby' to 'live'.

"Niner zulu, this is ground camp, Sunray in Bauviny for AF transport. Over."

The signal cracked, fizzled...

"Copy that Sunray. This is Sierra two zero bravo. Reading you loud and clear. Standby for AF transport link-up. Patching you now... Over and out."

"The signal went dead for a moment, then static again

and then Wagner could hear the sound of jet engines. The comms officer at the embassy station was piping the signal.

"AF Transport, this is Sierra two zero bravo patching your request for comm with Sunray at Bauviny. How do you read? Over."

"Five by five, Sierra two zero bravo. This is AF transport delta three three one. Passenger requesting comm channel."

"Copy that delta three three one, patching you in."

A moment later, Wagner was hearing Marie's voice.

"Mr. Wagner, can you hear me?"

"Hello congresswoman. Yes, I can hear you fine. Can you hear me?"

"Yes, yes… good. Mr. Wagner I am in the sky on my way. We expect to land in Langprabang tomorrow morning after a connection in Hawaii. I hope to be at the site by afternoon. I've arranged for a helicopter. Do you think you might meet me?"

"Of course. It'll be my pleasure…" Wagner was still groggy, but he knew this was the only chance he'd get. He cleared his throat. "In the meantime congresswoman, I must tell you that there is some concern here for your safety. The situation has gotten messy… There's been at least one kidnapping, possibly rape and the police chief assigned here by the Ministry of Defense is not cooperating. I mean to say, congresswoman, I cannot guarantee your safety, nor can I guarantee that any escort the Ministry of Defense may provide you, will be fit or even willing to protect you."

"These are harsh accusations, Mr. Wagner. But you needn't worry, Mr. Wagner, though I thank you for your concern. The ambassador has filled me in on your briefings to him of the situation. I will be providing my own security escort. Bred on apple pie and the good old red white and blue, don't you worry. Have you found this Thamu, yet?"

"Unfortunately no. We thought we had him," Wagner said. "But he appears to be moving."

"I see. Well, do what you can. If you're concerning yourself with my safety then make it a quick meet and greet. Find the man for me before I get there."

"I will do what I can, congresswoman."

"I know you will, Mr. Wagner. And I want to thank you for all your efforts so far. I've been reading up on some of the difficulties we've had in recovery missions like these in the past. We'll do our best. It's all Tom could've asked."

Wagner put the headset down and turned the comm station back to standby. Despite his objections—which he felt had been his duty to voice—he was glad Marie was arriving. It was his secret hope that a family member of the *peetyhoung*, that is a direct bloodline relation, might swing the villager's reluctance to part with the remains. Wagner knew blood relation and external culture could never trump the villager's spiritual beliefs and traditions— but he felt it might help to tip the balance. Wagner had an argument, in any case, prepared and quite well-rehearsed in his head. He hoped his argument, together with the pleas of a sister and the threat of Chantasith might all work together to sway Thamu and the villagers.

LIAM was waiting outside. He approached Wagner when he saw him come out. "Good news?"

Wagner nodded. "We'll have to see. Marie should be here tomorrow afternoon. She's somewhere over the Pacific as we speak. She will be in Vientiane tomorrow morning."

Liam shook his head and then pointed to path that lead away from the village to the rice fields and the camp where Chantasith's men were still set up. "What are we going to do about our friend?"

Suddenly the accusation of rape and the search for the girl returned to him. "It's time we have a talk with him," Wagner said. "Be ready in twenty… and get the translator," Wagner added as he returned to his tent for a shave and a quick breakfast.

Liam had already gone to see the translator and Wagner had barely enough time to finish breakfast when Chantasith and his band of four came walking up the path, heavy shotguns on their shoulders. Liam was at Wagner's tent.

"Sir! You'd better come out here."

A moment later Wagner emerged again from his tent. "What is it?" he asked Liam.

"Chantasith and his men are coming up the path."

"Good," Wagner said. "It saves us trouble of having to go confront him."

"He doesn't look happy," Liam warned.

Wagner looked at the Chantasith and his band of four coming up the path closely. He saw their military walk, their purposeful steps. He saw the guns strung over their shoulders too. Long barrels. He couldn't tell if they were rifles or shotguns.

"Understandable. It's hard to be happy about what's happening here," Wagner admitted. "Let's see what he has to say. I have some questions for him as well."

↑ ↑ ↑

IT had been one week now since they set up the camp. Chantasith was at his wit's end regarding this whole affair. He had 'checked out' of the whole business about cooperating with the Americans and the absurd opportunist politicians trying to run his show.

He was tired of being angry most of all. He found a release from it immediately after he decided he would take matters into his own hands. While the Americans and the politicians carried on with their meaningless and impossible game of appeasing everyone involved; he would do what he had set out to do. He understood now, that it had all been his error, so to speak. The eagle does not crawl on its belly like a snake; and if he attempts to do so, it is his own fault if he appears ridiculous. One thing was certain, the politicians and the Americans with their crooked, winding ways were snakes, and Chantasith and his men, clear-sighted and direct in purpose were eagles. And an eagle doesn't waste time with snakes. Chantasith went right up to Wagner.

"I've come to warn your team," he began. "To stay out of our way. We'll be out in the woods hunting and we don't want anyone getting shot by accident."

"Hunting?" Wagner echoed. Liam and Wagner looked at each other.

"That's right. Since you have no use for us, my officers and I will be taking this time off. We plan to be barbecuing," Chantasith added with a sly smile. "You're welcome to join us."

Wagner was biding his time. He wanted to catch Chantasith off-guard. Butter him up before throwing him in the pan. "The congresswoman will be arriving tomorrow. I thought you should know. She's a visiting state dignitary…"

Chantasith's brow was raised. There was a sardonic smile on his face. He turned to his lieutenant."

"What blind god gives power to woman?" he asked rhetorically. Chantasith reached into his pocket for a cigarette. He put in his mouth and lit it.

"Tourism is not my department," Chantasith said. "There are many guides at the airport happy to take care of your American woman for you," Chantasith said, turning to wink at his men. His men chuckled.

Wagner looked them over and sized them up. They were fearless and held his glance.

"You mean rape?" Wagner now interjected, seizing his opportunity.

Chantasith spun around and mumbled something under his breath.

Wagner pressed on. "Someone—it doesn't matter who—told one of my men that her aunt had been kidnapped and raped."

Chantasith spat on the ground. He seemed unphased. He looked at up at Wagner smiling. "Mr. Wagner, bring me a witness and I will make an arrest. In the meantime, try to stay out of my guns' sights," he added padding his gun.

"Is that a threat, Mr. Chantasith?"

"No, Mr. Wagner. Just a friendly reminder," he said laughing and turning to go. "It's just that you Americans look so much like our Laotian bamboo rat, we wouldn't want to make a mistake."

Wagner watched him walk off down the path and into the jungle.

"The gloves are off," he told Liam.

"It would seem so," Liam agreed.

"We need to find that girl that spoke to the translator last night."

"And the witness's wife. You forgot to mention…"

"No," Wagner corrected him. "I already confronted him on that, and only so that he'd know we were on to him. And that only to hopefully restrain him from further madness."

"What did he tell you?"

"What I expected him to tell me," Wagner confided. "That she had run off to be with her husband. But I believe this girl's aunt and the witness's wife are one and the same person."

↑ ↑ ↑

YAYA and Thamu woke and rose with the jungle. By the time the sun crested the mountain tops and the first rays broke into the valley, all birds were chirping, everything began stirring, even the trees it seemed took to life and no one would be too surprised if suddenly they uprooted themselves and began walking.

When Wagner and Chantasith were facing off at the village, Yaya and Thamu had finished their breakfast and were already gathering firewood for the day. Thamu was careful and he instructed Yaya along the way. He never picked from the same areas twice and never too close to the cave. "An experienced hunter," he told Yaya as he lifted a fallen branch to reveal the yellowed, matted grass beneath it, "would notice. He might start to wonder… If he were smart he'd be in hiding right now, waiting for us."

Yaya looked around, frightened at the prospect of someone hiding in the trees or behind a rock. Thamu laughed. "There's no one there."

"How do you know? How can you be sure?"

Thamu stopped. "Listen," Thamu instructed. "The deities speak to us through the animals and the jungle. What do you hear around us?"

"Nothing. There is nothing. It is silent."

"That's right. Now put your ears and your spirit over there and there and there," Thamu said pointing out in all directions."

"I hear," she whispered excitedly, "many small noises."

"Good," Thamu said. "Now keep listening." He took her arm and they began walking. "What do you hear?"

"The silence moves with us," she said.

"Good. You see, there is nothing else in this jungle disturbing its balance, its music, but us. As we move, the circle moves. At the edge, the animals crouch, return to their holes, the birds end their song, some fly away. The circle is perfect. If it were not, some of those birds and noises would enter our circle and we would know there is something else in this jungle the animals are running from."

"I don't know," Yaya said, unconvinced. "I am afraid, Thamu."

Thamu held her. "It is easier for a stranger to hide in the village than it is for him to hide in this jungle where there are a thousand eyes and ears and another thousand alarms cried for every step he takes… It is not just the foreigners. Even some of the villagers don't know this. Come, let's finish this and then I will show you. Something big is moving on the southwest side, and I wanted to see what it was anyway. We will find them and have eyes on them and they will never know we are there. We can get so close that I will tell you if they had mango or banana for breakfast."

"No, Thamu! It is too dangerous."

Thamu smiled. "Yaya, it is more dangerous to cover one's eyes and ears. For our safety, it is better to know than to not know."

Thamu released her. He returned to the wood pile he had collected. Together they bundled them tightly. "That's two," Thamu said. "Let's get another. You can carry one back and I'll carry two. Then we'll see what's happening."

⚊ ⚊ ⚊

BACK at the village, Wagner, Liam and the translator were knocking on every hut in search of the girl. Every hut they stopped at, they asked and everyone told them the same thing. No one else was kidnapped, no one else was missing. Only Thamu's wife…

Wagner was growing less hopeful. It had been three days now and if she had indeed been raped, she was also probably dead. Wagner was shaking his head. His jaw muscles contracted beneath his cheeks. He was grinding his teeth. But it wasn't anxiety welling up inside him; it was anger, even hate for Chantasith, his smug superciliousness. He wanted to choke that smile off his face.

"I fear the worst," he told Liam.

"Agreed. It doesn't look good."

"Alright, I want to talk to that old couple. I want to know why Chantasith singled them out and why he had that woman tied up."

"That's the old man with the rice fields at the edge of the village."

"Yes, I recognized him, too," Wagner said.

The three of them began making their way to the old

man's hut at the edge of the village. Then at the end of the path, they turned the corner and saw the low cane fencing that bordered the hut and the field. They could smell the jungle, lush and fresh coursing through the air. Wagner took a deep breath and took in the surroundings in the morning light. Not as flat as the cornfields of Iowa, not as dry.... It was more beautiful here. More variation, more for the eye to rest itself upon.

It was quiet in the village and approaching the hut all one could hear were the sounds coming from the woods behind it. The old man was there sitting on his rocking chair by his hut. He had been watching them approach in silence.

Liam and the translator stopped at the edge of the property while Wagner walked on. Wagner raised his hand and made a slight bow with his head when he was within six feet of him. He didn't need to move any closer. What he needed was to be in earshot. All the same Wagner, slowly moved closer. If he wanted the man to trust him, he needed the old man to be comfortable with having him in his space.

As Wagner approached the old man's head turned to keep Wagner's in view. The six foot old man, folded in his chair with his wrists resting on his knees was looking up at Wagner.

He motioned to a stool without saying a word. Wagner took it and sat down before the old man. "I don't speak Laotian, nor your tribal dialect," Wagner said in English. "I will call my my friends here," he said pointing to Liam and the translator, and then to his ears and mouth adding, "They will be speak and hear for me."

Wagner now paused and looked at the man squarely. It was important that he communicated to him that he was seeking his consent. "Okay?" Wagner asked.

The old man seemed to understand. "Oohh-kayee," he said.

Wagner called Liam and the translator over. Wagner spoke while maintaining eye contact with the old man.

"Thank you for receiving us," Wagner began. "I wanted to ask you some questions."

The translator repeated and the old man nodded.

"Did the police say why he bound your wife?"

The old man shook his head. "He says, no," the translator said.

"Do you know why he bound your wife?"

The old man pursed his lips. Wagner pressed on. "Okay," he said and took a pause. He forced a smile for the old man. "Why do *you* think he tied her up?"

"He says his wife has done nothing. Only a coward ties a woman up."

"Tell him I agree," Wagner said and rubbed his head. He shifted in his seat. He needed to get this old man to open up somehow. "The police chief says you know where Thamu is," Wagner said bluntly and rather blindly. He hadn't anticipated that his polite speech was a sophistication the tribesmen weren't used to. It was the simple and direct word that would unlock the man's mind for him.

"This is why he had tied your wife to the pole."

The old man had grunted, upon hearing the translator.

"Do you know where Thamu is?" Wagner ventured.

"The old man says he is never in the same place twice."

"Is he able to reach him? Tell him, I have a message for Thamu."

"He is listening he says."

"Tell him that four policemen have gone into the

woods with guns. They are gone looking for him. They are very dangerous men. They are no longer following the law."

Wagner waited for the translator to finish, but there was no reaction from the old man.

Wagner persisted. He thought it would be a show of good faith, if he refrained from asking the old man what if anything more he knew of Thamu whereabouts—and wanted only to get this word of warning to him.

"If you can, please warn him that the police chief's men are out in the jungle 'hunting' for him."

Wagner finally got a reaction from the old man, though it wasn't the one he expected. The old man had begun chuckling. The chuckling slowly rose in pitch and now he was laughing heartily and out loud. A moment later, he was speaking. Wagner waited for the translation.

"He asked 'hunting?'. And 'the city police?' Then he says the American—uh, you—are a good hen."

"Hen?" Wagner asked.

"Mother chicken," the translator specified.

"I see… Ask him why he says that."

The old man spoke and then stood up waiting for the translator to finish.

"He says, the city police cannot hunt Thamu. No one is a better hunter. They will never catch Thamu and if Thamu wants it, he will have all of them in a sack before noon. Now, he wants us to go with him. He wants to show us his rice field."

Yaya's father took Wagner and his men on a tour of his rice path. He'd been watching Wagner for some time now and he'd made up his mind about him. He could trust him. He went on ahead of them in his bare feet, slowly at first—he had been on his chair for some time and his old bones were slow to warm up. He reminded everyone not to step on the edge of the water ditches. "Mustn't break the mud or the water would escape."

"How long did it take you to build all these irrigation passages," Wagner asked.

The translator interpreted and reported back. "All his life."

They walked some more in silence. Wagner thought that had been the end of that conversation. Suddenly, the old man began talking and the translator was struggling to keep up.

"First, he clears up the flat land at the bottom," the translator was saying. Apparently, the old man was explaining how the rice fields were built. "He digs the passage on the next level up. The water will flow down the passage and out 'gates' to flood the field beneath it. The gates and water flow are controlled by depositing branches and twigs and stones to levee the water…. Then he starts again, up the next level. He digs another ring around it to collect the water flowing from the field above that will feed the field beneath it. He climbs up as high as he can. To the highest point of the creek. Then he digs a passage from the creek to the highest level. Then another to second level and another and another all the way to the bottom."

The old man paused and Wagner nodded as though to say he understood and was genuinely interested. He found it fascinating, in fact. These fields not only supplied the entire village, but allowed for trade with other villages for the surplus.

The old man went on, and the translator interpreted.

"Once the rice grows to the height of his knees, he blocks the branch passages and keeps only the main flow from the creek. He says it is "Heaven Creek" because it runs all year round and because of it the villagers never grow hungry."

At this point he turned to all of them smiling, and had said, "Sometimes, if you're lucky and smart, you can catch river crabs, fish and even shrimp in Heaven Creek."

Then they reached the end of the rice fields and there at the edge of the jungle forest, the old man stopped. "And these woods belong to no one but give us bamboo, mushrooms, medicines, animals for meat, fruits... and a place to hide," he added.

"A place to hide," the old man repeated, and then: "I know where Thamu is—or I know where to go so that he can see me and he'll come out to me. I can get a message to him if you need me to. But I am an old man and it is a very long walk to tell Thamu something he doesn't need to be told. Everyone in the village already knows. They are like elephants walking to the graveyard. Thamu will put them in their graves if he wants. But he is a good man, so we don't have to worry," the old man said looking at Wagner. "But when the time comes, and if, you need to send a message to Thamu, I might be able to help."

Wagner was gratified and thankful. "Thank you, Uncle," he said, in his Laotian, knowing that the appellation of uncle was a token of deep respect in Laos and extended beyond one's blood relations. "I will let you know. Thank you," Wagner said again and turned to go when he remembered.

"One more thing," he said. "There is a story of a kidnap and a rape circulating in the village, do you know anything about it?"

The old man was staring dispassionately at the translator. "Yes... Thamu's wife. She is missing. She was raped. Now, she is missing. She is dead most certainly. I would not want to be the man who meets Thamu in the jungle after he's raped and killed his wife."

Wagner and Liam looked at each other. All this time, they had been concerned for Thamu. Suddenly another stick of dynamite was thrown into the fire.

The old man had begun walking back toward his hut.

"He says, once blood is spilled on one side; there must be blood spilled on the other side. And now he must return to his chair. His wife worries if he is not at his chair."

They reached the hut and the old man regained his seat.

"Thank you for the tour of the fields," Wagner said. "It was most delightful."

They smiled at each other.

Wagner wasn't even three steps down the path and Liam came up to him.

"That's it?" he whispered.

"For now," Wagner said. "I don't know what he is to the villagers. Perhaps his age gives him some special respect… In any case, he seems to know where Thamu is—or is the only one who will say so—and we have his trust, I think."

"I wonder if the old man isn't a little too… set in his ways," Liam said, politely.

"You mean senile… You don't think Thamu can take Chantasith's men?"

"Five armed men against one unarmed man, alone in the jungle? Come on…"

"How do you know he's unarmed?"

"I just assumed."

"Ah!" Wagner said. "You see. That's the thing. The old man has no need for assumptions. He knows the situation better than we do, perhaps."

令 令 令

Chantasith and his men were sitting down to lunch by a ravine. They had scouted the southwest face of the mountain and would start on the northeast after a small rest. Though older, Chantasith had done well on the trek. It was the other men who had trouble keeping up. He had not only years on his men, but pounds also. They were now sprawled on the soft ground—two of them cooling their feet in the water—red in the face, still perspiring. But Chantasith was still on his feet and already good to go. His eyes were bright like the eyes of the feverish and he seemed to have the energy of a madman or of one possessed. He never felt so good.

"Don't get too comfortable boys," he told his men. "We'll be setting off in ten."

The men were lounging, resting their legs, finishing their lunches. One of the officers had started a conversation with his lieutenant and now everyone was listening in on it, Chantasith included.

"You don't think he'll give up the bones if we put a gun to his head?" Trayvong, the officer was asking. He was the youngest of the four and the cockiest. "I'm pretty sure I could make him talk," he said and laughed.

"He'll gladly martyrize himself," the Lieutenant said. "Death would be a ticket to glory. They would sing songs about him in the village for generations to come and he knows it."

"I don't get it," the officer confessed. "I mean, martyr? For the bones? No, I don't get it."

The Lieutenant looked over at Chantasith and knew that Chantasith was listening in. "The villagers believe the souls of those that get killed by accident transform themselves into spirits that can take the form of animals and sometimes human beings," the lieutenant explained. "Unlike those that die of old age or natural sicknesses; these dead must remain on earth. Those who die of natural causes return to their paradise world, but those who die suddenly, by accident or by mischief must remain to finish their work. It is the duty of the living to help so that the will of the gods is accomplished."

Some laughed. Chantasith scoffed. One of the officers spat.

"I heard them say that a giant cobra guards the remains," Trayvong went on. "Is that what they mean? They think the cobra is the spirit?"

"Possibly..."

"Then what happens if we kill the cobra?"

"I like the way you think..." Chantasith broke in, laughing.

The lieutenant smiled. "I suppose they'd be devastated. Their belief is that if the inhabitants of this world let harm befall its guardian, then the *peetyhoung* would sink into the lower worlds and there grow evil and powerful and then one day return to exact vengeance on those that let harm befall its guardian. They say the ghost becomes a stray and then a force of destruction bringing floods, droughts, airborne diseases of all sorts, storms, heat waves.... You know the deal. But it wouldn't make them give up their *peetyhoung*. It would probably only strengthen that savage's resolve..."

Chantasith was now clutching his stomach and laughing out loud.

"My good men!" he said with mirth. "I don't think I need to tell you to shoot any cobras or snakes of any kind on sight, without hesitation."

"No, sir!"

"Snakes and men have been mortal enemies since the dawn of time," Chantasith said and put on an air of gravity. "What would a villager do if a snake crawled into his village?"

"Kill it," one of the officers said.

"What would your mothers do if a snake crawled into her home?"

"Kill it!" two of the men shouted in sync.

"And so men... what would *you* do if a snake were to cross your path?" Chantasith asked Trayvong looking him in the eye.

"Kill it," he said.

"You would not let it live. You would crush its head under your heel. Why?" Chantasith asked looking around at his men one by one. "Because you are honorable men. Good men. And the serpent is the agent of man's oldest enemy. Part of a man's duty in this world is to rid it of snakes," Chantasith said with contempt. "Human snakes, *peetyhoung* snakes—whatever! A snake is a snake..." Chantasith was now visibly angry. He didn't bother to hide it.

"I tell you men," he said with burning intensity, "when you see that snake, kill it! None of this will matter in a year anyway, so shoot indiscriminately men!"

It seemed to his lieutenant that Chantasith was drunk. Of course, he knew it wasn't the case. But the police chief seemed elated somehow and out of character. The other officers in the meantime were smiling. Trayvong especially appeared to be enjoying the prospect.

"Snake hunting, hoorah!" he cried.

The Lieutenant ignored him. "What do you mean?" he

asked. "When you say none of this will matter—"

"That's right! None of this will matter in a year!" Chantasith repeated.

"Sir, what do you mean? What will happen in a year?"

"There are things you don't understand. There is a reason why the Americans are here now after all this time. And there's a reason why this Thamu will lose his *peetyhoung*, one way or another. I suspect they know it, too. That's why they are fighting so hard."

"I don't follow," the lieutenant said.

"This entire area," Chantasith said, turning in a slow circle with his arms outraised, "is to be developed next year. The villagers will be 'relocated'. You know what that means... The American team doesn't know it, but that's why they are here now. That's how it is with them—all secrets. Because it's an American company that will be developing the region. Not Laotian, not Vietnamese, American. A mining company, they are coming for minerals in the mountains. Even the mountains will be 'relocated' if you like. They will be blasting it and quarrying it until it's a pile of demineralized dust."

"A mining company?" the lieutenant echoed.

"Not just a mining company, but a town for the workers and a highway for the trucks, a slough to dump the sludge into the rivers... They'll need stores, plumbing, electricity... They're going to raze the jungle and there will be no room, no more place for the village or the villagers. The stupid ones will stay and work in the mines for the Americans. I've seen the deal go down. Even the trees were auctioned out to a lumber company. You see, the Americans were here three years ago, taking samples and mapping the area. They tramped up and down the mountains, dug holes everywhere. Took pictures... That's when they found the plane. Someone took a picture and sent it back. You could read the serial numbers off the plane's fuselage. Someone did some research and discovered it was a plane reported to have gone down in action but never recovered. No body either of course. It took some time, but about eight months later, they sent that Wagner clown over for the first time to confirm the crash site. They began asking about remains. They went to the village with translators to interview them for information. They soon found their witness. The Ministry of Defense has been cooperating with the Americans ever since. There's two things I can tell you, gentlemen: The Americans will have their mine and no witness, no village, no mountain, no dead man's bones and definitely no *peetyhoung* is going to stop them."

↑ ↑ ↑

ALL that time, unknown to Chantasith, Thamu and Yaya had been listening from behind a shrub. Yaya, frightened half to death, sat trying to control her trembling, while Thamu leaned back rested his neck against a rock and began picking his teeth with some straw he pulled from the ground. Yaya looked at him from time to time. Thamu didn't seem to care much about it all. It was only when Chantasith spoke that Thamu seemed to have any interest at all. That was the man that had killed Dee, he surmised.

After Chantasith and his men, resumed their mission, Thamu and Yaya made their way back to the cave by a circuitous route. Thamu had instructed Yaya all the way. And it was she in fact, that had led them to Chantasith. Thamu had told her to listen for disturbances and then move toward them to see if they intensified. "When the border of our silent circle touches the border of the disturbance, we stop, we hide, we move like animals," he had told her. This is what they had done, and they had crept right up to Chantasith and his men.

"We hunt wild pig the same way," Thamu said, munching on his straw, not even whispering, though speaking in a low voice. "It's better if they are killed without fear. The meat is healthier. They don't get the spirits of anger and fear in them."

Now they were well away from Chantasith and moving in the opposite direction. Yaya stopped Thamu.

"What is a mining company?" Yaya asked him.

Thamu shrugged his shoulders. "I don't know."

"You think it is true what they say?"

"What did they say, Yaya?"

"That the mining company will come and take away the village and the mountains and everything!"

Yaya was in tears.

"Of course not," Thamu laughed. "How can men remove a mountain? Even if they could, the deities would stop them before it could happen."

He held her and continued laughing for her sake; but he was not so sure about anything anymore.

XXXII

THE HOT SUN was getting low. It had been a hot afternoon and most people in the village had retired in doors or to the shade somewhere to sleep it off it seemed. Now they were emerging again. All day long, Wagner and Liam had waited in the village, planning for Marie's arrival and wondering, but avoiding talking about what their responsibility here was in Dee's apparent kidnapping, rape and possibly murder. Wagner couldn't help feel responsible. Liam did not remember Dee. He was a little more removed from the situation.

"I don't see how we can get involved," Liam said. "We have no jurisdiction. No body. No evidence."

"We can apply pressure through political channels and get the Ministry to bring Chantasith or whoever to justice."

"Perhaps," Liam said. He felt he was a lot more pragmatic than Wagner. But he had to be careful what he said. Wagner was his superior after all, even if he thought it was a little naïve to think they could change anything.

"We have to do something for these people. We came here and caused all this suffering. None of this would have happened if it weren't for us."

And that was a little naïve too, Liam thought. He

looked down the path snaking off the village to the rice pasture. It had become dusty in the hot afternoon. Villagers with their livestock tramped up and down that path. Pigs, cattle, goats, herdsmen, washingwomen, shepherds all crossing back and forth down the path to the nearby creek... and the dust they kicked up rose and fell covering the leaves and coating the greenery at its banks.

Most of the policemen had a good time of it without Chantasith around. They lounged about, smoked, played cards. Almost everyone was drunk by four. Chantasith had invited everyone into the woods for a day of sport and hunting. It was not an order—they were free to take their day as they pleased. It had been a steady six days and everyone deserved a day off anyway. Most men had no desire for hunting and dealing with the bugs and the heat in the jungle.

Chantasith returned to camp deprived of his prize game after his first outing, but not empty-handed. His men were carrying hare and a wild boar strung upon a pole they carried between them on their shoulders. The drunken men hailed them as heroes. Chantasith wasn't too displeased.

"Tell the cook to get a fire going," he said. "We're feasting tonight!"

Soon the men fell to eating and the sun was sinking behind the hills. Across the ways, in the village, Wagner's team were heating up cans of spaghetti in boiling water. The villagers watched on in curiosity. They were sure after much debate that it was worms in blood sauce.

⚑ ⚑ ⚑

The sun was sinking and now shining almost directly into the mouth of the cave. It was the time of day Thamu liked best—the time of day he found most peaceful. He was looking forward to this time of day, today most of all. With all the trouble mounting to the point of imminent crisis, it seemed, he was looking forward to a moment of serenity and communion with the jungle. But Yaya was still concerned. She fretted, was afraid and nervous and wouldn't stop talking.

"We have to stop them," she said. "Once the Americans have their dead soldiers they will have their mine machines eat the jungle and the village and the mountain," she was saying. "But if they don't get the bones, then they would not set their mine machines to overturn the graveyard. They must not find the bones," Yaya said.

"Yes, of course," Thamu murmured absent-mindedly. He was leaning back with his hands folded over his chest. He seemed to be staring vacantly into the horizon and Yaya wasn't sure he had heard her.

"Are you listening?" she asked him.

"The bones in the ground. No mine machine. Yes."

Yaya was shocked.

"Thamu! We may all die!"

Now Thamu sat up. "Yaya, don't go mad. The moon isn't out yet. No one is going to die… And I heard you—you think the bones of the dead will keep the machines away… But you are wrong, and there are no bones in the ground. It is up to us to stop the machines. The *peetyhoung* is nothing to the machines. The machines can't touch the *peetyhoung*. We do what we must for the village and our people, including the *peetyhoung*. But the *peetyhoung* cannot help us fight the mine machine; and the mine machine cannot see the *peetyhoung*. It is only the village that it is stuck in the middle. It is like when a storm comes and floods the village. The *peetyhoung* cannot help, he cannot stop it. And the storm does not see him. It knocks down the tree and sweeps the strong man off his feet but blows right through the *peetyhoung*."

Yaya was about to break in tears again, thinking of her dear father and mother and the rice fields and all the people in the village. Thamu saw that he had failed to comfort her.

"But you are right," he said. "That's why, they will never get the *peetyhoung*. It is well-guarded. We are well-guarded," Thamu corrected. "Every day we make sure: dry leaves and little twigs cover all the paths possible to reach up to where we are. Even if we were sleeping—"

"I want to see it…" Yaya suddenly said.

There was a question on Thamu's face.

"I want to see the bones of the *peetyhoung*. I want to see where it is hidden."

"We can't tonight," Thamu told her. "I want to go to the village and have a look at some things."

"The village? They will catch you."

"Catch me?" Thamu said. "They won't even see me."

"You will leave me alone?"

Thamu kissed her. "I won't be gone long."

☥ ☥ ☥

NIGHT had fallen and supper was done on both sides of the camp. Wagner and his men could hear the sounds of merriment coming from the police camp. It seemed they were having a party. "We'd better check it out," Wagner said.

"It almost sounds like they found the man," Liam agreed.

Wagner pumped his brows. "I hope not," Wagner said. "If he did, all this was for nothing. You wait here and keep an eye on things in case it's a diversion. I'll go alone."

CHANTASITH was sitting on a fold-out chair, smoking a cigarillo. Some of the Chantasith's men were wrestling and it seemed the others had taken wagers on who the winner would be. They stood about in a circle, framing the ring. The others sat about, watching and sipping their drinks. Chantasith was off to the side. Everyone looked drunk. Wagner walked into the camp and through it, making a bee line for Chantasith. No one seemed to care or notice. The place was littered everywhere with discarded paper plates, bottles and other garbage.

Chantasith looked up when he saw Wagner. He made no other motion. "The meat is all gone," he said. "But help yourself to some rice and fried bamboo shoots. It is quite good." If he could turn over in his chair he would.

Wagner smiled. "Thank you. Very kind... I wonder if I may have a word."

"The American wants words," Chantasith mumbled to himself. "Words, words.... Words are cheap Mr. Wagner. I offered you rice and bamboo shoots—that is something, that is money."

"It is about the witness's wife. They say she has been kidnapped and raped."

Chantasith could not hide his annoyance. He tried to stand up, but then thought better of it. He was too drunk. "First, Mr. Wagner, you tell me someone is kidnapped and someone was raped. Now, you tell me it is the same person.

It is hard to follow your American Hollywood stories, Mr. Wagner. They are filled with lies just like your films."

Wagner thought he could see fear in Chantasith's eyes. He knew he was guilty. "As chief of police, don't you think you should investigate?" he asked him.

"Did you witness these crimes, Mr. Wagner?"

"No, I did not," Wagner answered emphatically.

"Then bring me a witness and I shall open an investigation."

"Doesn't the disappearance of the witness's wife warrant an investigation?"

Chantasith laughed. "It's what I was trying to do until you and you're American cheerleader woman began interfering. You see Mr. Wagner. I can't help it if a wife decides to run off to join her fugitive husband. Find the husband and you'll find the wife. It's what I was trying to do. But my men and I are quite happy to take this holiday."

Wagner decided he'd press forward. "How could she have been raped if she has joined her husband?"

Now Chantasith was on his feet, drunk or not, standing nose to nose with Wagner. "You are beginning to annoy me, Mr. Wagner. You come here and interfere with my mandate and our laws and now you are trying to tell me how to do my job?"

Wagner had come this far. He felt it was time to go all the way. "Perhaps you don't investigate because you already know who the guilty party is," he said, while looking Chantasith in the eyes.

Chantasith was trembling with rage. With the alcohol, the insult to his pride, the bottled up frustration—he had gone beyond trying to hide it. He stepped to Wagner. With his nose pressing up against Wagner's, he shouted for his gun. Wagner could feel Chantasith's spittle on his lips. A second later, one of his men was handing Chantasith's hunting rifle to him. Chantasith primed the barrel and cocked it, all without taking his nose or his eyes off Wagner.

"And who would that be?" he asked him.

"If there's a guilty party," Wagner said and backed away. "I'm sure you know best who it is."

He turned and began making his way back to the village. Behind him, Chantasith had raised his gun to his shoulder. He brought his eye down on it and pointed the gun square at Wagner's back. "Pow!" he shouted and jerked his shoulder back as though the gun had fired.

The policemen, even the wrestlers who had disentangled their limbs to watch the sight, broke out laughing.

🐾 🐾 🐾

THAMU jumped silently down from the tree. He had been listening and could only get close enough to get a spattering of words. It didn't quite matter though, as he soon learned he didn't understand the strange language the two men were speaking. So he watched instead. And he thought he understood well enough from the body language what was happening. The situation was easy enough to read. At first they had camped together. Now the Americans had moved their camp to the village. It was clear the Americans were there to protect the villagers. For the villagers were now at peace whereas before everyone was fearing for the lives of their children. Also, when the police and Americans were camped together, there was order and quiet. Now, that the Americans had moved off, the police camp had fallen at once to drunken disorder. Thamu thought of dogs and knew how dogs behaved if the master was gone. Wagner was the only thing keeping Chantasith in control. It was clear to Thamu that Wagner was there to chastise Chantasith. Then he had seen Chantasith point the rifle at Wagner's back, he thought for a moment Wagner too would die.

He had already been to the village. He had stopped in on his mother. He had found her sitting in the kitchen. She was very old and had trouble remembering everything. She was happy to see him. Thamu kissed her cheek.

"They have taken Dee," she said.

Thamu was surprised to hear her speak lucidly. "I know," he said. "How do you know, mother? Did someone say anything to you?"

"You're my boy," she said, smiling at him again, proudly. "You look just like your father did when I married him."

Thamu kissed his mother one more time, and then snuck out. He stopped in on his own hut. He was careful to circle the village from all angles to see what if there were any men posted that he could not see. Only Liam was on guard duty it seemed. And he had his back to the village while he kept his eyes on the perimeter. Thamu walked right through his front door.

Though their marriage had been arranged as per village custom, Thamu had lived with Dee for many years—he would have to think to count exactly how many—and in that time a love and a respect had blossomed between them, if he could say that. In any case, he had come to know the woman that was his wife. From the state of the hut, he knew she had been taken. The kitchen had not been cleaned; the pots had not been scrubbed. Dee would never leave the house before cleaning her kitchen. She was always angry with him when he came in, in the afternoons and then just dropped his mug or his bowl in the kitchen.

He had learned to curb his appetite and wait for supper, or to wash after himself and replace the things he took so she couldn't tell the difference—as though it had been done by her hand. He watched and he learned. She drew a fresh pot of water from the basin they filled from the creek every day. She took a rag and first scrubbed the cups, then the bowls, then the pots. But not all at once. What she washed, she set aside. And then with another rag, she scrubbed them dry until they shone. Then she began the cycle again. Earlier on in their marriage, Thamu had thought he was the cleverer of the two and thought he could make many improvements. He tried washing the cups and the bowls and the pot together once; and then dry them all together. But when he did this, he found some of the spots had dried on to the cups and when he tried to scrub them dry, it just spread a film of grease over it and he was forced to wash them again. So, he had to retreat on his campaign of improvements once more.

He crept further into the house. The bed was made, but her morning shawl was on the floor. The clothes basket had been knocked down. Her working clothes hung neatly on the chair waiting for her. She had been taken in the morning, Thamu surmised. Three days ago, he judged by the state of the ripening mango on the table.

It seemed clear to him what had happened. Though he had feared the worst the moment the he had heard the news, it hit him only now, in earnest, for the first time. Thamu cried for his wife and swore he would avenge her death.

After that, Thamu had stopped in on Yaya's father. He promised the old man he would care for his daughter. After he had found his wife, tied to the pole, the old man asked Thamu to keep his daughter away from the village.

It wasn't safe, he said, with the police around. If they could stoop so low as to tie an old woman up, there was no telling what they wouldn't do to Yaya.

It was on his way back after stopping in on Yaya's father that he saw Wagner crossing the camp to confront Chantasith. Now, headed back to the cave and to Yaya, Thamu was careful to take a circuitous path. It was dark and night had fallen. Though he stepped lightly and cautiously, it was hard to tell what kind of trail he was leaving behind for the expert eye to track tomorrow morning. Broken twigs, disturbed leaves and muddy footprint.... It would be enough for an expert hunter like himself to track.

An hour or so later, he was making the last climb up the back side of the cliff. He found Yaya waiting at the summit for him.

"You're getting good," he said.

☝ ☝ ☝

NIGHT had fallen. Back at the village all the fires had been put out. The only lights still on were the battery lamp in Wagner's tent and the gas burner by Liam doing first guard duty again. The din from the police camp was also slowly dying. Wagner was in his tent on his folding chair before his folding desk on his folding computer. It is so quiet in between the little noises the night was throwing out that he could hear villagers, perhaps some of his own men, snoring.

He stood up slowly, giving his knees some time. His own legs had seen some hell in their day. He wasn't as young as he used to be. And for awhile, he stood there, on his legs. The image of those newborn calves still wet from birth struggling to stand came to him. He thought that probably everyone in the western world had that same image in their head. He saw suddenly how something so simple and innocuous as a National Geographic video could have conditioned everyone's mind all over the world. He turned off battery lamp and went to sleep.

IT was hell. Perhaps. He couldn't tell for sure, but Wagner thought he was dreaming of hell again. He heard the wailing and the howls of pain ring up in the night. An angel—no, it's Tom the pilot—was showing him how all these cries float up in the sky and collect on the roof to form clouds. Tom tells him this is how rain is made. He takes him up into the sky, faster, higher... the world is shrinking beneath him. Suddenly it was a little ball, no bigger than a marble. There in the middle of space was the American flag planted on a corpse.

"You're wasting your time here" Tom told him.

This was the sort of thing that would normally trigger Wagner's anxiety—the what ifs, the bifurcating paths and the notion that there was one right way only and all other ways were wrong." But he had matured since then, or regressed. He didn't care. He had outgrown these standards in any case. Forward, backward, right, wrong, good, bad... The world had made him, and he was in it for a reason. The best and only thing to do—the only possible thing to do—was to do what he had been made to do. The motive was internal, the direction came from within.

"I don't think so," he told him. "If I weren't here, I'd be home listening to the radio, looking for a mission like this one. Anyway, who's to say if it's a waste or not? You know the future?"

"That's not what I mean," Tom said.

Wagner suddenly felt foolish. "What do you mean then?"

"I mean you're running out of time."

† † †

THAMU lay on his mat in the cave. He was wide awake. Beside him he could hear the gentle purr of Yaya's snoring. He couldn't get the image of Dee's things lain askew in the hut. How unjust it was! Of all people to have to suffer for this—Dee should have been the last of them. A low-burning rage was simmering inside Thamu. He felt angry at the deities for not protecting Dee. At first, he had felt abandoned and sorry for it. He had felt guilty and he had searched his past for some transgression. Now, he felt they were heartless. He felt rebellious. He wanted to act in revolt. If it wasn't for Tom and the *peetyhoung*, he would go and dump the ashes on the policemen's heads. And as he thought everything over, another image returned to him again and again—that of Wagner and Chantasith talking. Thamu felt it somehow, intuited it. Chantasith had killed Dee—the Americans knew it. Now, he knew it too.

"The spilling of blood will not go unpunished," Thamu heard a voice say.

He opened his eyes, but it was no use. The cave was blanketed in darkness. There were no walls anywhere, no corners… he couldn't even see the entrance to the cave, nor the embers in the fireplace. All he could see was the snake that guarded the cave, shining luminescent like a glow in the dark stick.

"And you will be the agent of justice," the snake said.

XXXIII

THE MORNING WAS foggy. The clouds crowned the peaks and the mist seem to roll down them and spill across the valley. It would be some hours before the sun and its hot rays burned the mist off the air.

Chantasith and his men were already on their feet. They were awake earlier than usual. Chantasith was eager to get an early start. Marie was arriving today and this might very well be there last chance. He had his men before him, standing in file. Examining his men in the morning air in the dim light of dawn, reminded him of his military days. He liked it and wondered now why he ever left it. It seemed all the good men were in the military. Civilians were all sleepwalking pansies waiting for something to hit them. They were shaped by the world, but with men like himself and his team—it was the other way around: *they* shaped the world.

"That's right," Chantasith thought. "We shape the world and the pansies live in it. It's up to us—to me!"

"Men, you know our mission," he began. "Failure is not an option. Within hours the enemy will take the field and our time will be up. I need all of you with me today, at your sharpest and your best. We find him today, otherwise; the Americans will bring him out under escort and the matter will be much more difficult. We have a window of opportunity men. Let's use it!"

♠ ♠ ♠

THEY reached the bottom of the cliff just in time. The low noise of the helicopter had been getting steadily louder as though it was headed right for them. Thamu took Yaya by the arm and pulled her toward him against the banana tree. The broad leaves overhead would hide them from the helicopter. A moment later, the helicopter passed right over their heads.

"Don't worry," Yaya's father shouted over the drumming of the propellers. "It's carrying the American woman… the sister…."

A moment later they were all sitting down.

"So she has arrived," Thamu stated. "I wish they would all go away."

Yaya put her hand on Thamu's shoulder. "They have travelled too far to return home with empty hands."

Thamu nodded. "I know."

"Perhaps she will see that the *peetyhoung* is well-cared for. She will make offerings and find peace and return to her village," the old man said. "Things will return to normal. The American said they wanted only to talk," he reminded Thamu.

Yaya's father had left the village the morning following Wagner's speech and the American team's relocation of the camp to the village. He went to relay the message Wagner had asked the village to take to Thamu. "He is an honorable man," Yaya's father said of Wagner. "I believe he is speaking the truth."

"He is a traveller in a foreign land," Thamu reminded

everyone. "He may want good things, and his word may be true—but his words have no ears here to hear them. In his own village far away, he may be a great chief," Thamu said pointing at the river beneath him where some drift wood was floating by. "But here he is like the tree that has fallen off its roots and is carried by the river."

"The ground beneath him is like the water," Yaya said.

"He is far from his village. There is no place here for him to stand," Thamu added.

"A man with nowhere to stand cannot move things," Yaya's father agreed. "But perhaps the deities will help. We must appeal to them. So long as we do their will, they will protect the village."

Thamu nodded, but he was thinking of Dee and that the deities had already abandoned him. He must have made a mistake, he thought again. Somehow, he had displeased them.

↟ ↟ ↟

IT was time for Yaya's father to begin his trek return to the village now.

"Very well," Thamu said. "I will meet with them, tomorrow. You will tell them to take the northeast path. I will meet them."

The old man parted with Thamu, and then his daughter. Thamu and Yaya returned to the cave. Thamu was silent all the way. Yaya knew that Dee still lived in his mind and called to him. That morning, after rising, she had accompanied Thamu on his collection of firewood. She had put her arm through his. It was the first time she had felt that close to him. They were happy that morning and so she knew they could always be happy whenever they wanted. It seemed to her that they were two lovers, as simple as children, living alone in the woods by themselves and with no one to help them but each other—and the Americans and the police and the *peetyhoung* had all been forgotten, like a nightmare is when one opens the eyes.

The path had narrowed and Yaya took the trail behind him. Watching his back, his powerful step, thinking of that morning, it seemed to her that the jungle and the world came alive again. The crickets were chirping, the cicadas were blaring, every bird was singing a song, and the shrubs and the leaves, the underbrush were all moving with life and brilliance and color. A tear fell down onto her cheek. Up ahead, Thamu had stopped. He was standing on a boulder, his hand outstretched to her to help her up. She took his hand and he lifted her on to the rock. Thamu's other arm reached out and wrapped itself around her waist pulling her to him. "I have you," he said and Yaya's eyes welled up once more.

"I love you," she said.

Thamu put his hands on her head and stroked her long hair, black and resplendent like the night sky.

"You are love," Thamu answered and kissed her.

Thamu was holding her so tight that Yaya couldn't breathe. "I can't breathe," Yaya said laughing and crying.

Thamu let go. "I'm sorry," he said and Yaya saw that he was crying too. She put her hand gently on cheek and wiped the tear away with her thumb. "I don't want to go back to the village," she said. "I will stay with you."

YAYA had barely finished the words when they heard a cry and then a gunshot. Thamu wasn't sure, but Yaya was certain; that cry was her father's. They set off in its direction.

Thamu ran ahead. Without a sound, Thamu motioned to her still running. His right arm pointed at the origin of the gun shot. His left hand went to his chest and then made a big circle. The next moment he had disappeared up the hill and Yaya was already running down the valley in direction of the gunshot. Thamu was headed for the cave. Yaya jumped down the last stone and onto the bank of the ravine where the ground was flat and she could run fastest. Above her, Thamu had reached the cave and flown in and out of like a gust of wind, coming out a moment later with the bow and sack of arrows he used for hunting. He made a sharp left coming out of the cave and stopped for barely a second. There at the left of the entrance, he crouched and his hand reached down into the bush and pulled a rifle out from a behind a large moss covered stone. His feet were already running it seemed, before his hand had a chance to get itself free. Meanwhile, Yaya was still running. She could tell she wasn't far. She could hear voices. Thamu came speeding down the hill, his sack of arrows strung across his back and his bow in his left hand and the rifle in his right.

Yaya was crouched behind a tree when Thamu came up behind her. She pointed to a scene in a clearing by the path: Chantasith and his band of four had caught Yaya's father. Yaya looked worried. Thamu had a closer look. They had tied the old man to a tree. His pants were dusty as though he had fallen, otherwise he seemed unhurt.

"It's okay," Thamu whispered. "They have not hurt him and we are here now."

Yaya didn't seem impressed.

"We got here in time," Thamu repeated and turned

around to rest his back on the trunk of the tree. He needed to catch his breath and then a moment to think.

Yaya was fidgeting. Thamu saw her trying to get up to have a better look and pulled her down.

He put a finger to his lips and with his other hand patted the air softly as though telling her to slow down. Then he took the finger on his lips and put it to his ear. "Listen," he whispered and took out the rifle.

Yaya sat down next to him. She could hear Chantasith.

"You got away from me last time. But now there are no Americans—there is no one in fact," Chantasith was saying, "to help you. We're deep in the jungle."

Thamu was inspecting the rifle. There were two bullets in the cartridge. Thamu looked the barrel. It was clean and ready to go.

"Tell me where you were going, old man."

It was Chantasith again.

"I was returning to the village. Going home." Yaya's father answered. Yaya almost jumped at hearing her father's voice. Thamu reached out to her again. His head was nodding slowly. "See. He is alright," he said.

Yaya was listening. Her father's voice was steady.

Chantasith was laughing. "Then tell me where you are coming *from*."

Now Yaya's father was laughing too. Chantasith wasn't amused.

"You find this funny?" Chantasith said through his teeth. "Why don't you tell me what's so funny?"

"You sound like my wife," the old man answered. "Where have you been.... where are you going...."

Some of Chantasith's men were smiling. Chantasith looked on. "Now, I'm a patient—" he began to say, but Yaya's father cut him off again.

"I'm an old man now, but if I were younger…" the old man continued, "Maybe I'd take you as my wife. You know how to use your mouth, that's for sure."

One of Chantasith's men couldn't help it. He burst out laughing. The lieutenant kicked him. But everyone was smiling.

"But my marrying days are over…"

Chantasith took up his gun, and pointed it at him. "Not just your marrying days… old man. You'd better tell me what I want to know…"

Just a stone's throw away, crouched behind a tree, Thamu was handing Yaya the rifle.

"You have two bullets," Thamu said. "Just two," he repeated.

Yaya's father was laughing. "If I tell you, you will kill me…"

"We are policemen. We don't want to kill anyone. But you must answer our questions."

Yaya's father twisted his nose. "I know what you are. I know what you did to Thamu's wife."

"If you know that, then you know you had better answer my questions. Where are you coming from?"

"From seeing Thamu," the old man said simply.

Chantasith stepped back as though he was bowled over. "Finally!" he said. "Some sense out of these animals… So where is he now?" Chantasith asked.

"Who?"

Chantasith jumped up and had his hands on his throat. "Don't play stupid old man, I'm losing patience and running out of time."

"Thamu? He is probably here right now," the old man said. "With all the noise you make…"

Chantasith let him go and took a look around him.

For the first time, he felt hunted, like he had lost control of situation. Suddenly, without his police force and his job and the ministry behind him, gone rogue with his band of four, he felt vulnerable. It made him angry.

Yaya was holding the rifle and Thamu was getting up.

"The first shot," he was telling her. "You fire in the air."

Thamu explained his plan to her. She had two bullets. One bullet, she'd fire in the air. Then she was to run east and circle back to her father, while Thamu drew the men off to the west. "Then I will come back for your father." She'd have another bullet in the chamber. Thamu didn't need to tell her what to do with it. He knew she'd use it to kill Chantasith and save her father if she needed to.

Thamu closed his eyes and took a deep breath. "Ready?" he said.

"Ready," Yaya answered.

Yaya began crawling back from the tree. When she was far enough, she stood up and began running. Thamu stood up. A second later a shot rang out in the air. Thamu leapt out of the bush and ran across the path headed in the opposite direction.

Thamu stopped just for a second at the edge of the path and locked eyes with Chantasith. Thamu made sure Chantasith saw him and knew he was being taunted. A second later, he had leapt and disappeared back down the hill to where the ravine flowed and out of sight.

"That's him!" he heard Chantasith cry. "After him!"

The three men took off at once. His lieutenant lagged behind. "Go!" Chantasith cried. "What are you waiting for?"

"Sir, it might be a ploy to separate the team."

Chantasith was enraged. "A ploy? From a savage? Are you stupid man? What does it matter anyway if we catch him? And you're not going to catch him by standing here!"

"What if he comes back and you're alone?"

"Then you'll be right behind him…" Chantasith growled. "Because you are out chasing him and I'll be here waiting for him. We'll have him circled. Now go! I will keep watch over our prisoner."

↑ ↑ ↑

IT was easy for Thamu. The men weren't used to chasing and fighting like hunters were. They couldn't run and fire their guns. Meanwhile, Thamu had crossed the ravine with the men hot behind him, just like he had wanted. Now, he was climbing the opposite embankment that ran up the mountain. With every step he took he gained higher ground on them.

Chasing him, they had no idea they were being led. Thamu laughed with scorn. Even dogs new better. Hunting in packs. A leader would chase from behind while the rest of pack tried to circle in from the sides.

Thamu stopped. His back was flat up against a tree. He drew an arrow and put it to his bow. He waited… He closed his eyes. He thought of Dee. She had been devoted and loving. She was a strong, proud woman. Thamu would have to show himself worthy to have been her husband. He opened his eyes and held his breath and listened. Dry leaves crunching… and then again… and again. He stepped out from behind the tree and there he was, just trying to crawl up the hill, panting and red in the face like murder was some kind of game. Scrambling, the man reached for his gun. Thamu let his arrow fly and it struck him in the chest beneath the shoulder. His arm flew back and the man tumbled back down the hill, rolling over until hitting a tree. Thamu heard the crunch of broken ribs before a shot rang out and nicked the leaves to a tree at least ten feet away. The others had not seen him. He ducked back behind the tree and darted further up the mountain. Thamu was surprised that they kept coming. He hid behind another tree and attempted the same tactic. He lost all respect for these men when he was successful that second time. Even animals had more sense. He doubled back downhill without heed to caution and even took a third man out on his way. He knew the others would stumble about now, stepping gingerly everywhere they went for an hour looking for him before they finally gave up. Thamu was headed for Yaya.

↑ ↑ ↑

YAYA doubled back and returned to see her father alone with Chantasith. With her stomach to the ground and the rifle strung across her back, she began inching toward Chantasith.

She and Thamu had gone hunting together now many times. He had taught her everything he knew and she had learned well: How to approach your prey, when to pull your weapon, and how to fire it silently until it was too late... All this she used now. "It's in the breathing," Thamu would always say. "If you're breath isn't steady, your hand can't be. Breeeeeathe slooooowly," he'd tell her."

She wasn't going to pull the trigger unless she was sure the bullet would hit flesh and kill the beast. "A clean kill is best, most merciful," Thamu would say. It was clumsy and savage to make the animal suffer.

She could see her father. Chantasith was taunting him, but there was no risk to his life. She kept inching toward them, crawling forward on her front. It was time to get ready, she thought and pulled the gun strap off her shoulder. Perhaps she moved too quickly; maybe it was just bad luck. A bird flew off a branch at that moment and Chantasith turned around.

Yaya ducked and rolled to the side perhaps too quickly. Though she got herself clear of his sight in time, she had disturbed the brush. Chantasith noticed the ferns moving. He cocked his gun and began walking toward her. Yaya began inching back towards the ravine. She rolled down the slope when she reached the edge. But the ground was rougher than she thought. Though she tried to be as quiet as possible—"Be like the stones, be like the animals," Thamu had told her—the strap of the gun caught on a branch and it flew off her and fell to the ground. Her dress got caught in some brambles too. The buttons flew off her before her weight tore it off the thorns. Yaya continued to roll, but she was tumbling too fast and had lost control.

A minute later, Chantasith was standing above her with the rifle in his hand. Half-naked, bleeding, her breasts exposed and her hair laid all about her, Chantasith was smiling. He looked at Yaya's tanned thighs. Her breasts were full, the nipples dark and erect. He was laughing now. "This is too easy," he said aloud.

⚐ ⚐ ⚐

THE helicopter was landing at the edge of the rice fields. Wagner and his retinue were waiting there to welcome Marie. Wagner was sorry for the small size of the greeting party so he invited the translator along, who seemed eager to meet the woman who was "boss of American man" as the translator put it. "She's amazing," Wagner said. "She's eight feet tall and can pick a man up with each hand by the throat and hold them up like this." Wagner was holding his arms out front of him and raised them up while he winked at Liam. The translator's eyes were bugging out of his head. "Incredible!" he said.

Wagner and Liam were still chuckling when the helicopter finally pitched and touched ground and a very human-sized, middle-aged blond woman stepped out of the helicopter. "Meet my boss," Wagner said to the translator, with a wink.

By now, with all the helicopter rides back and forth and all the men tramping through the jungle, rumors about the Vinay Village and all sorts of strange happenings began spreading. Legends began sprouting and wild tales were told that reached ears as far as the city of Laungprabang. Some said a tribal man saved the life of an American spy pilot, pulling him out of a burning plane and that this man now had the secrets of the American empire and was hiding because he had too much power now and knew that they had to kill him. Others say the pilot fell out of the sky... just like that... and out of time too. He had come from the past and that a villager was hiding him in a cave and slowly nursing his recovery. Most dismissed the stories as wild fantasy, but now that even the government's own newspapers were announcing that an American politician was visiting the 'People's beautiful Vinay Village and mountains", people no longer knew what to think.

"Flight okay?" he asked her, as he took her hand.

"A little choppy, but we survived," Marie answered. "And how are you Mr. Wagner? You've been here a week now."

"Eight days, actually... Very well, congresswoman. It's nice to have you here. I've had the cook prepare some coffee and refreshment—"

"That won't be necessary, but thank you. I'd like you and your team to bring me up to date on the situation."

"Over coffee then," Wagner said, smiling. "It's a short walk back to the village. We've moved our camp there to protect the villagers."

"That bad?" the congresswoman asked.

"I have a plan that with your help may tip the balance," Wagner said.

"I'm eager to hear it. All the same, it's close to paradise, here. I was actually hoping the helicopter ride would last a little longer. I was enjoying view from on high. There are so many beautiful things to rest one's eyes on."

"Yes, I know I think I'm falling in love with the area," Wagner said. "I wish the circumstances had been different."

"I'm thankful at least that Tom's been waiting in a beautiful place…"

↟ ↟ ↟

YAYA was naked. She was lying on the ground before her father. Her hands and feet were bound. Yaya's father watched on in horror. Chantasith was laughing. "Your village women are all whores," he was saying. "I am going to do to your daughter what I did to Thamu's wife."

Chantasith lay the rifle down. Then, his own gun. He began undoing his pants. Thamu snorted again. No animal even eats out in the open. It is only those that travel in packs that do so, and Chantasith was without his pack.

Thamu sprung out of the bush. He was running as fast as he could, his bare feet carrying him silently. At the last minute, he let out a war cry the likes of which he had never screamed before. Chantasith turned around. Thamu jumped in the air, and coming down his fist caught Chantasith right on the jaw. Thamu landed, somersaulting and rolling and up on his feet the next second. The blow had sent Chantasith to the ground and broken his jaw. His teeth had fallen out of his mouth and his chin was covered in blood. He was squirming on the ground in pain. Thamu went an untied Yaya's hands. He was working on her feet when Chantasith let out a cry. With her hands freed, Thamu left Yaya to untie her feet. He stood up while he watched Chantasith do the same. The bleeding police chief, went for his gun. Thamu watched him pick it up. Then he kicked the rifle away, behind him. He turned to face Thamu, his gun pointed at him, the rifle behind him.

"I've been looking for you," Chantasith tried to get out.

Thamu said nothing. Thamu had an arrow in his bow. It was pointed square at Chantasith's right shoulder.

"You'd better be good with that—" Chantasith was saying when Thamu let the arrow fly.

Chantasith saw him release the arrow and fired the gun, but Thamu had already ducked and rolled to a position on his left. He was already reaching for his next arrow. The first had struck Chantasith on the shoulder. He was screaming in pain and his right arm fell limp. He switched the gun to his left and raised it to point at Thamu. Thamu saw it shake in his grip. His strength was failing him. Thamu lowered his aim. He was shooting for Chantasith's heart now. His aim was true, his hand was steady, but before he let go of the arrow, Thamu heard a shot ring out. His arm fell. The bow string went slack. His arms came apart and fell to their sides: the bow in his left and the arrow still in his right hand. Then the arrow fell from his hand and hit the ground just as Chantasith hit the ground face down in a cloud of dust. Yaya was standing behind him. The rifle in her hand was still smoking.

Thamu walked over still in a daze. Chantasith was dead.

↑ ↑ ↑

WAGNER, his team and Marie were all sitting outside on the fold out table Wagner had told the men to prepare. There wasn't much to offer, but Wagner made sure the best of their rations was put on display. He even asked the cook to enquire in the village if there was any fresh fruit or nuts to be had.

The entire village it seemed had come out—especially the children, who had never before seen such a strange sight: a woman with hair the color of gold! Word spread around the village like wildfire. The stories were again hard to believe: her skin which was said to be as white as milk, was supposedly made of pure moon pearl, and her hairs were strands of pure gold, each worth a fortune. Back home she was a queen and her husband the richest man alive.

Wagner tried to ignore the children who looked on with open mouths.

"Are they hungry?" Marie asked.

"No, it's the strange sight. They don't receive many

foreigners out here. They've probably never seen blonde hair before."

"Ah, perhaps I should wrap my head."

"I'm sure the novelty will wear off," Wagner said.

There was a pause and Liam, eager to make himself known to the congresswoman, spoke up.

"I hope you'll be okay with the animals," he said. "They're small and not much danger. You will see them: squirrels, frogs, lizards, insects... oh boy! the kinds of insects you expect to find pinned to photo board and on exhibition somewhere in a Jules Verne museum."

Marie was smiling. "Thank you... mmm... Liam, right?"

Liam nodded.

"I grew up in a farm," Marie continued. "In Iowa. I've seen it all. Bugs, animals, slaughter, birthing... you name it. But most importantly, I've seen the poverty and the isolation remote communities can feel. The mistrust they can have of state government as though it were an occupying force... It's certainly hot here," she said. "I think I'm overdressed."

"Mornings are wet and misty," Liam broke in. "But by midday the hot sun will have burned the fog away. It doesn't get as humid as the cities, but you'll still need mosquito repellant."

"Thank you, Liam. I'll make a note of that..." Marie said. "I'm sure you both understand how communities can be so isolated that they become self-sustaining—they need to be in order to survive. They've won the right to freedom by hardship and toil..."

"A government comprised of people living outside their community with no knowledge of or participation in it communal life is felt like an imposition," Wagner said.

"Exactly," Marie agreed. "I couldn't have said it better. It's natural that they'd be suspicious and resentful at first. Especially with Americans."

"Why is that, congresswoman? I mean, why do you single out Americans?"

"History, young man. You must study history. Not too long ago, a lie was fabricated in the United States government which soon told the nation that they were trying to prevent a communist takeover in the region. The attack started in the Gulf of Tonkin. The first wave of bombers were decimating."

"Then the Vietnamese returned to fight," Wagner added. "They fought bravely, using any tactic they could. They preferred to die than to be conquered."

"But there was no communist take-over," Marie continued. "It was a lie. The industrial-military complex as it has come to be called, had fabricated a war. They wanted a war that would never end. The profits would return to them every day, each day forever. The generals gave orders. They were never to seize key positions. They wanted the front to be static and the use of ammunition constant."

Wagner was disgusted and didn't mind showing it. He felt Marie had the same view on the question. "This was never Vietnam, just so you understand," he told Liam. "I mean, Laos had nothing to do with Vietnam. Laos was an independent and neutral country in the conflict. But we were all up and down in Laos, carrying on illegal operations. All along the north Vietnamese border. Those were some of the hardest hit areas."

"They didn't want to take Vietnam, you see," Marie said. "They waged a war on its borders. And even after they had bombed it to smithereens, they kept dropping bombs day and after day, because a few dirty people were making a lot of money off the taxpayer for each bomb that was dropped. If they took Vietnam, the war would be over and the river of profit would stop. No one wanted that! Meanwhile, people were dying on both sides. My brother was one of them."

"Not a pleasant chapter of our history," Wagner said.

"They seldom are. Speaking of unpleasant chapters…" Marie began, turning to Wagner. "Where is this police chief you mentioned? I expected to see him."

"I'm afraid. He can no longer be relied upon," Wagner answered. "He is hunting… ostensibly, trying to catch Thamu, our witness."

"I see…"

"Trying to kill him, we think," Liam added.

Wagner gave Liam a stern look as though to tell him to shut up. Liam sat back in his seat.

"Indeed?" Marie was saying.

"I am told that the man can take very good care of himself," was Wagner's attempt at recovery. "And he can't be found if he doesn't want to be found. I didn't want to overwhelm you with the particulars right off, but now that we're on the topic… There is someone I'd like you to meet."

Marie was listening.

"He is an old man here in the village. Revered not only for his age but his position in the community. He watches over the rice fields—their major crop. He can take us to Thamu, and with your help I hope to persuade them and the village to relinquish Tom's remains."

Marie was listening intently. "Can you explain to me, Mr. Wagner, again, why they refuse?"

Wagner uncrossed his legs and then crossed the again. He sat up, put his elbows on the table. It was a difficult subject and one hard to explain.

"I think… I think 'fear' would describe it best," he answered her. "They fear divine repercussions. They believe that 'deities' preside over the village and the villagers. Almost all of village culture, mores and rites are centered around either appeasing the deities or appealing to their mercy."

"And so what is they peetie… peetiesong?"

"*Peetyhoung*," Liam corrected.

"It is… perhaps the equivalent to our word 'spirit'," Wagner answered. "They believe the soul rests near its bodily remains. They must protect it from disturbance. It is their law, they say; and they believe destruction and more destruction will be levied against the village and the villager's heads if they disobey the deities."

"And so this Thamu is out risking his life to protect Tom's remains?"

"They feel responsible for it," Wagner said. "This Thamu was the first to find Tom, and so the duty of guarding his remains and so his soul falls to him."

A tear ran down Marie's cheek. "How touching… How beautiful! It's so nice to know Tom's been in such good hands all these years… I am deeply moved, Mr. Wagner," she said, reaching into her purse for a tissue.

"As are we all," Wagner agreed.

† † †

YAYA had untied her father and all three of them were returning to the village.

"It is no longer safe," Thamu told them and said he would escort them back until the village was in sight.

"Get started. I'll catch up soon," he said. He wanted to hide Chantasith's body from vultures and other carrion. He laid him down in the shade and covered him with banana leaves and branches and anything else he could find. He would come back and bury him later. The village would honor his dying even though he was an evil man, and they would pay their respects as was the law of the deities.

Thamu was catching up to them a minute later. Yaya was anxious and afraid. This was the first time she had felt so close to Thamu and now it felt like it was all slipping away.

"Why did this happen to us?" she asked upon seeing him come up behind them. "Why?"

Her father pat her hand.

"I don't understand," she said. "I hate this place! Why have they come for this pilot after so long!"

"Now, now," Yaya's father consoled. "Don't anger the deities."

"But why us?"

"We all live together. We are all one," her father said. "What happens to one of us, happens to us all."

Thamu was silent. He didn't know the reason for anything, but he understood the *peetyhoung* needed to live somewhere and that asking questions couldn't change what was.

"It is the law," Yaya's father said. "We must appease the deities."

"So far, they have not been appeased," Yaya argued. "Look at all death here. We are prisoners in our own village. If we just gave them the *peetyhoung*, this would all stop."

It did seem to Thamu that destruction and more

destruction would he heaped upon the village and the villagers' heads. Yaya was right. If he gave up Tom's remains, wouldn't the men go away? It seemed the deities who control everything desired the return of the *peetyhoung*.

"The destruction in our village comes by the hands of man," Yaya's father rebutted. "It is nothing compared to the destruction that would come if we anger the deities."

"It is different now that the sister is come to claim them," Yaya added.

They all nodded. "That's true," her father agreed. "But that is not for us to decide," he said looking at Thamu. "The deities will open the way for us as they always do."

Thamu was afraid that after having killed Chantasith, they would all have to hide from now on and forever. Chantasith was an important man. An important chief somewhere far away had sent him. But Thamu had not acted on anger. He had sought other solutions. The deities brought him to this juncture. This must be what they wanted.

The three of them continued, soon they reached the main creek that supplied the rice fields and from which most of the village gathered their water supply. All three of them were thirsty and all had a drink from it. Yaya's father, advanced in age as he was took the longest to kneel down and drink and rise again. Yaya and Thamu were alone for a moment.

"Do you remember when we were children?" Thamu asked pulling her toward him. "We used to play in this creek, you and me."

Thamu took her hand and pulled her toward him from where he stood below on the ravine's valley. The uneven ground had them standing eye to eye, facing each other, her chest against his. Thamu pulled her closer, and she felt his breath on her neck. Her chin was pressed against his now. Thamu ran his hand across her hair and down her back. They had always loved each other. But because Thamu was the chief's nephew his marriage had been arranged. Dee was the daughter of a neighbouring village chief and the marriage was important for everyone. But Yaya's father had never approved. Thamu was a married man and he had hoped the same happiness for his daughter.

But Yaya had kept away from other suitors all that time. She said she couldn't be with anyone else and that it was her fate to be alone. She swore and it was true, that Thamu and she had never lain together. She kept her love to herself and never had there been any sexual contact between the two of them. Her father said it didn't matter. The villagers would talk anyway and if she did not find a husband soon, they would label her lost, wanton… without dignity. Those last words, the old man had spoken with trepidation, and they were the words that incensed his daughter and fixed her resolve. He had regretted those words ever since. "So let them talk!" she had said, and his wife had agreed. "The chicken will cackle and fools will talk," she had said.

The old man found he was the odd man out. He was outnumbered. And now he saw them as they were, holding hands, eye to eye. Thamu was a widow. He had saved his life and his daughter's. He had won his right. He was pleased for his daughter.

The three of them walked home together in silence, enjoying a peace they had not known for some time.

THAMU stopped at the edge of the village. Yaya wanted to return with Thamu, but Thamu told her she should accompany her father.

"We have the Americans," Yaya's father said. "Do not worry. And with that devil gone, there is no one to hurt us any longer."

"He's right, Thamu," Yaya said. "We've won."

"Thamu, you are an honorable man," her father said. "We must end this bloodshed."

Thamu nodded in agreement. "Bring them here tomorrow. Take them down this path. I will meet with them here tomorrow when the sun is highest."

"I will tell them," the old man promised.

"And I will come by tomorrow in the morning to see you and mother," Yaya promised.

Yaya embraced her father and then returned to Thamu's side. She took his hand and together they watched the old man walk down the path to his hut.

YAYA'S father pushed open the door to his hut. His wife was by the kitchen, preparing tea. She didn't bother looking up. She recognized the shuffle and step of her husband as well as his voice.

"Did you see the woman?" she asked him.

"What woman?"

"With gold hair. They think she's some sort of queen. I think she looks like one of those fishes you'd sometimes bring home from the caves." The old woman shrugged her shoulders. "You know, the ones you said were white because they never leave the cave and the sun never gets a chance to color them?"

"Must be the foreigner… the sister."

"Yes" his wife said. "She's at the camp. Would you like some tea?"

"Very much," he said sitting down.

The old woman looked at the face she knew so well. That was an unusual response from her husband.

"Tell me what's happened," she said.

"Our daughter has found love."

"Oh, don't be silly!" she said chuckling. "Is that what's bothering you?"

"You will see. They will be married, soon. Thamu is a widower now."

"She will marry if she wants to. Don't you worry about that," the old woman said and poured out the tea.

"The police chief is dead," Yaya's father then added. "He had captured me. And then Yaya. Thamu rescued us. I don't know how many others were killed."

The old woman jaw dropped and she put her hand up to cover her open mouth. "Is Yaya safe?"

"Of course, of course…. She is with Thamu. He rescued us. He has courage Thamu and a good heart. I'm afraid I have been wrong about him all this time."

"You should go see the Americans and the woman if you want to end it," his wife said.

"Yes, I will see them tonight."

↟ ↟ ↟

LATER that night, the atmosphere in the village was completely changed and unlike anything Wagner had ever witnessed before. It seemed they were having a party. Marie had asked Wagner if the mood was this festive every night.

"No, this is unusual," Wagner said. He called Liam over. "Any idea what's happening?"

"It seems they are celebrating."

"Yes, but what are they celebrating? Is it a holiday?"

Liam shrugged his shoulders.

"Go find the translator and find out what's happening, please. Report back to me."

Liam went off in search of the translator, when the translator suddenly appeared behind them.

"They are celebrating justice and the passing of Dee to the spirit world."

"I see," Wagner said, turning around to see the translator and Yaya's father at his side.

"But why are they celebrating? That's odd," Marie said. "And who is Dee, how is she dead and why would they celebrate—"

Marie stopped, noticing that Yaya's father was staring at her. His wife had been right—the woman had the same white, smooth skin of an eel. He had never seen skin so white and nor so fresh. Wagner and Liam already looked strange enough, but this tall, pale, blonde woman was nothing like the old man had seen before. She spoke with authority which made him think that she was a queen back home, like his wife told him the villagers were saying.

"Thamu has killed the enemy. They are celebrating his victory," the translator said.

"The enemy?" Wagner repeated.

"Yes," the translator said. "He won't specify. He keeps saying 'enemy' and won't say anymore."

The old man didn't need to say anymore. Wagner thought he knew exactly what he meant; and if he was right, he was thankful that the old man was being vague with his words. Last thing he wanted was for his team and the congresswoman to get involved in local complications. As it was they could justifiably plead ignorance. And as far as Wagner was concerned, justice had been served.

"It probably means nothing," Wagner said, hoping to abate Marie's perplexity, and then quickly changed the subject. "Actually, this is the gentlemen I wanted us to see," he said, indicating Yaya's father. "He can lead us to our witness."

"*Actually*," the translator broke-in. He liked to mimic native English speakers. He felt like he had learned a new word. "*Actually*, the old man wants to see you, too."

"Oh?"

"He came and found me and said 'Take me to the American'. I asked what for; he told me to ask my wife what for and told me again to take me to you."

Wagner was smiling. "Well, you brought him. Ask him again now what he wants with me."

The translator asked Yaya's father again and the old man told them what Thamu had said.

"He says he will take you tomorrow to see Thamu. He says to meet him at his hut when the sun is highest in the sky. Then he will lead you up the path that runs along the creek and past the rice fields. He says Thamu will be waiting."

ᛏ ᛏ ᛏ

IT seemed there was nothing else to do but wait. Wagner had rehearsed the meeting and his argument a thousand times before.

Chantasith's lieutenant was one of the men that had survived. He had been delayed as he argued with Chantasith over whether he should stay or go. Those extra seconds may very well have saved his life. By the time he had crossed the ravine and was climbing the hill, Thamu had already taken out the first man, and was aiming for the man behind him.

He had returned to the camp and immediately inquired whether Chantasith had returned. Another one of their hunting party had arrived minutes ago. He saw the lieutenant and the two of them disappear into Chantasith's tent for privacy.

"Have you seen the chief?" the lieutenant asked.

"No. There at least two men down. Trayvong is out with a punctured lung. The arrow is still stuck in him. I dragged him back myself. He needs treatment."

The lieutenant was rubbing his forehead. What a mess this had become! "There's nothing we can do until morning. Give him some liquor. It'll help with the pain."

"What about the chief?"

"I don't know...." The lieutenant said. "He's either lost or dead. There's not much we can do about it."

"We have to tell someone, send out a rescue party... a helicopter—"

"Perhaps, but there is nothing we can do until morning. Just keep your mouth shut for now. Remember... we were out hunting, that's all. We'll figure something out in the morning. Hopefully the chief will be back by then."

THE sound of crickets invaded the night. Marie was on her back inside her sleeping bag. Maybe jetlagged, maybe too excited, maybe over-worried about the insects; she couldn't sleep. Her thoughts alternated between the last time she had been in a sleeping bag on a camping trip with her husband and children and a time much longer ago when she was still a child with her brother Tom. How she missed those days! Equally. The time when her boys were children still, innocent, smiling—how they looked up at her with those smiles, that love! And she missed those days with Tom very much, too. He returned to her now and again in her dreams. He always looked the same way—just the way he looked now, standing next to her cot, in full uniform and his driver's helmet over his head so that she never saw his face. She couldn't say why, but she was sure he was smiling behind his oxygen mask. Still, the dreams perplexed her and it had always haunted her that they had never found his body or his remains, that he was still lost somewhere in the jungle. She was glad this was finally coming to an end. A huge cricket, the size of an African elephant came stomping into the village. Big and blown up like a black balloon she turned to look and turning back, saw that Tom had gone. She looked back at the cricket and saw it was carrying him away. Tom was waving at her. Marie ran after them. Ahead of them were long, rolling green hills, like those she had seen on her flight over here. The bushes were all miniature banana trees and the grass were bamboo groves.

Down below was a small stream, a creek to be exact. The water was flowing down like bubbles in a boiling pot. The water was so clean and clear, that Marie was able to see the crabs and fish swimming along the bottom. She stood there watching them swimming beneath the water. They looked so peaceful to her as if caught up in a dream. Suddenly, the water began pulling back from the edges if it were all flowing down a drain. The creek was almost dry before long, with nothing but a circular puddle in the center of where she had been gazing. And there, as the whirlpool settled, the image of Tom's face, just as she remembered it the last she saw him, appeared. The water drained further and then not only was the creek gone, but so was the ground beneath her feet. Leaning over, she was no longer peering into water but down the edge of a cliff. Far away she saw the village, with all its huts standing on four poles looking like little boxes in the distance. Marie had vertigo suddenly. She felt filled with warm air and before she knew it she and Tom were flying across the valley and toward the village. She could seem them, walking about the village. When they drew nearer, Marie could see they were all naked. But where there genitalia should have been was only a smooth patch skin; and where there faces should have been, with noses and eyes and mouths, was the same patch of skin. It was horrifying.

"What does it mean, Tom?" she asked him. "Why are you showing me this?"

But Tom was silent. Instead of speaking, he flew down and joined them. And there standing on the ground in the center of the village, he became one of them and suddenly he too, was faceless.

XXXIV.

THE FOLLOWING DAY, Yaya arrived as she promised. She had tea with her mother and father. She assured them that all was well. Thamu had taken care of the bodies as custom required. Later, Thamu would take the elders of the village to the site and they would consecrate it as was customary.

It seemed everyone was waiting for noon. Yaya tried to keep herself occupied. While everyone was excited and dropped in on Yaya's father during the morning, Yaya was mostly concerned. She ran chores to keep herself busy and her mind off it. She brought a week's store of fire wood into the kitchen. So much so, that her mother had to tell her to stop. "There'll be no room to move about," she said. "Why don't you go outside and help your father," she said.

Everyone wanted to see Thamu, and at eleven a crowd had already gathered. Yaya's father was trying to explain to them that Thamu would not be able to see them today. But they wanted to know why; and then they wanted to know what the meeting was about, and who was going and if Thamu was coming back and whether the American woman would be staying with them.

Yaya was not as patient as her father. "Home!" she cried

with a finger pointing to the path behind them. "Now! Everyone go home! This is not a party and there is nothing here for you to do."

↟ ↟ ↟

BACK at the village, Wagner was preparing his men for the day ahead. Wagner had gathered them before the tent. He had to inform Liam and the team for the record and the day's official log of the plan: "This is day we've all been waiting for. Today we hope to accomplish what we came out here to do. It's been a rocky road and I want to thank all of you for your support so far. Marie Moorlock, the congresswoman and I will be meeting Yaya and her father at their hut. The translator will accompany us to facilitate. Yaya's father will be taking us up the path leading north out of the village. We will be walking towards some undisclosed location to meet with the witness, Thamu. Protocol requires that a visiting dignitary be accompanied by bodyguard and official escort. This is why the congresswoman has signed a waiver form absolving the government, the embassy, the Laotian government and any other third party of any liability. I have done the same."

"What about the translator?" Liam, who wanted to go as well, asked.

"The translator is neutral," Wagner said. "He interprets—that's all he does. He's Laotian so if anything, it works in our favor at least for our immediate goal."

"What is that goal, sir?"

"To gain his trust. We need to be appear non-threatening or the man will just disappear again. There will be no guns. There will equal numbers on either side:

there will be Yaya and her father on there's and Marie and myself on ours. One man, one woman... Nice balance."

"Tell me what you know about this tribe," Marie requested. "It would benefit all of us."

"They are simple, honest people. Mostly illiterate, they are great craftsmen and hunters. They honor truth and acts of heroism. Their tales are about great chiefs that fulfilled the will of the deities—almost like their gods—against great odds. The tribe's origins are a little bit of a mystery," Wagner paused. "This particular ethnic group was sent here in the fourteen century from south China. There was a civil war at the time with the Laoloum. Kun Cheng was said to be their leader. He sent troops to the lowland to fight the Laoloum. They say his troops had men from as far as what is Cambodia and Thailand today. In any case, it wasn't enough. The Laoloum won and some of these fighters were caught and taken prisoner by Laoloum soldiers. They were brought to the king. The king forced them to work in the palace doing manual labor—sawing wood, carving and cutting stone and gave them the name of Ka, which meant 'slave'. They've been called Ka ever since. A person of the Ka race is said to be a Khmu. In much the same way that someone from the US is said to be an 'American'. It may be a misnomer... Anyway, for five centuries or so, there wasn't much tension between the Khmu and the Laoloum and the Khmu remained slaves and were considered ethnically inferior. Then just as World War II was starting in Europe, a revolution broke out and the young Khmu joined the anti-royal forces. It was a full-on revolt. They joined with the left in their fought against the royal army from 1939 to 1957. Almost twenty years. There is still a lot of resentment, prejudice and hatred today on part of the royalists against the tribes because of this."

"Excellent summary, Mr. Wagner," Marie said in gratitude. "Excellent." There was a light in her eyes and she had an idea. "I don't think I could have hoped for a better briefing. You're information may have provided us with a fail-safe solution—an all-else-fails."

Wagner was curious, but he understood and appreciated the benefits of protocol. If Marie said no more, it was because now wasn't the place nor the audience for it. But Wagner was betting it was the same idea he already had. Two words flashed before him: "political refugee".

☝ ☝ ☝

IT was almost noon. Wagner decided it was time. Marie was ready. He called the translator. He told Liam to speak to no one. Rumors were flying around the village that Thamu had killed Chantasith. Wagner explained to Liam that the last thing they wanted was to be involved. "We know nothing. Say nothing. Chantasith is out hunting—that's all you know. You haven't heard rumors and you haven't an opinion. Are we understood?"

"Yes, sir, Mr. Wagner, sir."

Wagner, Marie and the translator set out for Yaya's father's hut. Wagner led the way, but Marie was eager to talk to him and she soon pulled up to his side. "Mr. Wagner, if I may have a word."

"Of course, congresswoman."

"I understand our witness has killed the 'enemy'," she began. "I understand that perhaps you are not telling me certain things and that it is for my own good."

Wagner nodded slowly, and listened carefully.

"I would just like to say one thing. If I'm right, you don't have to say anything. If I'm wrong, well there's no harm in you telling me so, now is there?"

She is very adroit, this congresswoman, Wagner thought. He nodded again, very slowly, very deliberately.

"I think," she said, "this might be the reason we haven't seen our famed police chief around."

Wagner was silent.

"I see."

IT wasn't long before they reached the hut and it seemed to Wagner that there wasn't much else to say. He was quite sure that he and Marie were of one mind on how to deal with the situation.

Yaya and her father were already sitting outside their hut. The old man stood up when he saw Wagner and Marie turn the corner. He appeared to shout something in the house and began walking down the path to meet them. His wife came out a moment later shouting and waving to them. Yaya turned around and blew her mother a kiss. The old man raised an arm but couldn't be bothered to turn around.

"Be home by tea!" she shouted.

"I've never missed tea my entire life. Not one day," he told Yaya. "Still, she tells me every day…"

Yaya took her father's arm in hers and squeezed it.

Wagner, Marie and the translator met them at the edge of the rice field. Marie felt a tenderness toward the villagers now that she understood how much they had suffered for her brother.

"Please," she said, turning to the translator. "Tell them, I am very grateful…" She waited for the translator to say the words, and then her hand went to her heart. "… And if there is ever anything I can do."

Yaya felt the emotion in Marie's words and she too was touched. But her father grumbled something, that the translator didn't catch. He kept walking.

"Follow me," he said. "We must hurry, or my wife shall have no one to have tea with and we'll all be crying over something more than the bones of the dead."

Yaya shook her head and smiled. The old man seemed to be in good humor. He began talking about his rice fields again. About how he dug the irrigation canals himself, just as he had told Wagner, and about the life in the village and how everything got done. The translator interpreted where he could. "In May the people plant," the translator reported. "Sometimes there is a marriage or more land is needed for whatever reason. Then they clear it. They burn a part of the forest and then work the soil by turning it over and pulling out roots. He says no one is allowed in the village in the afternoons except young children and elderly people—but maybe I misunderstood him. He says, chickens and pigs are kept in the village. Buffalo, horses, and cows feed far from the village and mostly run wild. Horses are herded because of the labor they perform. But buffaloes and cows were only useful to them on special occasions like feasts and marriages, when it was considered lawful to slaughter them for their meat."

"Tell him his village is very beautiful," Marie said. "And the rice fields look well-tended."

They went on walking and talking in this way, and the mood was light. The old man kept them entertained with his stories and information on village life. He was telling them a story of a buffalo that had come to the village once because Thabo, Thamu's uncle, the greatest chief of their village that ever was, as the old man regarded him, had killed a buffalo stag together with some other boys by tripping it up, and then dropping a large stone on its head. It was Thabo's eldest sister's wedding and Thabo wanted to catch the buffalo himself. Not knowing any better, they killed a calf. They dragged the stag back to the village. Its parents followed the scent and then went berserk on the village. They had to kill them too. The old man was saying he had never eaten so well in his life and chuckled as he began listing all the different buffalo dishes he had that year. He was reminiscing on his favorite, which his wife hated to make he said, when Marie suddenly let out a cry.

Thamu had jumped out of brush and into the path directly ahead of him. He had the rifle that fired the shot that killed Chantasith strung over his shoulder.

Yaya broke from the group and ran at once to his side. Thamu's arm went out to receive her but he never took his eyes off Marie. He had never before seen such a being—and it was that intense gaze that had startled her.

Thamu satisfied himself that the strange creature was real. Birds came in many colors and sizes and so did human beings. The strangest thing however, was the resemblance to his *peetyhoung*. She looked just like him—the nose, the mouth, but like an angel: skin like ivory and hair like gold. But Thamu was now looking around, and behind everyone... He seemed to be making sure they hadn't been followed. It had been some days now that he had been living in the wild, and he had got used to it.

"It's okay," Yaya whispered.

Thamu listened and watched a second longer and then appeared convinced. He looked back down and nodded at Yaya's father. Then his eyes fell on Wagner. Wagner had been there when it all began. Thamu felt a kinship with him. He thought that in his own strange way, this American had struggled and suffered as much for the *peetyhoung* as he had.

"That's Thamu," Wagner told Marie. "That's our witness."

🕊 🕊 🕊

MARIE leaned in. "Let's not bring up the remains for a while and just get to know him, if you don't mind."

"Absolutely," Wagner said. "I agree."

Marie laid out a picnic blanket she had brought. Marie and Wagner had agreed he'd bring whatever refreshments he could spare from the rations with him. Wagner had brought apple juice boxes, some crackers and salted nuts. Marie began laying all these down and then took a seat, inviting everyone to sit down with her. Thamu and Yaya's father seemed uncomfortable with the situation, but Yaya reminded them sternly, whether it was right to refuse the kindness of the foreigner and whether or not they wanted to end this.

Thamu sat down on the dirt, afraid touch the blanket. Yaya's father walked over to a stone in the shade and said he would sit there. Getting up and down to the rough ground would be too much for his bones. Then he grumbled that the blanket had too many colors and patterns and that it was cruel to make blanket out of birds. Yaya laughed and told him it wasn't made of feathers but colored yarn.

"It's death to the parakeet all the same," the old man said. "You can't just take a bird's colors away and throw it on the ground."

Thamu was accepting a cracker. He was hungry and his hunger won out over his reticence. He had never before

- 280 -

seen such food. The buttery light cookie melted in his mouth. He was looking at Yaya, smiling. He gave her the last bit of his cracker for her to try.

Marie was observing them and was touched by their simple act of sharing. It seemed so natural, so unaffected to her. Thamu watched her face for a reaction as he bit into it. He knew Yaya would love it.

"I want to thank you for all you've done for my brother," Marie said and waited for the translator, before continuing. "I am so sorry for all the trouble this has brought you and your village. We didn't know it would lead to so much suffering, do you understand? All we wanted was for my brother to return home."

Thamu said nothing. The concept of gratitude was a little foreign to the villagers. Everyone had their duty to perform and everyone knew what their duty was and performed it. There were no favors. Thamu looked at Wagner and then the old man in the distance, wondering if there was something he was supposed to say or do. Wagner smiled at him. The old man seemed to be nodding off and was no help. Yaya gave him another cracker. Thamu stuffed it into his mouth, which to him seemed the wisest thing to do. He was looking at Yaya again, smiling.

Some more pleasantries were exchanged and then Wagner cast a glance at Marie who gave a quick nod in response.

Wagner cleared his throat and the translator perked up. "Thamu, Wagner said, addressing him. "It is good to see you alive and healthy."

Thamu smiled.

"We were all worried…" Wagner said drawing a circle around the group. "This is Tom's sister….sister of the *peetyhoung*." Wagner repeated for emphasis.

Thamu nodded as though to say he understood. He showed them his empty hands as if to say, "Thamu has no sister," but did not speak the words for the translator to interpret.

Wagner continued. Understanding the culture and limited vocabulary, he replaced thanks and gratitude and more appropriate terms. "Tom's sister, Americans and villagers say Thamu great hunter, great chief. Tom's sister has big heart for you. You uncle to *peetyhoung*. Big friend to brother."

Wagner waited. The translator was smiling. Wagner appeared to get the gist of it. The translation had never been so easy. It was almost word for word.

Thamu smiled again. He put his right hand on his left shoulder and spoke for the first time. Wagner looked at the translator.

"He said, 'Law,' and then 'Thamu happy for sister'. He promises to take good care of her brother."

Thamu was smiling. "Thamu guard *peetyhoung* well," he repeated to the translator. "All my life. *Peetyhoung* Thamu's brother, too," he said, looking at Marie.

Marie looked at the translator and when she heard the words, her eyes welled up with tears. She held them back and tried to speak without choking. "Thamu, you are a dear, dear man."

The translator interpreted, "Thamu is friend."

Marie continued. "Thamu, Tom's father is old and dying. His wish is to see his son rest before he passes. Do you understand?"

"He says, '*Dooy*,' which means, 'yes,' he understands. He says, he will be happy and feel great honor to show your father where Tom is resting."

They had to explain to him that Tom's father was sick

and couldn't travel. Thamu said he was sad that he would have to wait until the old man was healthier. Then they said he would not get healthier and Thamu said they should appeal to the deities, perhaps they would help.

Wagner saw that the conversation was going nowhere. He offered Thamu and then everyone else some apple juice. "Fruit water," he told Thamu. "Apples from my country."

Thamu turned the juice box around in his hand. Wagner said, "I'll show you." He held up his juice box. Thamu and Yaya watched intently. Even her father who appeared to be dozing, opened an eye. Wagner removed the straw from the wax fastener. He waited for everyone to do the same. Even Marie played along. Then he tore the corner off the plastic wrap with his teeth and removed the straw. He held it up for all of them to see and then waited until they were all holding the straw up. Thamu and Yaya were fascinated. Wagner couldn't help but smile. Then he showed them the small circular aluminum perforation at the top for the straw. Taking the sharp point he pushed until it broke the membrane. Then he held up the juice box with the straw in it, almost triumphantly as if to show that had been the entire point. He waited again and when all of them had their straw in their juice box, Wagner put it to his mouth and made a loud sucking noise on the straw. Thamu watched. He looked at Yaya and then his straw. He brought the juice box up to his face, first smelled the straw and then slowly put his lips to it. A moment later, he was smiling and nodding. "*Di, di*," he said.

Wagner laughed. "He says, it's good," he told Marie.

Wagner began: "Thamu, in my village we have a law. When a man dies he is put to rest near his home and family. Do you understand?"

"*Dooy.*"

"He says they have the same law," the translator explained. "If a man dies outside the village and it is not too far, then they send men out to bring him back. If it is too far, then the men burn him in a pyre and return with the ashes. It is rare that something like that happens, he says. Sometimes men go out far and disappear. They are lost and we never find them or hear about them."

"Thamu, we have come to bring our villager back home," Wagner said. "Do you understand? This is why we are here."

Thamu began speaking. Wagner and Marie waited for the translator.

"The *peetyhoung* is a traveller. We didn't know his village or how to tell his people. He was the first to find him he says, so the responsibility fell upon him."

"Thamu, I understand your law dictates that you must protect the *peetyhoung*," Marie interjected. "What if it was *you* that took Tom home? Wouldn't that be okay? If you had known how to find the *peetyhoung*'s village that day twenty-two years ago, would you not have tried to bring him home?"

Thamu said, "It was the Law."

"Then it is no different now."

Everyone waited. Yaya looked at Thamu in panic.

Thamu spoke. "He says, 'Thamu does not know the way to Tom's father. Thamu does not know first step. Thamu is lost before he begins trail. Thamu cannot take Tom to his village.'"

"We will go together," Marie said.

Thamu looked at her and then at Yaya and then at Wagner and back at Yaya.

Yaya was looking back at him. She had put the juice box down. Her face had crimsoned; she was angry and afraid. She thought she knew more about the world than Thamu who cared only about the village and hunting. The voyage was long and dangerous. He might never return.

"I am a congresswoman, damn it," she said as an aside to Wagner. "And if I can't manage to get him political asylum, would good is the US government?"

She kept her eyes on Thamu who was looking at Yaya. "And your wife, of course," Marie said, mistaking Yaya for Thamu's wife.

Yaya burst out in tears. Thamu reached out to comfort her. He gave her a look that let her know that he would maker her his wife soon enough and that all that would change.

"My daughter will miss you," her father said, with his eyes still shut and laughing.

"I will not leave her," Thamu answered.

"Ah, well… those are the words that all tragedies begin with."

"Papa!"

Wagner leaned in. "Thamu, I understand that the police chief… had an accident. I don't know what happened, and it is not my business, but I think that the police will blame you and if we don't end this right now. They may send more and more men to the village, and then to the jungle to look for you. It is best if they knew you were somewhere they couldn't go. They would forget about you soon. We understand there is prejudice…" The translator had no word for prejudice and Wagner corrected himself and began again. "We can offer protection. In my country, sometimes when people attack someone from one village, the second village can give them home and security. Most importantly," Wagner added. "You can accompany the *peetyhoung* and see him to his final resting place. Would that fulfill the law and appease the deities?"

Thamu said nothing. He rose and took Yaya's hand.

He turned to Marie and Wagner and said he would return to the village tonight with an answer.

Wagner, Marie and the translator left them and headed back to the village. Their hopes were high. Yaya's father was the first to speak after they were alone.

"They are right," the old man said. "What they say is just and what they want is lawful. They offer to take you with them. They make the way easy."

Yaya's eyes were watering. Thamu was pondering.

"I will come to the village tonight," he said again. "And I will know my mind and speak it."

⚐ ⚐ ⚐

WAGNER went to relieve Liam of his post on guard duty.

"I'll take over for a while," he said.

"Thanks," Liam said. "How did it go?"

"Good, I think. We'll know for sure tonight. We might have some passengers with us on our return home," Wagner said. "We might not. But either way, I think we're getting our pilot home. Any activity from our friends?" Wagner asked meaning the police.

"Nothing," Liam told him.

"Chantasith?"

"Strangest thing. No hunting today. There all just sitting about."

"Good. Hopefully, it'll stay that way. We'll be out of here tomorrow morning at first light and you and I will be having drinks at the embassy while we wait for transport out of here. Get the team to start packing the inessentials. I want us ready to move in the morning. Pack it all up, except the tents and the sleeping gear and whatever we need for tonight."

"Yes sir!" Liam said. He was glad to hear they were finally getting out of here.

"And bring the comm officer over. I'll be putting in a standby request for a helicopter."

𝓲 𝓲 𝓲

THE sun was setting. Yaya's family's hut was full of people. Everyone wanted to know what was happening and if Thamu was going to marry the woman with the gold, blond hair. There had been a rumor going around that she was the pilot's brother and loved her brother so much, she was marrying Thamu. When Yaya's father, absent-mindedly hinted that Thamu might possibly be going with them, everyone burst out before the old man could finish, as if confirmed in the rumor. "So, it's true!"

Yaya was in a rage. She grabbed a broom and wanted to chase the crowd away. "You are all fools!" she said. "No one is going anywhere and no one is marrying. Your spirits are as filthy as your faces. Step off my mother's property!"

OVER across the way, past the winding ravine the valley and on the other side of the hills, Thamu was headed in secrecy to where the *peetyhoung's* mortal remains were preserved. He turned off the path for the last stretch of climbing. Alone, Thamu bent down to a stone laid over the base of the tree trunk. He removed the stone, and saw the snake coiled about an earthen jar, rise up from the hole with its tongue slithering in and out. Ashes, teeth and bones were in a little earthen jar. Thamu kneeled before the snake and closed his eyes. In his mind he could see that it had grown to the size of the tree. Thamu addressed it in his native Khmu:

"You are free to return to your home in the world of spirits. You are released from guardianship. The deities have sent his sister and villagers to bring him home. You and I have served him well."

Thamu, with his eyes still closed, reached into the hole and pulled the jar out. He opened his eyes to clean the jar. He began wiping the dirt off its sides with the sleeves of his shirt. Then he went to cover the hole again and noticed the snake had died.

"Travel well," he said.

Thamu began his return to the village. He would sleep that night among his people for this first time since all this began.

XXXV.

THAT NIGHT YAYA laid her cheek on his chest. Thamu had asked Yaya's father in marriage, and though it was not official, he would take her to Tom's village wot him and go with the Americans. Yaya's mother cried all night. Yaya slept like a child. Thamu lay awake all night thinking of how strange life was and so full of surprises—of the strange journey he was about to embark upon now and what new surprises there wouldn't be awaiting him. Most of all, he felt happy with Yaya. He had not forgotten Dee and said he was leaving his land, his hut and all his animals to Dee's family. Now that he had decided to be Yaya's husband, he would work in the rice fields with her father as soon as they returned from their voyage. "You'll be old and we'll be dead," the old man had grumbled, if you ever returned.

They rose and made preparations. Marie came to the hut in the morning and had breakfast with them. She brought honey and fruit preserves that were sweeter and lighter than anything they had known. Wagner could not be there as he was making preparations. He explained to them yesterday that they would be leaving as soon as they could tomorrow. They were to pack what they needed. Thamu said all he needed was his bow and arrow and that he would catch the rest once he was there. They all smiled, even Yaya. Thamu didn't understand, but he was told he would not be able to bring his bow and arrows.

He sat at the table now, with the earthen jar of Tom's remains between his legs. He never let go of it for even a moment, keeping assiduous watch. Again, Marie was touched by his devotion to it.

He was bringing nothing with him, he said. All he needed was his bow and arrow. Marie asked him about clothes. Thamu was wearing his traditional black cotton pants. He had his best shirt on, but as with most of the village men, he was barefoot.

Yaya was wearing a traditional Khmu dress and though she was wearing traditional slippers made of woven bamboo, Marie knew they wouldn't survive the trip. She looked forward to shopping for them once they returned to the capital. How delightful it would all be, she thought. She was already dressing them up in her mind.

↟ ↟ ↟

THE sun was getting higher in the sky. A crowd had come out to the hut to see Thamu and Yaya off. There wasn't much shade to be had around the rice fields, and soon everyone was glistening with sweat in the hot sun. Even some of the policemen had come out to witness the event.

Soon, they were hearing the distant roar of the propeller engines. They had needed two helicopter: one for Wagner's team and the supplies; and the second for Marie, her men, Thamu and Yaya.

Yaya embraces her mother dearly. Then her father.

Tears are in her eyes. Thamu waves to everyone. They all let out a cheer.

Now the American, Wagner, is saying that Marie, Yaya and Thamu will be going first. There is not enough room for both flying machines to land at once.

Thamu helped Yaya in and then took a seat next to her. Thamu watched Marie strap herself in and then watched as the co-pilot did the same to Yaya and then himself. Soon, the machine lurched like a strong wind had blown it across the field and before Thamu knew anything, he was flying.

He looks out from the window, thinking back upon his uncle Thabo and the first time he met Tom his *peetyhoung*, His uncle would never imagined it would all finish like this. "Guard this *peetyhoung*," he had told him. "He is not like the others and your destiny is tied with his."

He pressed his fingers tightly against the earthen jar carrying his *peetyhoung*. He had kept his word. He turned over and looked at Yaya. He could tell she was afraid, but happy. They were amazed that they were flying. What a marvel it was to see their village beneath them.

Thamu removed one his hands from its hold on the urn and reached for Yaya's hand.

Yaya took his hand and was no longer afraid.

ABOUT THE AUTHOR

SOMSY CAMVAN was born in 1954, a son of Khmu tribe parents and horse traders. Somsy spent the early time of his life a small village in north Laos. His father sent him to live with a relative in the capital city Vientiane in his late teens to receive an education. After finishing his training in Communications, in 1974, he worked for the government-owned newspaper, "*The People's Voice*" He was held for questioning in 1979 for suspicions of collaborating with the anti–Government group. Fearing for his safety, Somsy escaped to Canada via Thailand in the late 1980s, where he has been living since in a quiet country home, in the province of Quebec. His work of historical fictions include *Blanket Coffin* and *The Other Side of Mekong*.

www.ingramcontent.com/pod-product-compliance
Lightning Source LLC
Chambersburg PA
CBHW020542020726
47494CB00006B/1882